"Do you like Ms. Johnson, Daddy?"

"Sure, Billy. She's a nice lady." Nick was touched by the sadness in his son's eyes. "Why do you ask?"

"Uh, I just thought maybe..." Billy was silent for a few seconds, then he mumbled, "I miss Mom."

"I know, son. We both do." Nick placed a hand on the boy's shoulder.

When Billy didn't respond, Nick continued. "I would give anything if I could bring her back."

"What *really* happened, Dad?"

"Billy, she drowned. You know that."

Billy looked up at him, eyes narrowed. "Yeah, sure," he said and walked away.

Nick stood and watched him go. *So much for his father-son talk.* Well, he'd just have to try again. Nobody ever said being a single father would be easy.

ABOUT THE AUTHOR

Bringing Up Father is the second Superromance novel from the writing team of Margaret Masten and Saundra Pool. The two live in Morton, Texas, where they teach at the same elementary school. They both dreamed of writing but found, as Margaret puts it, that "writing is not as simple as nonwriters believe." It was Saundra who suggested they collaborate and the successful partnership was formed.

Maggie Simpson

Bringing up FATHER

Harlequin Books

TORONTO • NEW YORK • LONDON
AMSTERDAM • PARIS • SYDNEY • HAMBURG
STOCKHOLM • ATHENS • TOKYO • MILAN
MADRID • WARSAW • BUDAPEST • AUCKLAND

ISBN 0-373-70608-1

BRINGING UP FATHER

Bringing up FATHER

PROLOGUE

THE LAST FEW MEETINGS of the Corpus Christi Senior Citizens' Quilting Club had been fairly dull. Nothing much out of the ordinary had happened since my neighbor, Susan Bradley, married the man who'd introduced her to her brand-new grandson. Now, I was about to make my fellow quilters sit up and take notice.

"Betsy's met the man she's going to marry," I announced loudly, seeing with satisfaction that everyone stopped what they were doing and gave me their full attention.

"Isn't she the old-maid schoolteacher?" asked Bertha Clark.

I stood up, sucked in my breath and clenched my teeth. Not too hard, though. I didn't want my dentures to pinch. Betsy—Elizabeth Ann Johnson—was my favorite granddaughter. I'd been worried about her for years because she spent far too much time at work and not enough time hunting for a husband. Fortunately, before I could light into Bertha and defend Betsy, Virginia Black asked a question.

"She's only in her early thirties, isn't she, Agnes? Quite beautiful, too, I hear."

"She was thirty-three in December." I looked down my nose at Bertha as I spoke. "In this day and age, thirty-something isn't old. In any event, all that's about to change. She's met Mr. Right. They will get married and we are going to make her a wedding ring quilt for a wedding present."

"Is it that nice young dentist she's been dating?" Virginia asked.

"Robert King? Gracious, no." I shook my head. "That pot of water's been on the stove long enough to boil, and nothing's happened."

Bertha nodded her agreement before asking, "Well, who is he, then?"

"He works at the Gulf Coast Aquarium. His name is Nick Lupton."

Virginia peered over her reading glasses. "Did you say Nicholas Lupton?"

"Yes, do you know him?"

"I've known him since he was a child. If I must say so, he's handsome enough to make a married woman slide her left hand in a pocket." Virginia blushed.

For her to say something so out of character meant this Nick was good looking. Seeing as how I hadn't met him yet, I took her at her word.

Era Sullivan, the quietest member of our group, spoke up. "My neighbor works at the aquarium and she's as nutty as a fruitcake. Keeps her blinds closed all the time like someone was going to see something they shouldn't."

We all ignored that remark because Era didn't have room to talk. She was becoming a little strange herself.

Virginia paused while threading her needle. "Have they set the date yet?"

"Not exactly. In fact, Betsy doesn't know she's going to marry him yet." *I sat back down.* "His son Billy is a pupil at the school where she's the assistant principal and that boy is a holy terror. He's given Betsy fits all year, and his dad won't do anything about it. I feel she's taken on Billy as a special project because he reminds her of her little brother."

Bertha said, "I didn't know you had a grandson."

"Don't anymore. Jake died when he was nine." *Even though that had been fifteen years ago, I still got teary-eyed just talking about it, which is why I seldom do.* "I think that's why Betsy has taken such an interest in this boy and," *I added,* "his father."

CHAPTER ONE

BETSY WAS STEAMED! With long strides she quickly covered the fifty yards from the parking lot to the ramp leading to the Gulf Coast Aquarium. Today she refused to let the beauty of the sparkling white building distract her from her mission. She was going to give Nick Lupton a piece of her mind and no one was going to stop her.

She paused in front of a blue-topped gazebo debating whether to cut into the long line of ticket buyers. Finally, she decided against it. She wasn't going to buy a ticket just to get a few minutes of time with the director of animal husbandry, so she hurried up the wide concrete ramp. Her blood was pounding through her veins in time with the rushing water cascading down and around the arched double entry of the aquarium. She hardly noticed the deafening roar, the refreshing mist of the water or the pleasant May temperature. She was more aware of her own temperature, and it was boiling.

She was going to have to control herself or no one would call Mr. Lupton up front to see her. Slowing her pace and assuming a professional facade to match her red and black business suit, Betsy walked to the information desk.

"Hello." She leaned forward across the countertop and smiled broadly at the balding uniformed man on the other side. He laid down the colored brochure without taking his eyes off her. "I need to see Mr. Nicholas Lupton. It's about his son. Could you please direct me to him?"

The volunteer readjusted his trifocals. "Yes, ma'am. Is he expecting you?"

"I'm sure that he is." It was only a little white lie. Mr. Lupton surely realized that she would follow up on her letter.

"Ma'am, I can't take you into the work area—it's for authorized personnel only, you know—but if you'd give me your name, I'll certainly page him to come to the desk to meet you. If he's here, that is. He may be out fishing today."

"Thank you so much. Tell him that Elizabeth Johnson, assistant principal of Hodges Elementary School, needs to see him." She wanted to add that Nick Lupton apparently did a lot of fishing because he'd been out the previous time she'd come out here to see him, too.

Her red-tipped nails tapped a staccato rhythm on the countertop while she waited for him to appear. She studied the suspended models of swordfish and sharks swimming in an ocean of air above her head. They looked the way she felt—out for blood. Nick Lupton's blood.

It was high time, she decided, that the man was made to understand what parenthood encompassed. He was old enough to know better. Yet he devoted more time to marine life than he did to his own son's life.

She was still surveying her surroundings when a tall, lean man separated himself from the stream of people entering the exhibition area and walked toward her. She recognized Nick Lupton even though he didn't look like the well-groomed professional who'd given the Earth Day presentation at school a couple of months ago. He was wearing cutoff jeans and a partially buttoned chambray shirt with a white starfish embroidered above the left pocket. However, he still bore a certain air of authority, and the sight of him did something to her heartbeat. Her anger dissipated as he strode toward her, a mild level of concern clouding his eyes.

"Ms. Johnson, good to see you...I think. Has something happened to Billy?" He extended his right hand in greeting. His index finger was wrapped in gauze.

"No, Billy is fine." Careful to avoid hitting the injured finger, Betsy held out her hand to receive his warm grip. "What happened to you?" She nodded toward their still-clasped hands before extricating her own.

Obviously embarrassed, he held up his finger and grinned. "Carelessness. I cut it trying to get a hook out of a fish's mouth last night."

"You went fishing last night?"

"Yes, ma'am, I did, until about eight." He seemed compelled to add, "Fishing's a regular part of my job. After I got back in last night, it took a while to sort out the catch and put the fish in quarantine."

Didn't he know that spending time with his son was part of his job, too? Where was Billy when his father was out so late? That, though, was really none of her business. No, she decided, it *was* her business. She suspected Billy wouldn't be having the problems he was if his dad spent more time with him. Careful to avoid an accusatory tone, Betsy asked, "Why do you have to go fishing so often? I mean, aren't there other employees who do that sort of thing?"

"There are, but I prefer to supervise the fishing because it's important to get new specimen for the aquarium, to replace the little fish the big ones eat and to catch food for the fish we've already got. We want to feed them fresh food as much as possible."

"Okay, point made," she grudgingly acknowledged.

"Would you like me to show you around?"

"Another time maybe. I'm here about Billy, today. Is there someplace we could talk in private?" She didn't think the foyer of the aquarium was a good place to say what she had in mind.

"Yeah, sure. Follow me." Nick unlocked a camouflaged doorway and led her into the interior of the aquarium. "Watch your step," he warned, indicating a concrete lip that would prevent water from flooding the public areas should a leak spring in one of the water tanks.

"Isn't this area for authorized personnel only?"

"It is. I just authorized you."

Betsy stepped over the lip and followed him through a maze of gray pipes and beige tanks. She studied his broad shoulders and lean legs. Although his straight blond hair was beginning to thin at the crown, there was no denying that the man was very attractive. She'd thought that a couple of months ago when she'd first seen him at school on Earth Day.

Then the problems with Billy had mushroomed, and Nick Lupton had failed to respond to the school's written notices, nor had he returned a telephone message. She wanted to know why.

In his small cluttered office, he nudged the only chair toward her, then propped himself against the edge of the desk near an outdated computer, crossed his arms and faced her. "Okay. What's wrong this time?"

You, she wanted to say, but realized that it would have a double meaning. Not only was he a problem as Billy's father, but the tight quarters made her acutely aware of him as a man, creating another problem. Her knees were mere inches from his bare legs. She twisted sideways in the chair to increase the distance between her and this very attractive man. "Mr. Lupton, Mrs. Bradley, Billy's teacher, has tried to keep you abreast of Billy's problems this year. While his behavior improved for a while, he's an unhappy little boy who—"

"What makes you think he's unhappy?" Nick interrupted.

Betsy was startled by the combativeness in the man's voice. She hadn't really gotten started yet. She hadn't even mentioned his ignoring the letter she'd written to him advising him of Billy's problems. "Because he said so."

"Oh."

"He also said he doesn't do his classwork because he doesn't want to. I can't tell you why he doesn't want to, but I can tell you what his lack of effort has resulted in. He has fallen so far behind that he needs to attend summer school. That's what I've come to discuss with you."

Nick cupped his chin in a hand, one finger stroking his rigid jawline. "How far behind?"

"He's failing math and language arts," Betsy answered. "Have you had a chance to look at his achievement test scores that we sent out last week?" Nick hadn't come for the parent-teacher conference to have the scores explained to him.

"Those scores aren't valid. I know my son, and he's bright."

"I know your son, too, Mr. Lupton, and he *is* bright. However, school work is judged on output, not what either one of us thinks he is capable of doing. In math, for example, he's quite far behind." Betsy considered telling the man she thought Billy might be depressed and that was what was affecting his school-work. But judging from Nick Lupton's body language, she thought better of it.

Nick hesitated, seemingly considering what Betsy had suggested. "Do you think a tutor would help? I hate for him to have to go to summer school."

Secretly, she thought a tutor would be fine, but she didn't trust the man to follow through. He hadn't done much for Billy lately and there was no reason to think he would now. "Sometimes tutors work rather well, but Billy really needs to be with other kids, which brings up another concern."

Nick raised an eyebrow. "And what's that?"

"Billy is lashing out at his classmates like he did at the beginning of the year."

"In what way?"

"He does things like elbowing them when he walks down the hall, holding the doors to the toilet stalls closed so kids can't get out, grabbing and tearing up papers." Betsy was listing only highlights of Billy's bulging discipline folder. She hoped it was enough to allow Nick to get the picture.

"What are the rest of the kids doing to him?"

"The other children aren't provoking Billy's actions, if that's what you are implying." Betsy paused, realizing that she needed to let this man know that she wanted to help his son. "Mr. Lupton, I really don't mean to be presumptuous, but Billy acts like he's angry at the whole world. Is there a reason for him to be so angry?"

"Not that I know of, and if he is, it's a family matter." Nick raised himself to his full six feet and leaned toward Betsy. "Are you through meddling, Ms. Johnson?"

Irritated, Betsy raised herself to her full five foot ten in her two-inch heels and met his sea green eyes. "If it means not trying to help Billy, then the answer, Mr. Lupton, is no, I'm not."

THAT WOMAN WAS a barracuda! Hours later, after all the aquarium's visitors had left, Nick was still muttering to himself as he locked the chemicals cabinet. Like a barracuda, Betsy Johnson didn't give up very easily. Well, she could sure as hell give up on this one. He was a capable, competent father who made appropriate decisions for his son, and nobody was going to convince him otherwise.

She'd remained cool and calm, although he'd noted her struggle to do so. Under other circumstances, he would have welcomed her visit, remembering the envious glances from the guys when she'd followed him into his office. Too bad her gorgeous blue eyes had turned so cold in their assessment of him.

He thought he managed rather well as a single parent. Billy went to school clean and well dressed, had plenty to eat and he was never left alone. The sitter picked Billy up after school, except for the few months he'd had to leave Billy at his parents'. Billy had understood.

Nick had seen to it that all kinds of gadgets and games filled his son's room. Thinking about it now, he realized that he never saw Billy actually playing with any of the games. Mainly, the boy lay on his bed and watched TV. Nick shrugged when he remembered his mother telling him that it wasn't healthy for Billy to spend so much time alone. Being alone could prevent the child from developing lifelong social skills, his mother had warned.

Of course, one of the first things he intended to do when he got home was look up those test scores. He didn't believe in standardized testing for children, so he'd never opened the envelope from the school, but he wasn't going to tell that to Betsy Johnson. For some reason, he had no desire to sink any lower in her estimation.

WHEN NICK SWUNG his Jeep into the circular drive-way in front of his house, the setting sun's rays glinted into his eyes. It was only eight, the earliest he'd been home in several weeks. Janie, his housekeeper and baby-sitter, would be surprised. Seeing her car sitting in the driveway reassured him that he was a good father. Still, he resolved to have a talk with Billy tonight.

"Billy, Janie," he called as he entered the silent foyer.

A slender young woman emerged from the kitchen wiping her hands on a towel. "Good evening, Mr. Lupton. You're home early tonight. I've cleaned up the dishes but saved you some food in the microwave. Are you ready to eat?"

Nick sniffed the aroma and realized he was hungry. "I sure am," he said, realizing how lucky he was to have Janie as a housekeeper. She was dependable, a good cook and seemed to dote on Billy. "Where's Billy?"

"He's in his room…he's a little out of sorts." Janie hesitated, then added in a low voice, "Mr. Lupton, before I leave, I'd like to discuss Billy with you. I've wanted to for some time now."

Not again. Tonight he wished, more than usual, that Vicki was still alive to share some of the decisions concerning Billy. Not that raising Billy had ever been a joint effort. Soon after Billy's birth, Nick had learned that Vicki had preferred to do things her way and did not welcome his suggestions. As a result, he had left most of the parenting to her. And he had to give her credit. Billy had been well behaved and happy while she had been alive. "What about Billy?"

Janie's dark eyes matched the tone of her voice. Troubled. "He won't do what I ask him to. In fact, he's, ah—" she searched for the correct word "—well, he's becoming a brat. I'm sorry, Mr. Lupton, but something is going to have to be done if you want me to stay with him this summer. I'm not prepared to put up with his smart-mouthing indefinitely."

Momentarily, he wondered if Betsy Johnson had gotten hold of Janie. "What's he saying?"

"Oh, things like, 'You're not my mother and I don't have to do what you say.'"

"I'm sorry about that, Janie. I'll have a talk with Billy about manners. I'm sure it's just a phase he's going through."

"I certainly hope he gets through it soon. He's been in this phase all year."

"All year?" That couldn't be. Nick might have been wrapped up in his own grief but surely he would have noticed if his son had been misbehaving for that long.

"Yes, Mr. Lupton. I've told you about the times he stormed into his room after I got on to him."

"Oh, oh, yes. Well, thanks for reminding me. I'll talk to him about that, too." Nick recalled that Janie had periodically mentioned incidents when she'd had to discipline Billy, but Nick had never considered any of them to be of consequence.

Passing through the hallway after Janie left, Nick stopped and stared at the closed door to his son's room before he gently rapped on it. There was no response, so Nick opened the door and peered inside. "Billy, you asleep?" The slight figure of his son was sprawled on the Dallas Cowboys bedspread, the little boy's eyes trained on the TV screen. "Billy?"

"Hi, Dad. How was work?" he said, looking at his father.

Nick went over and sat on the bed. "It was fine. You know how it is."

"Yeah, I know."

Nick fumbled for the words to say to his son. He really didn't know how to talk to a ten-year-old. But he did know that he couldn't hit Billy with both Janie's and Ms. Johnson's complaints. He'd take care of them one at a time. "Say, Billy. Guess who came to see me today?"

"Who?"

"Ms. Johnson from school." Nick watched his son's eyes shift back to the television. "You know what she wanted?"

Billy shrugged his shoulders.

"She thinks you need to go to summer school."

"I don't wanna go to summer school," he muttered. "I know all that stuff."

"That's what she thinks, too."

Billy's eyes flickered in the dim light given off by the television set. "She does? Then why should I go to summer school?"

"Well, she thinks math is a trouble spot for you. I thought you were pretty good with math."

"Kinda. Some of it, maybe."

Nick was somewhat surprised that Billy wavered. "What parts give you trouble?"

"I know my facts, but, Daddy, fourth-grade math is hard. I hate all that stupid stuff. I'll bet you'd have trouble with it, too."

"I might. But if I did, I think I'd want someone to help me learn it." He noticed that Billy's fingers were tightly interwoven, with his thumbs chasing circles around each other. "Do you want us to have a look at it now?"

Billy shook his head. "Not right now. I want to finish watching this show."

Nick glanced at the screen. He had no idea what show his son was watching. "Mind if I prop up on the bed and watch it with you?"

"I don't care," Billy said, a big grin spreading across his face as he moved over to give his father room.

AFTER BILLY HAD gone to sleep, Nick grabbed his weathered briefcase off the desk and spread legal forms over the large dining-room table. For several months he'd been trying to donate a shark that was outgrowing its tank to an aquarium in Mexico. The international paperwork was a nightmare.

By ten, he had developed the full-blown headache that had been threatening all day...or at least since his meeting with Betsy Johnson. He massaged the back of his neck a few times, then stood up and put away the papers he'd been working on.

The slow, hot shower and a couple of aspirin helped him feel better physically, but he knew he wouldn't be able to fall asleep anytime soon. For two years now, no matter how much he desired it, sleep had been a reluctant companion. He lay naked, spread-eagle on the king-size bed and studied the ceiling, just as he'd done so many times since Vicki's accident. Night after night he'd lain here and stared up until he knew every crack, every dimple.

Tonight, joining all the old ghosts, a new one emerged. Ms. Johnson had only been trying to help his son, and he'd verbally attacked her for making him feel inadequate as a father. He ought to call and apologize. He glanced at the digital clock. Only a few minutes after ten-thirty, too late for a polite call. He argued with himself for a few seconds before deciding that his reason for calling justified the late hour.

He rolled onto his abdomen and stretched across the bed until he could reach the phone book on the headboard shelf. He ran his finger down the directory several times before he decided that E. A. Johnson must be her. A smile spread over his face. *E. A.* If anyone needed an unlisted phone number, Elizabeth—could it be Ann?—Johnson did. He bet irate parents called her all the time.

He punched in the numbers and counted five rings. Inwardly, he grimaced. Maybe she was already asleep. Just as he was about to hang up, he heard a low voice float over the wire. "Hello."

"Ms. Johnson?" Nick's misgivings about his impulsive call intensified as he thought the huskiness in her voice could be the result of sleep.

"Yes."

"This is Nick Lupton. I hope I didn't wake you."

"And if you did?"

He pictured her sitting in bed, her black, disheveled hair draped over a shoulder as she leaned toward a nightstand phone. "Then I guess I owe you two apologies."

Laughter greeted his ears. "No, Mr. Lupton, you didn't wake me. What can I do to help you?"

"I've thought about what you said today."

"And?"

"You were right." He settled back against a couple of goose-down pillows and pulled a sheet up over his legs. "Billy will go to summer school."

"That's great. I'll get the information in the mail to you right away. Then, if you have any questions, let me know."

"I already have one." Who was he kidding? He'd called Betsy Johnson to hear her contralto voice which was as enticing now as her body had been when he'd met her in the spring.

"What's that?"

"Will you come back to the aquarium to let me give you a tour? I need to do something to show you that my behavior is not always so boorish."

"I'd love to. Thank you very much."

He placed the receiver in the cradle and curled one arm behind his head. How could she be so nice after he had behaved so badly that morning? He remembered how she had stood in his office and met him eyeball to eyeball. She hadn't been intimidated in the least. He liked that.

CHAPTER TWO

"COME ON, Billy." With his palm planted firmly in the middle of his son's back, Nick guided Billy through the metal double doors of the elementary school. His son had been nothing but difficult since he'd been told he was going to summer school. After enduring weeks of his temper tantrums and silent sulks, Nick was tempted to take the easy way out and cancel the whole idea. Only Janie's threat to quit had made him stand firm. That and the thought of facing Betsy Johnson's ire.

"I'm coming." Billy shrugged Nick's hand off his back and moved toward the protection of the wall. Nick joined him to get out of the way of the crowd of children and parents milling about.

"It's going to be okay, Billy. Six weeks is all, then you'll have a lot of free time." Wanting to placate his sullen son, he added, "You get in there and show your teacher that you could teach the class if you wanted to." They were meaningless words, he knew, because he'd worked with Billy the past week and found that Ms. Johnson was right. His son did have trouble concentrating on math.

Since neither he nor Billy's mother had ever had trouble with math, Nick wondered if Billy's problems might be the result of poor teaching. So he decided to tutor Billy on his own. He discovered that the boy hadn't retained one blessed thing during the week Nick worked with him. It was as though Billy didn't have a brain cell in his head. Nick sure knew why he hadn't become a teacher.

The air-conditioned hallway provided relief from the already heightening early summer's heat. Pausing, he unfolded the information sheets Ms. Johnson had sent him and looked at the floor plan of the open-concept school. Though he'd been here in the spring for Earth Day presentations, he did not know the layout of his son's school. Vicki had always taken care of Billy's education.

He refolded the papers and stuck them in his hip pocket. Schedules and classroom assignments were posted outside the office housed in the central core of the building.

After depositing Billy in the correct classroom, Nick started back down the hall somewhat disappointed that he hadn't bumped into Betsy Johnson, when he heard a voice call out. "Mr. Lupton?"

Nick turned toward the source and saw the assistant principal clothed in a mass of swirling white fabric. She looked like an angel, except, of course, angels didn't adorn themselves in gold jewels and dusky eye shadow.

"How nice of you to bring Billy to school," she said, coming toward him. She didn't break her stride until she buried her slender fingers in his extended hand.

"Ms. Johnson," he said, "it's good to see you again."

A warm smile flooded Betsy's face. "And I'm relieved to see you again. For a few minutes this morning, I was afraid you'd backed out on me."

"The thought did cross my mind a time or two," Nick admitted. "In addition to Billy's objections, it's going to be wild around our place for a while handling the logistics. Janie Gonzales, my housekeeper, is taking classes at the college, Billy's here and I'm working."

"It'll all work out. You'll see. Billy's trying to convince you not to send him is to be expected, but he'll be fine in a day or two. If he has any problems, I'll let you know."

Nick didn't doubt that for a moment.

"Hi, Miss Johnson." A little girl stopped and hugged Betsy.

"Hi, Amanda. I'm so glad to see you. Did you enjoy your vacation?"

"It was only a week," the little girl moaned.

Nick watched while Betsy returned the embrace of several other children, all the while listening to what they'd done while they'd been out of school. That she remembered all their names amazed him.

Finally, she said, "Why don't all of you go on to class now, and during recess I'll go outside with you." Obviously pleased with her promise, the children scurried down the hallway.

"You're going out during recess?" Nick asked skeptically.

"Sure. That's when I learn all their secrets." Betsy gave a little boy one last hug, then she turned her full attention to Nick. "During the summer, we are much less formal."

"Do you work here all summer?" Until he'd received her letter, he hadn't known that schools were even open during the summer.

"Just to the middle of this month. Then I'm off until the first of August." When she waved to a passing student, her gold bracelets jingled as though they shared her enthusiasm. "I'll have some free time for a change."

"Sounds good. What do you plan to do?" He didn't know her well enough to ask such a personal question but he wasn't quite ready to say goodbye. Betsy, the woman, intrigued him. There was something flamboyant—nearly exotic—about her which attracted him. Ms. Johnson, the schoolmarm who interfered with him and Billy, was another matter.

"I thought about doing something different like robbing banks, getting a job at a strip joint or hiring out as a mercenary, but decided those all sounded rather dull." She cocked her head to one side as if she were thinking. "So, I'm going to hang out with my family, and maybe do a little diving."

He didn't catch her last words. His mind had taken off at the mention of the strip joint. Before he could stop himself, he was staring at her and visualizing her performing in the spotlight on a tiny stage. She was built for the job. Tall and lean with curves in all of the right places.

"Mr. Lupton. I was joking."

She didn't appear the least bit embarrassed by his gaze. Nor did she appear to be flattered. No. What she looked was downright self-assured.

"Too bad. I might have taken up cruising topless bars." He shrugged as if disappointed. "And the name's Nick."

"Nick." The way she said it was like a caress.

Before he could respond, out of the corner of his eye he saw a young boy hurrying down the corridor toward them. He looked closer. Billy.

Betsy turned to see what had diverted his attention.

"Daddy," Billy exclaimed hopefully, "I forgot to bring paper and pencils. I guess I can't stay."

Betsy laughed. "No problem, Billy. I've got some in my office that you can borrow."

"Oh," Billy groaned.

"Thanks, Ms. Johnson," Nick said. He should have checked Billy's backpack. He'd assumed supplies were in there.

She smiled at him over the top of Billy's head. "Well, we'd better go get that pencil and paper and get you to class." She reached out and laid a hand on the boy's shoulder. "Are you still interested in the Kemp's ridley turtles, Billy?"

Billy looked up. "No, ma'am. Well, kind of, but I've been checking out the river otter."

Betsy raised a naturally arched black eyebrow and looked at Nick. "The river otter?"

He offered an explanation. "It's another threatened species."

"DAMN!" Two weeks later, Nick watched Betsy Johnson and his son crossing the patio toward him. He glanced at the dead bird in his gloved hands, then twisted his arm to read his watch. Twelve-thirty. How the devil could he have lost track of the time? He was supposed to have picked Billy up nearly an hour ago.

Betsy stopped three feet in front of him and looked at him with cold, blue eyes. "You forgot. This is the second time, Mr. Lupton. I called but was told you couldn't be disturbed."

"I didn't realize the time. We've had a crisis here this morning." Nick didn't want to argue or explain in front of Billy or the volunteer standing nearby. "Mary Alice, would you do me a favor and take Billy up to the lobby and get him something to drink?"

"Why, of course, Dr. Lupton. Come along, Billy. Let's see if we can find a lemonade." Knowingly, the gray-haired lady shrugged, then draped her arm around Billy's shoulders and guided him away.

As soon as the elevator doors closed, Nick turned to the woman who was obviously expecting some kind of answer from him. He thrust the lifeless gray gull he was holding toward her as though it explained everything. "They've been dying all morning."

Her icy gaze began to thaw. He could tell she was struggling to come up with an appropriate response. Finally, she took a deep breath and answered in a less confrontational tone than he'd expected, "That's terrible." Nodding toward the gull, she asked, "What happened? What's causing it?"

"Hell if I know. That's why I'm down here...not taking any calls...and apparently not doing any good, either. This is the third one." He laid the bird on a table and sighed. Leaning against the counter's edge, he crossed his arms, and faced Betsy. "Look, I'm sorry about forgetting the time. I'm sure Billy was frightened, but I won't forget again."

"I know emergencies happen, but—"

A short, red-haired man holding another large bird interrupted them. "Nick?" he called, trying to balance his unwieldy cargo. "You might take a look at this one, too. It looks like the same thing. I tell you we're having an epidemic."

Nick reached out and relieved the man of the limp bird. "Thanks, Tom." He tilted his head sideways toward Betsy. "Tom, this is Ms. Johnson, Billy's principal. Ms. Johnson, Thomas Taylor, one of our marine biologists." After the perfunctory introduction, Nick turned to examine the pelican.

Tom and Betsy stood on either side of him peering over his shoulders while he examined the bird for any visible sign of trauma. He knew what he would find. Nothing.

Something was killing the birds, and he didn't have a clue what. The blood samples he'd sent to the lab had come back negative for deadly bacteria or viruses, contrary to what Tom had thought was causing the deaths.

Nick felt sick to his stomach. These birds had been sent to the aquarium to be nursed back to health. But he'd failed them. He'd only felt this inadequate once before. Long-repressed images of a blond woman gasping for breath suddenly flashed before his eyes.

Vicki.

He blinked several times trying to wipe the painful pictures from his consciousness. Tom's concerned voice penetrated the fog that was beginning to close in on him. "What did you find?"

Refocusing on the bird, Nick shook his head. "Nothing." He leaned his head back, took a deep breath and cursed no one in particular before he dug into a tray on the edge of the table and pulled out two scalpels to perform a necropsy.

He quickly made incisions and removed the tissue specimen he needed. "Take these up to the lab and have Chester do a histology and analysis," he instructed Tom after putting the samples into separate glass dishes, which he labeled. "They've got to show something." He said the words out loud as if to convince himself.

Tom hurried toward the elevator, nearly bumping into Billy and Mary Alice when they stepped out.

Billy scampered up to Nick and frowned at his dad's blood-covered hands, then looked at the crumpled remains of the dead birds. "Yuck! What happened?"

Nick explained to Billy what had been going on. "And now we're checking for poison, though I can't see how that could have happened. We take too many precautions."

"Le'me see, Dad. I wanna check 'em out." Billy tiptoed forward to get a better view.

Nick guided his son away from the counter. "I think it'll be safer if you kept your distance, Billy. The birds could be diseased."

Betsy had stood quietly behind him as he'd worked. Now she spoke. "Mr. Lupton, I can see that you're busy. Would you like me to take Billy back to my place until you're through? I think we're both in the way here." She paused and looked at Billy. "If Billy's agreeable, that is."

"No, I wanna stay here and watch you, Dad," Billy pleaded.

"Billy, I'm really swamped. You'll have to stay upstairs in my office or go with Mary Alice, okay?"

For a second, Billy looked as if he wasn't sure what he wanted to do. Then he sighed and glanced up at his principal. "Naw. I'll go with Miss Johnson."

"I really appreciate your offer, Ms. Johnson. Mother is out of town and Janie has a big test tomorrow. I was planning on keeping Billy here today, but this hasn't turned out to be the most opportune time."

"I can see that. Billy and I will find something fun to do." Betsy pulled out her card and laid it on the counter. "Here's my address and telephone number if you need to call. Are you ready to go, Billy?"

"Yeah, I guess."

When she and Billy stepped out of the aquarium into the bright sunlight, she lowered her sunglasses, which had been serving as a headband, into place. "Are you hungry? There's a place not far from here that makes a mean hamburger."

"I don't like hamburgers."

Betsy raised an eyebrow as she looked at the boy. "Maybe they'll have other things." She led the way to a small café where outdoor tables overlooked Corpus Christi Bay. A waitress clad in shorts brought them menus.

Billy ignored her and without even picking up his menu stared at the immense aircraft carrier docked a short distance away.

"I see they have barbecue and tacos if you don't want a hamburger," Betsy suggested.

"I'd rather have pizza."

"They don't have pizza, but you have the three choices I gave you." Betsy fixed him with her gaze.

"Tacos, I guess." He shifted in his seat to get a better look at the ship.

Betsy turned to see what he was interested in and after giving their order to the waitress, she said, "Billy, it's too nice to hibernate indoors today. Let's do something special. Is there anything you would like to do?"

"I don't care."

"There must be something." She nodded toward the aircraft carrier. "...like touring the *Lexington*."

"Could we...really?" Billy leaned forward. "I've always wanted to check it out but Dad never has the time to take me."

"We'll go as soon as we finish eating."

Billy's mood took a definite turn for the better. He wolfed down his tacos and two sodas before asking, "Are you finished yet?"

"Almost."

"If you aren't going to eat those potato chips, can I have them?"

"Sure." She pushed the paper plate heaped with the ridged chips toward him.

Billy took a handful, then stood beside the table to get a better look at the *Lexington* while he popped them into his mouth one at a time. "She's called the 'Blue Ghost.' Did you know that?"

Betsy did know, but pretended not to. "Really. Why's that?"

"Because during the war, the Japanese kept on claiming they sunk her and she kept coming back." He changed the subject when he saw Betsy get out her purse. "Will you let me pay out?"

"Sure." She handed Billy a couple of bills and watched him go to the counter and pay their check before they headed the few yards to the ship. As they trudged through the summer heat, she vowed to make Nick aware that he was going to have to make room in his life for his son. The man was not doing a good job as a father. She could sympathize with him—his job did demand a lot, and being a single parent was difficult. But for the sake of the boy, he was going to have to make adjustments.

After Betsy purchased tickets, they walked up a wide ramp that led to the center of the hangar deck. Betsy wondered if Nick even knew what he was missing. Why did one never appreciate how important something was until it was gone?

A gray-haired World War II veteran with the posture and dignity of a young naval academy cadet met them. "Just follow the arrows. The tour takes about two hours," he said, handing Betsy a brochure and pointing to the bow.

"Can I have that?" Billy asked Betsy and reached for the tour map.

"Only if you promise to be my guide." She handed him the map, noticing how he stifled a satisfied look as he studied it. "Reading maps is hard work, isn't it?" she said.

"Aw, it's easy. I'll help you sometimes." Billy took off toward the bow. "It says we start over here."

Betsy had to hurry across the metal deck to keep up with the energetic boy. Billy reminded her of Jake, her younger brother who had died when he was nine. When Jake was alive, they had fought all the time, but when he was gone, there had been a big hole in her life that had never been filled. Her parents had adjusted on the outside, but to this day, whenever the family got together, there were things that just weren't mentioned, places that no one went, circumstances that were avoided. Christmas had never been the same.

Shaking off the beginnings of melancholy, she followed Billy up narrow stairs to the flight deck. Then they followed the arrows through the ship that had recently been turned into a museum. Yes, her goal for the summer was to make Nick a better parent and in turn make Billy a happier child.

"Come on, Miss Johnson," Billy encouraged her when she paused to study a brass compass. "There's lots more."

Everywhere, signs saying Do Not Enter kept the tourists out of harm's way. Except Billy.

"Boy, Daddy would love this." Billy ducked under the yellow chains and started up a ladder that was clearly marked off-limits.

The poignancy of Billy's yearning for his father cut into Betsy's heart at the same time as she grabbed his hand and pulled him back. "You aren't supposed to go up there," she reprimanded.

"But I want to."

"We don't always get to do everything we want."

"My daddy lets me," Billy protested.

"I'm not your daddy." Her voice was firm but she couldn't help sympathizing with Nick. Suddenly she had a much clearer picture of what the Lupton home must be like. Nick probably compensated for Vicki's death by being over permissive. Billy needed a little discipline. No, he needed a lot of discipline wrapped in love. Before it was too late.

IT WAS AFTER five o'clock when Billy and Betsy got back to her house. Billy walked into her spotless living room, looked around, picked up the television remote and began flipping through the channels.

Betsy chose to ignore him while she checked her mail and played her telephone messages.

She smiled at the sound of Robert King's voice. "Honey, I've been trying to get a hold of you for days. Where've you been hiding? Let's go diving in Cozumel for the weekend. All the gang is going. I should be home in an hour. Give me a call. Love ya."

Robert was such a sweetheart. Too bad he didn't make her heart beat one bit faster, she thought as she changed clothes, then loaded breakfast dishes into the dishwasher before she joined Billy in the living room. He lay sprawled on the carpet, still clicking through the channels at a rate of one every five or six seconds.

Without looking up, he asked, "Who was that man?"

"An old friend."

"You going diving with him?"

"I might."

"Are you going to marry him?"

"*That,* young man, is none of your business. Here, let me have the remote, please."

"I'm not through with it."

Betsy bent over and took the device from his hand. "You've had your turn. Now, it's mine." She stretched out on the cushioned sofa and wriggled her toes. Her feet ached to the bone from the afternoon hike over hot metal decks.

Billy mumbled something under his breath when she changed the channel to the news but Betsy ignored his little snorts.

After several minutes, he said, "There's nothing to do around here."

"You could do your math homework."

"I left my stuff at school."

"Isn't it in your backpack?" she asked.

"No." He ducked his head. "I thought I'd get to help Dad at the aquarium, so I left it in my desk."

"Well, you can come in a little earlier tomorrow and get it done." How could a person chastise a child like Billy without destroying what little spirit the boy had left? She wasn't up to it.

"Would you please hand me my hairbrush on the end table beside your chair, then why don't you recite the multiplication tables through the twelves while I listen to the news?"

"Big deal. That's not much to do." Nevertheless, he stood up, picked up the brush and brought it to her.

"Thank you, Billy. After the news is over, we'll find you something to do." She took the brush and started brushing her hair, allowing it to feather over the arm of the sofa.

Billy recited a few of the multiplication tables as he stood and watched her, a faraway look developing in his eyes. Then he asked softly, "Can I do that?"

Betsy was surprised but caught herself in time not to show it. "Yes, if you'd like."

Taking the brush from her extended hand, Billy walked around to the end of the sofa where she couldn't see his face. She felt him carefully draw the bristles through the strands.

As he brushed, he seemed to forget his earlier bad humor caused by having to listen to the news. After a while, he twisted her hair into a knot atop her head, then let it fall back over the arm of the sofa. He brushed the mane to one side of her head then the other. Finally, he awkwardly braided the strands of hair and walked around to face her.

When he appraised his creation, he giggled and said, "You don't look like Miss Johnson."

"Who do I look like?"

"You look like a witch," he said. "But a pretty witch."

"Thank you, I guess, if witches can be pretty."

He lifted the braid, then paused. "Your hair's longer than my mother's was," he whispered.

"You used to brush your mother's hair, didn't you?" she asked gently.

"Yeah. She's dead, you know."

"I know, Billy. You must miss her a lot." Betsy turned toward him, but he moved behind her where she couldn't see his face.

"Yeah." Clumsily, his fingers worked at undoing the braid he'd created. "My dad let her die." His voice was completely unemotional. He could have been talking about the weather.

"I'm sure that's not true." Betsy's heart ached for the boy. How did a ten-year-old cope if he believed his father was to blame for his mother's death?

"It is, too. I heard him tell my grandmother and I heard...." He stopped as if he were afraid to reveal too much.

"Maybe you heard him say something when he was just upset and blaming himself in some way. I'm sure he didn't really mean whatever you heard." She rested her weight on her elbow and reached out to Billy.

He backed away from her. "My dad doesn't say things he doesn't mean." Dropping the brush onto an end table where it clattered to a rest, he plopped down in a chair, rubbed his eyes with the back of his sleeve and stared at the television screen.

This time she didn't try to comfort him.

CHAPTER THREE

NICK LUPTON TOOK the three steps to Betsy's front porch one at a time, leaned against the beige brick and pressed the doorbell. She had a nice place. Even in the moonlight filtering through the palms, he could tell that the lawn was mowed and the flower beds tended. Wearily, he massaged the back of his neck, wondering if she and Billy had had a better day than he.

When the doorknob rattled, he took a deep breath and straightened the kinks out of his long limbs. He knew he looked haggard with his wrinkled clothes and disheveled hair.

Before getting out of the car, he'd checked himself in the rearview mirror to make sure he didn't have blood or worse on his face. What he'd seen didn't please him. Short brown stubble sprouted from his chin and dark rings circled his tired green eyes. Today, he looked every bit of his thirty-eight years plus some extra.

He was stifling a yawn when the door opened. "Sorry it's so late."

"You needn't apologize. I didn't have anything planned tonight." Betsy brushed a strand of hair out of her face and smiled. "When you called, you said it might be after ten before you got here." She held open the door and motioned, "Come on in."

He followed her inside and looked around at the graciously decorated living room. Green must be her favorite color, he decided. A dark green-and-salmon-print sofa and love seat formed an L in the center of the room. The arrangement and colors evoked the outdoors. Neither rustic nor contemporary, it was warm and comfortable, with the comfort enhanced by a warm spicy smell drifting from the kitchen. His stomach growled audibly.

Betsy smiled. "Sounds like you haven't had supper. Billy wanted pizza so that's what we had."

"That's the food of choice this month. Next month it will be something else."

"There's some left. Would you like a piece?"

He raised a hand in protest. "No, that would be an imposition. It's late."

"Nonsense. I'll just have to throw it out since it won't be any good tomorrow. How about some iced tea to go with it?"

"I shouldn't put you to the trouble, but it sounds great. I haven't stopped since eight o'clock this morning." He chose the sofa and sat down. "Where's Billy?"

"He's asleep in my room," Betsy called from the narrow galley kitchen off the living-dining room. "Do you take sugar?"

"Lots." Nick leaned back, envying Billy for being asleep. The sound of Betsy moving around in the kitchen blended with the comfort of the sofa. He closed his eyes.

When Betsy returned to the living room with a tray holding two tall glasses of tea and a plate of warm pizza, Nick was sprawled with his legs crossed at the ankles in front of him, head against the back of the sofa. Hearing her approaching, he opened one eye then the other before raising himself to an upright position. He started to get up.

"No, no," she said, motioning him to stay seated. "Just stay on the sofa."

"Thanks." He savored the aroma, then took a big bite out of the pizza she handed him. It was delicious, but a liver sandwich would have been good at that moment, and he hated liver. After swallowing, he asked, "Did you have trouble getting Billy into bed?"

"Not much." Betsy took a seat beside Nick.

He raised a questioning eyebrow. "It's a struggle every night at home. He can dream up a thousand and one things he needs to do or ask."

"That's probably because he doesn't want to be separated from you. It's understandable, considering what he's been through." She added, "Of course, tonight it helped that he was so tired he couldn't keep his eyes open."

Nick shook his head in disbelief and said, "What did the two of you do this afternoon?"

"We toured the *Lexington*. It was fun, except for all the walking. That ship must have ten miles of metal decks. I was so glad when we got to the fantail. Billy let me stop there for a soft drink at the snack bar, but he slurped his down in record time. He didn't want to waste a minute."

"Did you see it all? The ship, I mean."

"Are you kidding?" Betsy waved her hands back and forth. "Up and down, back and forth. Billy had the map and he planned to see everything printed on it. We even went to the sick bay, which is where my feet needed to stop."

He glanced at her shoeless feet. "Did you wear those red shoes you had on this morning?"

She was surprised that he remembered the sling-backed heels she'd been wearing when she came to the aquarium with Billy. It seemed too long to have been that morning. "Unfortunately. From now on, I'm carrying a pair of tennis shoes in the car trunk for such emergencies."

He leaned forward and flipped through the illustrated book about the ship's history lying on the coffee table. "Did you get this today?"

"Uh-huh, while Billy looked at everything in the ship's store."

"I know Billy must have enjoyed the day." Nick closed the book and sat back. "He's mentioned several times that he wanted to go."

"Then why didn't you take him?"

"I haven't had the time." Nick took a gulp of tea and set the glass on a ceramic coaster on the end table. "Anyway, he got to go. That's what's important."

"It isn't the same, Nick. He wanted to share it with you."

Staring at the cover of the book to keep from seeing the censure that he was sure was in her eyes, Nick gritted his teeth. She was trying to make him feel guilty. Again. "When Vicki was alive, she didn't want him out in crowds like that," he explained, even though he didn't think it was any of her business.

When Betsy touched his bare arm softly to get his attention, he looked up. Her voice was only slightly above a whisper. "I see. Have you talked to Billy about how he feels ... toward you ... about his mother's death?"

Nick stiffened. "Do you ask the parents of all your students such personal questions? Or am I being given preferential treatment?"

Choosing not to respond to his question, Betsy withdrew her hand from his arm and sat up straighter. "Billy has some misconception that you. ..." She paused, apparently searching for the right words. "He said something this afternoon—"

"I'm sure he said a lot," Nick interrupted. "Just tell me what's bothering you."

"It really isn't my place to say."

"I can't believe that's going to stop you." He leaned back against the sofa in frustration. "You tell me I'm at fault, but you won't tell me what I'm doing wrong."

"I didn't say you were at fault. Stop putting words into my mouth." She leaned toward him. "I only said that you need to talk to Billy."

"If I'm going to get another lecture on parenting, I'll leave now." He made a move to get up.

"Please hear me out. All I'm asking is that you talk to Billy." She hesitated, then continued, "He blames you for his mother's death in some way. Now, you can call it meddling if you wish, but he needs some reassurance that he's mistaken."

Nick felt as if he'd been hit as he slumped back against the sofa. "Where did he get that idea?"

"He said he heard you say something to your mother."

Nick never really talked to Billy about Vicki's death. He'd just assumed that because Billy never brought it up, he was dealing with it in his own way. The boy had shied away and refused to talk the few times Nick had tried to bring up the subject. He should have tried harder. "I guess you're right, Ms. Johnson. I should talk to him if that's what he thinks."

"Good." She changed the subject. "And how about dropping the Ms. Johnson. If I'm going to call you Nick, please call me Betsy. A couple of weeks ago, you offered to show me through the aquarium. Does the offer still stand?"

"Sure . . . Betsy."

"Would any day be okay?"

"Probably. Just give me a call, and as long as we don't have another day like today. . . ."

"You said you thought you were onto something about the birds when you called earlier this evening," she said.

"I may be." He turned to face her. "Betsy, until I'm sure what happened, what I'm about to tell you is just between you and me."

"Of course."

"The birds got hold of some trichlorothon, a pesticide we use." Just saying the words out loud made his skin crawl.

"Poison?" Betsy frowned. "How on earth could—"

"I don't know—yet. We keep all chemicals like that under lock and key."

"You think someone purposely poisoned them?"

"I want to believe it was an accident, but I don't see how it could be."

"Could it have gotten in their food by mistake?"

"I don't think so. Chances of the food's becoming contaminated are almost nonexistent. The first thing we did this morning was pull the food and check it."

"You didn't find anything." She said it as a statement of fact.

Nick sighed. "It was clean. The food preparation area is almost sterile. Sue, our nutritionist, disinfects it at the end of every day. It's far cleaner than any home or restaurant kitchen."

"If she cleaned it last night, couldn't she have erased any evidence before you got a chance to look it over today?"

"Perhaps, but Sue wouldn't do—"

"I don't mean that she would knowingly destroy evidence. My question was rhetorical."

Nick nodded. He had considered the same thing. "Birds get sick almost immediately. If they had been poisoned yesterday, they would have started dying within a few hours."

"But it could have happened?"

"Yes, but I would expect to find some trace of poison. None of the pans, tubs, nothing had any residue."

"Does Sue have any help in the kitchen?"

"Yes, sometimes the volunteers help out, but they're very careful. None of them would ever do anything to hurt the birds. They treat the birds like abandoned babies."

Betsy shook her head. "Maybe it was just a freak accident and won't happen again."

"I have to believe that. I stayed for a while tonight to see if any more birds became ill, but none did, thank goodness."

"I don't know what to say. I know you must care for the birds . . . and the fish."

Nick thought of all the species housed at the aquarium and smiled. "Someday I'll tell you a story or two about their antics. They're so interesting to watch, and I want everyone to have a chance to enjoy them as much as I do. That's why I've worked so hard to make the aquarium a reality."

Betsy nodded and leaned toward him, indicating her interest as he continued, "I supervised the acquisition of animals. I've dived to the deepest parts of the Gulf all in search of the perfect specimen." He paused and took a deep breath. "And today I realized how easily it could all disappear."

Betsy's warm eyes searched his face. "I do understand."

Nick shrugged. He'd said more than he'd intended. He wasn't much for sharing personal feelings, but she was so easy to talk to. She acted as if she really did understand and care.

"The aquarium is lucky to have a man like you." She reached over and squeezed his hand. Her fingers were almost as long as his, and they closed firmly around his hand. "I'm glad I could help a little by taking care of Billy today."

Her warm touch was reassuring. Emotions he hadn't felt for months formed tiny cracks in the dull lifeless plain where his heart had once been. Emotions he wasn't ready to feel. He had to get away from Betsy Johnson. He needed to think.

Unable to think of anything appropriate to say, he followed Betsy's cue. "Speaking of Billy, I'd better get him and let you go to bed."

THE NEXT MORNING Nick walked through the quiet aquarium, enjoying the peace. He breathed deeply of the marine life aroma and closed his eyes. He imagined himself in the Gulf waters. He liked being here in the early-morning silence before the crowds arrived. It gave him time to appreciate the life abounding in the tanks.

The night had been long. He'd tossed and turned, first with worry for the birds, then with unwelcome thoughts of Betsy Johnson. The woman was like both ends of a magnet, pulling him to her and pushing him away. No, it was guilt that pushed him away. He'd been glad when morning had arrived, and it was time to leave for work.

As he slid the key out of the lock to his office, he caught the flash of light as the automatic timer activated the lights in the tanks. Seven a.m. As he did every morning, he poured water through the small drip coffee maker and waited for it to brew before beginning his early-morning rounds.

First, he had to check the birds to see if they had all survived the night. Of course, Steve, the night-duty operations manager, would have called him if anything had been amiss. Sipping his coffee from a ceramic mug, he strolled through the paths that would be crowded with noisy visitors in a few hours. His silent tennis shoes didn't signal his presence even though his heart roared in his ears as he approached the birds in the Marsh, Dune and Bay exhibits. The cacophony coming from the hungry fowl was deafening. They were fine.

By the time Nick got back to his office, Tom and two other divers had shown up to clean the tanks. Nick stuffed his hands into his pockets and rocked back and forth on his heels while they prepared their gear. He didn't like what he was going to have to do, but it was his job. "Guys, when you finish, come to the conference room. We need to have a staff meeting."

Tom nodded as he pulled a blue and yellow wet suit from the rack. "About the birds?"

"Yes."

"How'd you find things this morning?"

"No problems."

Tom twisted to roll the neoprene suit up his body. "It was just some stupid accident. It won't happen again."

"We have to make sure it doesn't." Nick really wanted to accept Tom's reasoning that the poisonings had been the result of someone's carelessness. But whose? And would it happen again?

By eight-thirty, nine people had assembled in the conference room. Along with Sue, Tom and a couple of volunteers who helped with the birds, Chester the chemist, two marine biologists and a couple of divers who usually fed the fish, were sitting around the laminated table. Nick stood with one foot propped on a chair.

"I'm sure by now everyone is aware of what happened yesterday," Nick said watching the expressions on each person's face as he talked, not sure what he was looking for there.

Tom nodded. "I saw the same type of thing when I worked at a vet research center. I might have been of more help if you'd asked."

Nick wanted to ask him why the hell he hadn't said something before now, but he figured that this was just more of Tom's exaggerations about his exploits. The others in the group ignored Tom, as well.

Nick continued, "We don't want to alarm anyone, but we have to be extra careful. We don't know how the birds got the poison. One possibility is a visitor fed the birds something that was contaminated."

Tom interrupted. "The birds wouldn't take food from a stranger."

"That's probably true in most cases. But we have to consider every possibility. The next step is for each of us to fill out a Lost Animal Incident Review. I'll call you into my office one at a time this morning to go over where you were and what you did yesterday morning after coming to work."

"Sounds like you suspect one of us," Chester said.

"To the contrary, Chester. I don't suspect anyone on this staff. This is just routine, and a log of your activities is for your protection. I've already got mine written."

While the staff wrote their reports, he talked, partially to deflect any feelings of accusation. "Today is a fast day, so none of the big fish are being fed, maybe eliminating the chance of them getting poisoned. But the birds have to have food. Though we have volunteers in the marsh, we need the staff to take a turn watching the area for a while, just to be on the safe side. I'll make up a schedule."

Mary Alice raised her hand. "I'll volunteer to watch the other volunteers." She smiled at her pun.

Nick left the staff room with Chester, then hurried to his office where the telephone was ringing. He picked up the receiver and held it between his ear and shoulder while he flipped through the incident logs in his hand. "Nick Lupton here. May I help you?"

"Betsy Johnson here, and yes, you can help me." He could almost hear the laughter in her voice as her words echoed his. "Your secret is out. It seems Billy has told everyone in summer school about the dead birds. Every kid here wants to come to the aquarium. With whom do I need to talk about setting up a time for a tour?"

Nick tried to shift his thoughts from his problems to the even more disturbing woman on the other end of the phone. "For that whole troop I saw the first day?"

"No, just the students who have made real progress. Maybe twenty—tops. This will be a reward."

"Oh. Well, that sounds like a good idea." He wondered if Billy would be one of those rewarded.

"When you got to work this morning, were there any more sick birds?"

"No, everything's fine."

"That's a relief."

"And thanks again for taking care of Billy yesterday."

"You are very welcome. We had a good time." She changed the subject. "Now, who makes arrangements for tour groups?"

"Renee Vaughn is our director of educational programs. She can help you."

"You're kidding. Renee Vaughn who used to teach? We taught together for several years until she got married and moved away."

"If it's the same Renee, she moved back. She's worked here since the aquarium opened three years ago."

"I'll give her a call and set up a time." She paused. "Maybe I'll see you then...if you help with the tour."

After he hung up the receiver, he thought about what she'd said. The prospect of leading a crew of ten- and eleven-year-olds anywhere for two hours would probably be something like taking an unleashed Saint Bernard through a curio shop. Not something he'd relish doing. On the other hand, he wouldn't mind an excuse to spend time with Betsy.

He looked at the detailed Lost Animal Incident Review he'd been studying, then tossed it down with the others. There was over an hour unaccounted for on Tom's sheet. He'd have to call him and get an explanation.

Nick's thoughts returned to the woman who'd just hung up. She affected him more than he wanted to admit.

CHAPTER FOUR

"RENEE, it's wonderful to see you!" Betsy hugged the aquarium's education director then glanced over her shoulder to make sure her cosponsor was having no trouble corralling the twenty eager students who had earned the field trip. Then she turned her attention to her old friend. "How have you been?"

"Really well." Renee smiled broadly. "It's great to see you again, too. By the way, what's this I hear about you being a principal?"

"It's assistant principal, but, still, can you believe it? Me? The rebellious teacher who was always in hot water with the administration?" Betsy rolled her eyes in remembrance. "I've reformed. But, my news isn't anything compared to yours." She indicated Renee's enlarged abdomen. "When's the baby due?"

"In four long, hot weeks."

"Are you going to work until then?" Even though she thought Renee looked radiant, Betsy had noticed the swollen ankles.

"I was hoping to work until the delivery, but now I'm not so sure. Since Junior here is taking up more than his share of the breathing room, I'm having to slow down a bit." Renee breathed deeply as though to prove her point. "In fact, Dr. Lupton was scheduled to relieve me today and lead your tour group."

"Oh?" The thought of seeing Nick pleased her.

"But he called right before you got here and begged off," Renee continued. "He got hung up with a guy from Mexico about a shark, so I'm going to be your guide, after all. If we walk slowly, I'll do fine."

Although Betsy was glad to see Renee, she felt a quick stab of disappointment. She'd anticipated seeing Nick Lupton again, at least for a few minutes. And it had nothing to do with Billy's behavior.

"I understand those unexpected occasions. They're always cropping up at school," Betsy conceded. She'd see Nick another time. After all, he had again suggested a private tour of the aquarium. She'd remind him if need be. "Well, are you ready to get started?"

She and Louise, the other sponsor with the group, organized the students, giving them strict instructions about what they could and could not touch. Betsy was concerned that Billy, in particular, hear the rules because she feared he'd try to show off in front of the others. Satisfied that the students understood what was expected of them, Betsy stepped back to allow the excited children to follow Renee to the Living Shore exhibit.

Once there, Renee explained to the students, "This is the only exhibit where you can actually touch the animals." She picked up a mollusk shell and handed it to a little girl. "Inside this shell lives an animal that didn't make the shell. Can any of you tell me what it is?"

"A hermit crab!" Billy blurted out, not giving anyone else time to think.

"That's right. As a hermit crab grows larger," she explained, "it has to find a new shell for its home. So it may end up with several shells in a lifetime." After answering other questions about the crabs, she patiently answered more about sea urchins and starfish.

Just as the group was leaving the exhibit, a shrill voice screamed out. Everyone whirled around and saw a hermit crab clinging tenaciously to a little blondhaired girl's palm.

Renee cleared a path until she reached the little girl. After glancing at the child's name tag, she instructed, "Here, Amanda, just gently put your hand back in the water."

"No! Get it off!" Amanda refused to move her hand that was extended stiffly in the air.

"Crybaby," Billy sneered. "You scared it." He elbowed one of the other boys, and they both snickered and repeated the taunt. "Crybaby, crybaby."

Renee guided Amanda's hand into the pool. As soon as the child's palm was lying still on the surface of the water, the crab turned loose.

Betsy walked up behind Billy and whispered, "That's enough." She'd talk to him later.

Order restored, the group continued through the Sea Turtle exhibit where a more subdued Billy explained about the endangered Kemp's ridley. "That there is Tripod," he said, pointing out a large turtle. "He's called that because he only has three legs."

The other students gathered in close to listen. "What happened to his other leg?" one asked.

"A shark got it." Billy made a snapping motion with his mouth, obviously enjoying the spotlight. It was a change to see him getting positive attention rather than being disciplined for causing trouble, Betsy thought.

"Do you get to come here every day, Billy?" another kid asked.

"Yeah. I get to help feed the fish and nearly all the birds." He was practically swaggering as he led the way to the Island of Steel exhibit with Renee following close behind. Betsy, positioned in the middle of the group, hoped he didn't betray her trust.

Billy stopped and pointed. "This is the biggest tank here. It holds like about one hundred and thirty-two thousand gallons of water." Judging from the kids' faces, they were suitably impressed and Billy continued, "It's supposed to look like the bottom of an off-shore oil platform. That's where lots of fish gather in the ocean looking for food and a place to hide. There's over a hundred fish in this tank."

Amanda, who had been walking behind Billy listening to his comments, looked into his face with awe. "Gosh, Billy, you know a lot."

Betsy leaned toward Renee and whispered, "Looks like you may have lost your job."

"Child labor laws protect me," Renee answered wryly. "But, Billy probably does know as much or more than I do about the fish."

Betsy followed Renee and the others around a corner of the glass tank to get a better view. Suspended in the right side of the exhibit was a tripletail, and, on the bottom, near a barnacle-encrusted platform leg, swam a nine-foot nurse shark.

"Wow, look at that shark," one of the boys said excitedly. "I betcha that's as big as the one in *Jaws*."

"No, it's not," another child contradicted.

The children's ensuing argument about sharks amused Betsy and distracted her from where she was walking until she heard two men talking animatedly in Spanish. Looking up, she spotted Nick and another man standing in front of the tank. The man was pointing at the biggest shark.

When Nick glanced her way, she smiled and nodded.

"Betsy, come on over. This is Señor Salinas from Mexico City. He's come to see about the shark." After a few minutes of polite conversation, Nick excused himself and Betsy from the other man for a moment.

"I meant to help with this tour, but I got detained," Nick said. "How's it going?"

"Really well. Your son has taken over." She nodded toward Billy and his rapt listeners.

Just as Nick glanced toward his son amid the other students, Billy saw him.

"Hey, Daddy!" Billy started toward him. "Hey, guys," he said to the group of children tagging along beside him, "this here's my dad."

Nick greeted the kids.

"Mr. Lupton, Mr. Lupton," a shy little voice beckoned from the back of the group. "How come you're giving away a shark like Billy says?"

Nick's eyes sought out the youngster. "Because, son, sharks outgrow their tanks in captivity. We don't have the room to keep him."

"That's kind of like the hermit crab," Billy pontificated.

"If he's already nearly too big, can we feed him, then?" another child asked.

"Can't today," Nick said. "It's a fast day."

"Huh?" A freckle-faced kid wrinkled his nose.

"To fast means not to eat. We try to mimic their natural environment where they are more active and have to hunt for their food. Since they wouldn't find food every day in their natural habitat, we don't feed them every day. Twice a week we let them go hungry. How'd you like it if your parents didn't feed you twice a week?"

There was a collective groan. "That would be mean," one voice said.

"For you, maybe, but it isn't for the fish," Nick answered. "It helps offset the high-fat frozen diet we feed them. And I'm not talking about Fudgsicles."

Betsy watched Nick's face as he talked to the kids. He was good with them, mixing humor with information. She wondered why he couldn't be the same with his own son. If he would take some of that firmness and decisiveness he showed with other children and transfer it to Billy, she would be well on her way to achieving her goal for the summer.

Billy beamed with pride as Nick finally excused himself. "You kids have a good time. Now, I need to get back to Señor Salinas."

Looking at her watch, Betsy knew the tour was nearly over when Renee clustered the children into a couple of elevators and directed them to the lower level and onto the patio that sprawled up to the marsh that lay along two sides of the aquarium. There, she gathered the students into a tight little group. "Listen, carefully. The last section we'll see contains the river otters. It's a new exhibit and not quite finished."

"Wait'll you see this." Billy herded the kids after her.

"Students, watch your step." Renee indicated a narrow boardwalk as she continued her dialogue. "We're doing some construction for the otters. Even though they're relatively large creatures, they're also good escape artists. It's almost impossible to build an exhibit that they can't get out of."

Billy added, "Yeah, my daddy said that they can get through any hole they can stick their head in."

Renee paused to allow the group to assemble close to her. "These otters came to us from Missouri where they are still plentiful. Here in Texas, we don't trap them in the wild because they're rare. These otters lost their home because it was being developed for tourism."

As the students mumbled about the destruction of habitat, Renee started across the makeshift walkway to where the otters were temporarily housed, when she stumbled. Her cry alerted Betsy who watched in horror as Renee clawed at the air before her body tumbled slowly to the ground.

"Renee," Betsy yelled as she pushed her way through several students to reach the writhing Renee.

By the time Betsy reached her, Renee was lying on her side with her legs pulled up. Her hands clutched at her stomach. Betsy knelt and listened to Renee's labored breathing. "Billy, go inside to the front desk to get help." As an afterthought, she added, "Get your dad, too."

Billy broke from the group and dashed to the elevator. "Ohhh, it hurts." Renee rubbed her abdomen. "I think I've done it."

"Try to relax, Renee, and don't move," Betsy instructed. "I've sent for help."

Louise took up the slack for Betsy and led the curious students away from Renee into an empty courtyard. Betsy appreciated Louise's taking charge of the children. Although they were Betsy's responsibility, she knew they were in no danger. Renee was.

While Betsy held Renee's hand and wondered how long it would take help to arrive, Mary Alice hurried up.

When she saw Renee lying on her side in obvious distress, she stopped. "Oh, no! You poor thing." Mary Alice knelt next to Betsy. "I just came in for the day, and I heard Billy calling for his daddy. He said there'd been an accident. I thought...I mean...Renee. Oh, dear, this is awful."

Mary Alice's presence seemed to calm Renee, but Betsy didn't look up until Nick strode across the concrete toward them. "Thank goodness you're here," she said, glancing into his eyes. They were dark with concern.

"Help's on the way." He surveyed the scene before him. "What happened?"

She could feel the heat from his body as he squatted on one knee to give Renee comfort. It gave her comfort, too. "She tripped and fell."

AFTER THE SOUND of the ambulance siren faded into the distance, Betsy watched Nick hunched over the boardwalk, studying each plank leading up to the place where Renee had stumbled. She wondered what he was looking for.

Seemingly satisfied, he rose and came toward her. "I'm sorry that your tour turned out this way."

"So am I, but it's not the tour I'm worried about. I'm worried about Renee. Where is the ambulance taking her?"

"Spohn Hospital South." Nick stopped, then added, "I'm going to check on her as soon as I can get things settled here. Would you like to go with me?"

"Yes, I would, but I have to help Louise get these kids back to school first." Betsy looked toward the students who were happily sipping the soft drinks that Mary Alice had distributed to them.

Nick glanced back toward the boardwalk, then consulted his watch. "I'll pick you up at school. Say, in thirty minutes?"

"I CALLED the hospital just before I came over," Nick told Betsy as he held the door open for her to get into his Jeep. "Michael, Renee's husband, was already there," Nick explained. "He said that it looks like Renee may have gone into labor."

Betsy shook her head in dismay. "I was afraid of that. Thanks for inviting me to go with you to see her."

"Glad you wanted to go. We'll take Billy home," Nick said as his son climbed into the back seat.

"But I wanna go with you," Billy whined.

"Hospitals aren't any fun."

"But I wanna." Billy leaned forward into the narrow space between the adults.

"Billy, I don't think that's a good idea. You'd be bored in no time."

"No, I wouldn't. Pl-le-ease, Daddy."

"They won't allow you past the waiting room. You're too young."

"Come on, Daddy."

"Janie's expecting you."

"I don't wanna go home." Billy was still arguing in a whiny voice when they pulled into the driveway of a large two-story Spanish-style house.

"Be back in a second," Nick said to Betsy.

Betsy had sat silently through the discourse, biting her tongue and wishing she were somewhere else. The beautiful bay surrounding the point of land where the house sat wasn't enough to take her mind off the unhappy duo plodding down the walkway to the large double front door, still arguing.

She had seen Nick's address on Billy's file but hadn't actually realized where the house was situated. She was surprised. Somehow, she had pictured him living in a less showy setting.

In a few minutes, Nick came out of the house and climbed into the driver's seat. "I apologize for Billy's behavior."

"Why didn't you just tell him no?" Betsy asked as they backed into the street. She could see Nick bristle at her question.

"I did." Nick looked at her as though daring her to dispute him.

"No, you didn't."

"I thought I did," Nick persisted.

"No, not really. You left yourself wide open for an argument."

"Vicki always said a child should be reasoned with, not commanded."

Betsy knew she was treading on thin ice, contradicting his late wife. Still, she thought he should have been firmer with Billy. "There's nothing wrong with explaining things that need explaining, but sometimes you just have to say no."

"All right, have it your way. But let's drop it. Okay? I'm not in the mood for a lesson in parenting."

He could use several lessons in parenting, she thought, turning to stare out the window at the passing houses. She didn't understand this man. How could such an intelligent person allow himself to be manipulated by a child? Did he really believe he could help Billy deal with his mother's death by simply allowing the child to behave as he pleased?

HOURS LATER, Betsy watched Nick as he stood with one hand propped against the hospital window jamb. The orange hues of the setting sun backlit his finely chiseled profile as he studied the horizon. Beneath his controlled exterior, the hint of a frown threatened. She could tell he was nervous and doing his best to hide it.

Each time he raised his cup to take a sip of coffee, the muscles of his well-tanned arm rippled in reaction. Turning from the window, he straightened his body in an effortless, catlike movement. She watched, fascinated with the way he moved. But more, she was impressed that he was concerned enough about a co-worker to come to the hospital instead of ascertaining Renee's condition over the phone.

Glancing at her with eyes hiding any emotion, Nick tossed the empty disposable cup in the trash, then looked at his watch. "It's been almost two hours since we heard anything. Do you think something's wrong?''

"I don't know," Betsy admitted. "You probably know more about childbirth than I do. I've never had any children."

"Yeah, but you're a woman and women are supposed to know about childbirth. You know, instinct and woman-talk."

Betsy didn't respond, but instead watched as Nick paced the carpeted floor before he stopped in front of a framed blue infant's suit. He stared at it for several moments. "Vicki was in labor for a long time with Billy. It was rough."

"I'm sure it was." Betsy couldn't think of any other response.

With a sigh, Nick sat down beside her on the vinyl sofa and picked up a nearby *Field and Stream*. He flipped through it before tossing it aside and leaning his head back against the wall. He stretched his legs out, one arm resting on his abdomen, and closed his eyes.

Betsy wondered whether he was remembering another time he had sat and waited. She wanted to reach over and take his hand but didn't because she was afraid she would be intruding. But she wanted to help. "Did you go in the delivery room with your wife?"

"Yeah, Vicki went for all that natural stuff," he said, opening his eyes and looking at Betsy. "We even considered delivering the baby at home. Thank God we backed out of that." He grinned at Betsy, shaking his head at the memory. "Anyway, we did attend natural childbirth classes and thought we had all the answers." Nick rubbed his hand over his jaw. "After six hours, I started asking the doctors to give her something for the pain, but she refused. I don't know that I would ever want anyone I loved to go through that again."

"From what I've heard, most women think that it's worth it." Betsy looked over at him. "Did you and Vicki want any more children?"

"We'd discussed it," he admitted. "But Vicki said that one child took so much of her time she didn't want another. She was a really conscientious mother. She was always there for Billy. Until she died, Billy had never spent a night away from her. I thought it might have been good for him to have a brother or sister."

Betsy thought so, too. Then, wanting to direct the conversation away from Vicki, she brought up something that had concerned her earlier. "I saw you looking at the board where Renee stumbled. Was something wrong with it?"

"I'm not sure. It looked as though it might have been purposely loosened. I passed over that walkway yesterday several times. It didn't seem wobbly then."

"Surely, it was an accident. I can't imagine anyone deliberately wanting to hurt Renee."

"I doubt Renee was the intended victim."

Betsy remembered Renee saying that Nick had been scheduled to lead the tour. "If this mishap was planned, you were supposed to be the victim?"

He nodded. "I think so."

"But why? The most that could have happened to you would have been a sprained ankle or skinned knee."

"Maybe that was all that was supposed to happen." Nick leaned forward. "Anyway, I have the area closed off until I can get back and check it out. There's probably nothing to it. Just a little more bad luck."

"What about the saying that 'trouble comes in threes'?"

"Don't say that. If the birds are counted as one incident, we're only at number two." Nick ran his fingers through his hair. "You know what concerns me the most? If the birds were poisoned, then—"

"Renee's okay," a voice interrupted him.

Nick stood up. "That's great," he said to the young man dressed in green scrubs. "Betsy, this is Michael."

Betsy smiled. "Yes, I met Michael at his and Renee's wedding. It seems that I have an ability to show up for the special occasions. And the baby?"

Michael looked tired, but he smiled at Nick and Betsy. "We have a baby boy, Michael junior. He'll have to stay in the neonatal unit for a few days. The doctor said he's a little jaundiced but thinks he'll be okay."

Betsy sighed with relief. "Thank goodness."

Nick offered his hand to Michael. "Congratulations to the two of you. Since things are under control, and it's been a long day, Betsy and I should get going. If you need anything, call."

Nick was dog-tired as he eased his Jeep over the speed bump guarding the asphalt parking lot in front of the school. Security lights cast an eerie glow over the deserted block. Only Betsy's car was still there.

"I should have suggested that you leave your car at my house or we should have taken it by yours," Nick said as he surveyed the vacant surroundings.

Betsy stifled a yawn. "I thought of it, too, but neither of us had any idea it would be this late before we got back here."

"It's been quite a day." He swung his long legs out of the Jeep and went around to where Betsy already stood in the narrow space between their vehicles gazing up at the summer sky.

"The weather is so balmy and peaceful. Just look at the stars twinkling overhead. It's a beautiful night for a baby to be born," she said.

"Yeah, it is." He leaned one hip against the hood of her car, crossed his arms and studied her in the early-evening dusk. She looked as fresh now as she had earlier. The rhinestones studding her turquoise denim dress twinkled as she swayed. Nick was mesmerized. She didn't need the flashy clothing even though it fit her personality. The light shimmered off her long hair making him want to reach out to brush it away from her face. "Beautiful," he said, and he wasn't talking about the night.

She looked up at him, her eyes sparkling as much as the stars above them. "Do you believe that each child has a guardian angel to watch over them?"

"I suspect that every parent of a ten-year-old believes it."

"Well, Michael junior got his tonight."

"I think he must have gotten his early. Someone was already watching out for him."

"Nick, I know you're worried about Renee, but she'll be fine. It was an accident. But—" Betsy seemed to have a new thought "—will you have to do more tours...now that she's out?"

"Nope, remember that I only do VIPs on occasion. For general tours, personnel's already lined up a temp." He remembered that the woman hired for the job planned to be out of town until the week before she was scheduled to substitute for Renee. "Damn! She can't come in. Not for another three or four weeks."

"Oh, that's terrible." Betsy shook her head. "Maybe she'll reconsider."

"No, she's away. And this is our busiest time of year."

"Everything will work out. There's Mary Alice and other volunteers. Plus, more tours could be designated as VIPs," she teased. As she turned to insert her key into the lock, she added, "Wish I could help."

He reached out and caught her hand in his. "Oh, but you can." Nick was pleased with the idea that flashed through his mind.

"I can?"

"Sure. How would you like a summer job? Just three or four weeks."

"You're kidding? I don't know anything about aquariums."

"You can read up. If you'd be interested, I'll talk to Sammie in personnel tomorrow. It might not pay as well as stripping, but it's a lot more respectable . . . for a school principal."

CHAPTER FIVE

June meeting of the
Quilting Club

"WELL, did she take the job?" Bertha asked at our next club meeting while she dug through her sewing kit for her favorite thimble.

"Of course," I said, unable to conceal my pride. "In fact, she's going to be a real asset to the aquarium. Just you wait and see."

"I suppose," Bertha sniffed. "Of course, you can't overlook the fact that she'll be near Nick. I'm sure she didn't."

"I would hope not," Virginia offered. "They're both attractive people. And single."

"Perhaps, but I've noticed how brazen some women are when they go after widowers." Bertha took off on one of her tirades. "Why, the man down the street from me—before his poor wife's body was even cold—the ladies were lined up bringing him pies and offering their condolences. Ladies who'd never even met his wife."

I shot Bertha a withering look. "Betsy doesn't have to chase a man. There are plenty asking her out. For instance, Robert King has been after her to marry him *for years."* *"Years"* may have been stretching the truth a little, but I sure wasn't going to let Bertha imply that my Betsy was a wallflower.

Virginia came to my rescue. *"I'm sure she doesn't. Betsy, being the type of person to help people, would attract Robert and Nicholas, too. Nick undoubtedly needs her help."* Virginia got a distant look in her eyes and smiled as she held up her needle and adjusted the thread length. *"Then, too, I would think the aquarium offers the prospect of adventure."*

"Or at least a break from routine," I added. *"She went by the aquarium yesterday. She said everyone was so nice. A volunteer named Mary Alice—she's about our age, I'd say—offered to show her around. Betsy said she was really helpful."*

Era looked up from her quilting. *"They said she never did get over being jilted at the altar."*

"What did you say?" Sometimes it was impossible to follow Era's line of thought.

"Mary Alice," Era said, her needle stilled. *"She's the neighbor I was telling you about. They said her beau just went off and left her to have the baby in shame."*

The other three of us looked at one another, not sure who or what Era was talking about. *"You're saying this Mary Alice has a child?"*

"No, not anymore." Era looked puzzled as if she was surprised at what she'd said. *"I haven't seen that girl in over thirty years."*

"What happened to her?" Bertha asked. Bertha liked to gossip as much as she liked to discuss her health.

Era pursed her mouth and wrinkled her forehead, then shook her head. "I can't rightly recall."

When she began to fuss with the knot in the end of her thread, I knew that she'd said all she was going to on the subject. You can't put much credence in what Era says. Lately, she'd been getting things all confused.

Virginia redirected the conversation. "Has Betsy said how Billy is doing in summer school?"

I felt a certain amount of pride in telling about Billy's success, since I knew I had had a hand in it. "He improved enough to go on a field trip to the aquarium. Betsy says things are looking up."

CHAPTER SIX

"YOU SURVIVED the Sea Schoolers I see." Nick stood in the doorway to the resource center where Betsy was cleaning up after the last of the four-year-olds had left.

The sound of his voice made her stomach lurch. With the exception of adolescent infatuations, no man had ever discomfited her the way he did. "So, what did you expect?" Betsy slid the last book onto a shelf, then ran her fingers through her hair.

"Success," Nick answered. "I hid outside in the hall and watched part of your program. You did a good job."

Betsy cocked her head and looked at him. "Hid, did you? Well, I thought it went well." She didn't tell him that it took her three days to prepare the lesson. "Have you ever done any of the educational programs?"

"No. Not for me. I have a hard time keeping adults tuned in." Nick chuckled. "However, it was obvious you wanted to lose everyone's attention when that little boy wanted to know what the sea horses were doing."

Betsy moaned, rolling her eyes upward. "Sea horses! Sea horses should have been innocent enough. Teachers often have them in their classrooms along with gerbils and other animals for students to learn about. Why today, of all days, did they decide to mate?"

"You whipped those kids through the mating dance of the sea horse awfully quick."

"If it were only kids in the room, it wouldn't have been so bad. Some of them wouldn't have even noticed, but a few of the parents had gaping mouths. Funny thing, though, everyone wanted to get closer to see for themselves."

Nick laughed. "You should have seen the bored-looking woman in the back. Her head jerked up so hard she probably got whiplash when that kid blurted out—loudly—that the sea horses were making babies. I wouldn't expect her little girl back next week."

"I've only been here three hours and already you may be losing guests."

"Don't worry about it. You handled it well. But it *was* funny."

Betsy knew an account of the incident would spread to the aquarium's personnel before day's end, and she'd be subjected to friendly gibes as a result. She was glad that Nick saw the humorous side, anyway.

"What else is on your agenda for the day?" Nick asked.

"Lots. How to entertain two-year-olds is first. Conquering twenty-second attention spans may be quite a challenge. Then, I plan to study Renee's notes about the diving expedition to the Flower Gardens coming up next month. I'm really excited about that.

Until now, I've been put off by the eight-hour boat ride out. It's a lot easier to get to the other reefs.''

"That's exactly what makes this one special—its inaccessibility. Unlike many reefs that have heavy diver traffic, the Flower Gardens are in pristine condition. Absolutely breathtaking."

"Do you go there often?"

"I haven't been in a while." The sudden change of expression on Nick's face, which she couldn't really identify, kept Betsy from pursuing the subject.

"It's sad that our presence can cause harm to the reefs. If only people would be more careful."

"That's true," Nick said, nodding in agreement. "Now, tell me, have you run across any problems or concerns with your job that I can help you with?"

"No, but I am curious about the Fourth of July celebration. Mary Alice said it's big, big, big. I don't know what to expect."

"She's right. It is." His expression eased and some enthusiasm reentered his voice. "I've got some pictures at the house of past celebrations if you want to see them."

"Great. Anything I can learn in advance will make me feel better."

Mary Alice, clad in aqua polyester stretch pants and a flowered tunic, came into the room. "Did I hear my name mentioned?"

Betsy walked over and draped her arm around Mary Alice's shoulders. "This woman has been my life's blood the past three days, and, yes, you did hear your name when I mentioned the celebration on the Fourth.''

"Oh, yes. The Fourth." Mary Alice appeared lost in her thoughts. "Vicki always did most of the planning, didn't she, Nick?" Mary Alice said abstractedly.

"Yes," Nick agreed.

"It's just not the same without Vicki." The corners to Mary Alice's mouth turned down as she shook her head.

Silence. Betsy wished Mary Alice hadn't mentioned Vicki.

Nick cleared his throat and said to Betsy, "The reason I came in here was to tell you that we're loading the shark to send to Mexico this morning. Mother's bringing Billy to watch, and I thought you might like to observe the process, too."

"I'd love to." Not only was she interested in the shark, but it would be a way of getting out from under the cloud that Mary Alice had unknowingly caused. Mainly she wanted to be near Nick and watch him work with the shark.

"Let's go then." After they arrived at the wet area, Nick looked around and asked one of the two divers standing there, "Where's Tom?"

The diver replied with a shrug of his shoulders, "I haven't seen him this morning."

Nick swore under his breath as he surveyed the situation. "That leaves only us three. We're going to be a man short." He turned to her and pointed overhead. "You can watch from any place on the walk above the tank."

As Betsy watched Nick choose from a row of matching black and blue wet suits, she wished she could join in the dive, but knew it was impossible. Besides, she didn't know as much about capturing a shark as a shark would know about capturing her.

Tom, face flushed, came rushing in a few minutes later. "Sorry I'm late." He looked at the preparations under way. "You know, this would have been easier, Nick, if you'd arranged for a helicopter. When I worked at Sea World, we always moved the big fish with a chopper."

An exasperated look marred Nick's handsome face. Betsy could tell he wanted to discuss Tom's tardiness but refrained from doing so in front of the others. Instead, he said, "A helicopter would have been too expensive and wouldn't have been able to carry the water needed to transport this large a shark all the way to Mexico." He turned and started toward the dressing rooms.

Tom pursed his lips and turned to Betsy as he took his suit down from the hanger on the wall. "Did I mention that I used to photograph sharks underwater?" He didn't wait for her reply. "One almost got me off the coast of Australia once, but I managed to get my knife out . . . it was a bloody battle."

"No. I don't believe you've told me about that."

"When we have more time, I'll tell you all about it," he said over his shoulder as he hurried off.

Betsy wondered why Tom was late as she watched him head to a dressing room. His face wasn't as flushed as it was when he'd first come in, but he'd nervously checked his hair with his hands to see if it was in place while he talked to her.

Billy came dashing in the room, breaking into her thoughts. "Did I make it in time? Where's Daddy?"

"Hi to you, too, Billy. Yes, you did, and he's getting his wet suit on," Betsy answered. "Do you want to watch with me from the top? If you're nice, I promise not to push you in."

Billy's face froze momentarily, then he flashed her a grin. "You're teasing. You wouldn't push me in even if I was mean—would you?"

Betsy ruffled his hair. "No, Billy, not even if you were terrible. Where's your grandmother?"

"Grandma's staying downstairs. I think it makes her nervous to watch," Billy confided.

"You're going to join us, aren't you, Mary Alice?" Betsy turned and was surprised to see the older woman slumped in a chair, rubbing her knee. "What's the matter?" she asked, walking over and laying her hand on the woman's shoulder.

"Nothing's wrong that youth couldn't cure. My arthritis is acting up, is all. I don't think I'm up to climbing those steps today."

"You're sure you're okay?"

"Really, it's nothing. But I think I'll go sit down in a comfortable spot for a spell." Mary Alice headed off just as the divers assembled at the foot of the concrete stairway that led to a catwalk around the largest tank.

Nick walked over to his son and squeezed his shoulder. "Glad you made it, Billy. We're just ready to start," he said, then took off.

"Come on, Miss Johnson," Billy urged, nudging her. Dutifully, she clambered up the steps with Billy, then hung back as Nick and the other three divers stood around the ledge at the top of the tank and discussed what each person was going to do.

Four men that Betsy had not seen before climbed up the steps hauling a fiberglass and nylon stretcher to the side of the tank.

"That's what they're going to carry the shark on," Billy explained.

The divers sat on the edge of the tank and slid into the water as unobtrusively as possible. It was fascinating to watch them swim among the large predators. Nick patiently stalked the two-hundred-and-twenty-pound shark that was their target. She had to admire the finesse with which Nick slid the net over the shark's head.

Immediately, the other three divers grasped the flailing shark around the middle. The animal proved too strong for them, twisted out of their clutches and swam away.

"Damn! It got away," Billy hollered. He slapped his hand over his mouth and looked up at Betsy.

"Do you think that was bad enough for me to throw you in the tank?" Betsy asked with a straight face.

"No. I'm sorry, Miss Johnson. It just slipped out. I won't say that word again. You won't tell Daddy, will you?"

"It depends on how you behave from now on." Betsy realized Billy was serious and decided to quit teasing him. "No, I won't tell your daddy unless you say it again. Now, let's watch."

Nick signaled one of the divers to watch the other sharks in the tank.

"Daddy doesn't want one of them to sneak up on him from behind," Billy said without lifting his eyes from their focal point.

Betsy held her breath as Nick and the shark circled each other. Nick neared the shark and dropped back again and again as the shark swerved and glided through the tank. Betsy wished this was over.

"We can see better over there." Billy pointed out the far side of the tank.

Betsy wasn't sure she wanted to see better, but followed Billy to where he had pointed. The divers cornered the shark, and again Nick slid the net over its head and the divers converged on the captured beast. This time, the shark didn't resist as strongly, and the divers swam it to the side of the tank where the stretcher was waiting. Quickly, they slid the stretcher under the shark, and pulled it up on both sides of the animal.

As Betsy released her breath, Billy took off for the stairs. "I'll meet you at the truck, Miss Johnson."

Betsy wasn't ready to go to the truck, wanting instead to watch the entire process, wanting to make sure Nick was safe. She relaxed when he climbed out of the tank to check the animal for any sign of injury before it was strapped in and hauled away. Betsy walked a few feet behind as Nick followed the men carrying the stretcher to the waiting tank trailer.

Billy was jumping up and down at the truck when they got there. Betsy pulled him out of the way as they watched the men put the shark in the trailer equipped with pumps and oxygen for the long overland haul between Corpus Christi and Mexico City. Betsy was amazed at the efficiency that kept the shark out of the water less than five minutes. She was pleased that all had gone well for Nick.

ALL HAD NOT gone well. The next afternoon, Nick received a long-distance call from Señor Salinas informing him that the shark was dead on arrival. What had happened? Nick wondered as he waited for the truck driver to answer his phone somewhere in a hotel room in Mexico City.

"Hola," a sleepy voice answered.

"Jose?"

"Sí."

Nick switched to English when he was sure he had the right party. "What the hell went wrong?"

Instantly Jose was alert. "Damned if I know. All the pumps were working, everything appeared to be fine."

"Have you dumped the tank?"

"No, thought you might want a water sample."

"You thought right."

"Salinas already took one."

"Good. I'll see you day after tomorrow."

After hanging up the phone, Nick sought out Tom and found him feeding the river otters, which wasn't normally one of his duties. "Tom, would you come into my office as soon as you finish that."

He was reading the employee logs when Tom stuck his head in the door. Nick laid down the papers and leaned back in his chair. "The shark didn't make it."

Tom's eyes widened as he shook his head. "Why not? What happened?"

"I don't know yet. Salinas is doing a necropsy. I was hoping you could shed some light on what might have happened. There's an hour missing here in your Lost Animal Incident Review, and yesterday when we moved the shark, you were late."

Tom's face got red. "Are you accusing me of doing something to the shark?"

"No. I just want to know where you were."

"I wasn't killing anything. I can tell you that." He turned and stalked out of the office.

Nick leaned back in his chair and massaged the back of his neck. In his years as director of animal husbandry, he had never encountered such a string of what appeared to be unrelated accidents. Accidents?

He suspected that someone was deliberately trying to engineer the accidents. He'd go to the police with his suspicions, but he could just imagine their reaction. Some birds were dead, but he had no evidence that anyone had poisoned them. An employee had tripped on a loose board. The cops would put all their manpower on that one. Now a shark had died somewhere between Brownsville and Mexico City. He had nothing to go on but his own instincts. No motive. No suspects.

Even though Tom got on his nerves, he didn't think the man was guilty of foul play. But who?

BETSY WAS WATCHING the river otters play in what would soon be their newly completed enclosure near the outdoor marsh, when she saw Nick approaching. He looked tired and her heart went out to him. So far, they hadn't actually worked together but he had been available to answer questions, and she'd had plenty of questions.

She had been surprised to learn that he was considered one of the nation's experts on marine life. He was so modest about his accomplishments. She smiled as he neared her. "Hello, how has your day been?"

"I've had better." He looked at the otters rather than her.

"What's wrong?" She studied the side of his face nearest her. Tiny lines radiated from the corner of his eye, lines she hadn't noticed yesterday.

He turned and looked at her. "The shark died in transport."

"Oh, no. What happened?"

"I don't know yet."

"I'm sorry, Nick." She laid her hand on his sleeve, knowing she couldn't ease his pain. "You took so many precautions."

He closed his hand over hers and held it against his arm as if drawing comfort from her. "Apparently not enough. This was number three." He managed a halfhearted smile. "Didn't you say trouble came in threes?"

THERE WERE NO more mishaps the following week, so Nick left the aquarium earlier than usual on Friday to spend some time with Billy. He felt guilty leaving but knew that Billy needed his time as much as the animals did. Besides, he was tired of the twelve- and fourteen-hour days.

"Hey, river rat," he called to his son, wondering how long it had been since he'd called him that. "Wanna go work on the sailboat?"

Hardly before the words were out, Billy tore down the hallway with a grin plastered across his face and shoes in his hands. "Yeah, le'me put these on."

They went out to the backyard and walked down to the dock. Nick was glad he'd gotten home at a decent hour. Side by side, he and Billy polished metal and oiled the teak trim of the white boat as they talked.

Thinking about what Betsy had told him, Nick knew he needed to patch up his relationship with Billy before his son doubted his love. Now would be a good time to bring up Vicki's death, but he'd been dreading having the talk. Billy was just beginning to relax with him.

"Daddy?"

"Mmm?" Nick looked up from his task.

"Did you ever find out what killed the shark?"

"Yeah. Some chlorine got in the water in the transport trailer."

"How?"

"I haven't been able to find out. That's why I've been working so much." He didn't want to discuss the aquarium's latest incident. "We need to get this finished," Nick said. "I need to shower before Ms. Johnson gets here."

"What's she coming for?" Billy's polishing slowed down.

"She wants to look at some pictures of the aquarium's Fourth of July party."

"Oh." Billy studied his father. "Do you like Miss Johnson, Daddy?"

"Sure. She's a nice lady." Nick got to his feet, touched by the sadness in his son's eyes. "Why do you ask?"

"Uh, I just thought maybe...uh, I don't know." Billy stopped and looked out over the bay. He was silent for a few seconds, then he mumbled, "I miss Mom."

Nick hardly heard the faint words, but his heart registered the emotion. "I know, son." He walked around to stand beside Billy. Laying a hand on his son's shoulder, he said, "I miss her, too."

When Billy didn't respond, Nick continued, "I would give anything if I could bring her back."

"What *really* happened, Daddy?"

Nick flinched when Billy stressed the word really. "Billy, she drowned."

Billy looked up at him, his eyes narrowed in an accusing manner. "Yeah, sure."

"That's the truth." Realizing the time of reckoning had come, he squatted on one knee in front of his son and grasped the little boy's shoulders with both hands. "Billy, look at me. I don't know what you think you heard, but I didn't want your mother to die."

"She told you!" Billy grew rigid.

"Who?"

"Miss Johnson. She told you what I said."

"She thought it was best that I knew so I could help you."

"I don't need any help." Billy twisted away and ran up the dock toward the house.

Nick stood and watched him go. So much for his father-son talk. It was quite obvious that Billy didn't believe him about Vicki. Boy, he'd made a real mess of things.

He followed the same path Billy had taken up the wooden steps to the backyard. He went into the house and paused in the kitchen to get a drink of water, then filled a glass for Billy before he headed upstairs. He tapped on the closed door to Billy's room.

"Leave me alone," came a muffled sound.

"Okay, Billy. Later." Nick headed down the hall to the shower. He felt soiled in more ways than one.

He was still dripping wet when Billy called from the hallway. "I'm going to spend the night with Grandmother. Bye."

"Wait, when did this come about?"

"I called her. She's here now to pick me up."

Nick threw on a cotton robe and followed Billy down to the den, drying his hair with a towel as he went.

A tall, elegant woman stood looking out the glass wall that faced the bay. He crossed the room and gave his mother a kiss on the cheek. "Hello, Mother."

She raised an eyebrow and frowned. "Billy said that he needed a place to stay for the night because you were having a guest."

Nick glared at his son for putting him in a predicament. He didn't want to tell his mother that Billy was manipulating them. "It's not quite the way it sounds. Ms. Johnson, the assistant principal at Billy's school, has been doing some summer work at the aquarium. She's just dropping by to pick up some pictures. I think Billy was just missing you and Dad, so that was as good an excuse as any."

She smiled and laid a protective hand on Billy's shoulder. "He never needs an excuse to visit us. We love to have him."

"I know, Mom, and I really appreciate it. I'll pick him up in the morning."

Nick wished he'd handled the discussion about Vicki's death with more finesse and given Billy the reassurance the boy needed. Being a good father wasn't easy, Nick realized, but he was determined to undo the damage he'd done.

Tomorrow.

CHAPTER SEVEN

As BETSY STOOD on the steps of Nick's house and waited for someone to answer the doorbell, she looked around and wondered about the life that Nick and Vicki had led here. The green lawn, lined with tall palmettos, multicolored bougainvillea in pots and scattered oleander defied the salt air. Betsy didn't like to think of Nick with Vicki. Maybe she shouldn't have suggested coming by for the pictures Nick had promised to let her see. But he had seemed pleased.

Her back was to the door when she heard it open. She turned slowly and faced Nick. She was more attracted to him than any man she'd ever met. It wasn't just his lean good looks, but the way he moved with purpose when he didn't realize she was watching, and the way his smile began in the corners of his piercing green eyes then traveled to his mouth when he was amused.

"Afternoon, Betsy," he said in an uncharacteristic drawl. "Come on in." He stepped back to let her enter, then he closed the large carved door behind him. "Straight ahead."

She paused briefly when she stepped into the immense den. An entire wall overlooked Corpus Christi

Bay and the Gulf of Mexico. She walked straight to the windows where she gazed at the breathtaking green expanse. "What a beautiful view."

"I enjoy it." He nodded in agreement. "Would you like something to drink? Margarita?"

"Mmm. That would be perfect. Where's Billy?"

"He's spending the night with my folks."

She hadn't realized they would be alone, but was delighted. Did he want to be with her as much as she wanted to be with him? "You didn't mention that this afternoon."

"Billy wasn't angry with me then."

She watched as Nick squeezed the fresh limes. So much for her hopes that Nick had planned for them to be alone. "What happened?"

Nick flipped the lime peels into the trash. "We had the little heart-to-heart you'd suggested. I'm afraid I didn't handle it very well, and he got angry."

"Oh, Nick. I'm sorry."

"It's not your fault. The fact that we even discussed it at all is a start. I hate to admit it, but you were right. Billy blames me for his mother's death." His gaze met hers in a moment of agonizing silence. "I owe you one for letting me know."

"I just wish things had turned out better. But don't give up."

"I won't." Even though the problem with Billy had Nick concerned, he was glad Betsy had come. She understood. Her presence made him feel better. It was impossible to be unhappy in the same room with a woman as beautiful as Betsy in her bright sundress. While he finished the drinks, he noticed she seemed nervous as she walked around the room and studied the photos and plaques on the walls.

She stopped in front of an award. "What is this one for?"

"I don't remember." He joined her and looked at the piece of wood and brass. Her body was mere inches from his and the softest scent of flowers and musk teased his nostrils.

"These don't mean anything to you, do they?" She turned to look at him, her head cocked slightly, and a look of incredulity on her face.

"They're not alive. It's the animals that are important." When he handed her the pale green grass filled with lime ice, her fingers covered his briefly. The contact set every nerve in his body tingling. He watched her raise the stemmed glass and lick the salt off the rim with the tip of her tongue. His own mouth was suddenly dry and he fought the desire to draw her into his arms and taste her soft lips.

She stepped back but held his gaze over the rim of her glass as they each took a sip. "Umm...delicious."

Tearing his eyes from hers, he looked at the drink in his hand then back up to her bare neck and shoulders. He felt an uncontrollable urge to touch the velvety skin exposed. Tonight she was more than Billy's principal, more than a colleague. She was a desirable woman.

Betsy was suddenly aware of the warmth in the room. Men had never made her nervous, but then no man had ever bowled her over before. She could almost feel Nick's gaze as it caressed her skin and she wanted to feel his touch, as well. He fixed her with his gaze as surely as he invaded her heart. To diffuse the growing tension she forced herself to ask, "May I see the pictures you were going to show me?"

Nick set his drink down. "Certainly. I'll get them right now." He walked over to a row of built-in ceiling high white shelves and removed a photo album from among several.

Taking a deep breath to regain her composure, Betsy settled in the center of the heavy Spanish-style sofa eager to see the pictures. Nick sat beside her and pointed to the first picture in the album. "This one was taken the year the aquarium opened."

She tried to ignore the effect he was having on her heart beat, as he explained the events connected with the picture. Studying the photo of Nick surrounded by a group of people in black ties and evening gowns, Betsy searched the faces, wondering if one of the women was Vicki. She wanted to know how his wife had looked.

"And this is a shot of the first Fourth of July celebration we held. Look at the back and you'll see Mary Alice and Renee in their lawn chairs waiting for the fireworks."

When Betsy moved closer to see the background, the fabric of her dress settled along the edge of his thigh. As he showed her picture after picture, she was aware that only cotton separated them. Her ability to concentrate was impaired by his nearness and her fear that he might not share the feeling, and the fear that he might.

"Thank you for taking the time to show them to me," she said, moving away and leaning back against the arm of the sofa. She needed to put distance between them. "Would it be possible for me to take them tonight to study?" She might be able to focus on them if she were alone, but not while she was with Nick.

"Keep them as long as you like." He picked up her empty glass. "Let me get you another drink."

"No thanks. I ... probably should be going." The words didn't sound convincing even to her own ears.

"It's only a little after eight and you haven't seen the sunset yet." He poured himself another drink and walked to the window.

She joined him. "This is a wonderful view of the horizon. Trees and houses have a way of obstructing the colors of sunsets." The sun, hidden low in the western sky behind them, cast its golden glow over the gentle waves.

"Would you like to go outside?" Nick asked, setting his unfinished drink on a nearby table.

"For a little while. You really can't get the effect of the Gulf without the wind in your hair."

Nick smiled as he opened the door and took her elbow to guide her down the steps. "Do you sail?" he asked when they reached the dock.

"It's been a while." She ran her hand along the stainless rail of a thirty-six-foot yacht trimmed with freshly oiled teak.

"Sailing has always been important in our family. But there just doesn't seem to be enough time anymore."

"I understand that. I used to spend a lot of time on or in the water, sailing and diving. But this past year has been live, eat, dream and sleep school. Come to think of it, scratch sleep," she added dryly, then brushed her hair out of her eyes. "I've only gone diving once this summer. And I haven't been on a sailboat in over a year."

Nick walked alongside his boat, unaware that he was inspecting its hull as he went. "Billy loves it."

"Then, taking Billy sailing would be a good way for you two to patch things up."

"I would if I had the time. . . ." He stopped himself before he made the excuse. "Okay, I'll make the time. Would you like to join us?"

"Yes, I would like that." Tucking her hands behind her, she leaned back against a pier and watched multicolored sails crisscross the bay. It was so peaceful.

For a while, Nick stood a short distance away as he, too, watched the passing vessels. But when she looked over and smiled, without a word he came closer and placed the palm of his hand on the weathered wood that supported her head, his body almost touching hers. With the heat of him at her side, she watched the dusk deepen until she could only faintly make out the outline of the boats sailing in the bay seeking out their berths.

She felt his fingers as they curled around a stray strand of hair blown by the wind across his hand. Turning to face him, she caught her breath at the longing in his eyes.

"You're wonderful," he said as he combed more of her hair through his fingers. "Even when you're reading me the riot act."

"I have never read...." Her protest died when his fingertip brushed her lips.

"Shh. Don't argue." He stepped forward, filling the narrow gap between them as his hand cupped the back of her neck and urged her nearer.

"I wasn't—" She stopped her denial, wanting him to kiss her. An ache settled around her heart and rose into her throat as she lifted her head and waited for him to lower his. At first, she felt only his warm breath mingled with the warm breeze from the bay tease her bare shoulder and neck before he sought her moist, waiting lips.

He brushed her lips with his before cupping her face in gentle hands to hold them both steady while he trailed kisses along her forehead and nose until she gulped at the yearnings she felt deep within her. When he wound his arms around her, engulfing her in his warmth she knew this was where she belonged. This was the man she wanted to share the rest of her life with.

He deepened the kiss, surprising her with his intensity. Primal desire built in the pit of her stomach until she moaned and leaned into him. What gentleness there had been, changed to raw passion. He pressed her against the pier with his body as his hands grasped her to him. She returned his kisses with equal passion until they were both lost in a world of their own making. Just when she thought there could be no turning back, Nick stopped and stepped away, leaving a void where he had been.

Startled by the ensuing chill, Betsy asked, "Nick? What's wrong?"

"I'm sorry, but I can't—"

She searched his face until she caught a glimmer of light reflected in his eyes. She knew. Guilt. Raising a finger to his lips, she stopped him. "Don't say anything. Please." She couldn't stand the thought of his saying something that would put a wedge between them forever. She slipped away from the wooden post. "I'll show myself out."

Tiny lights hidden along the walkway guided her physically but not emotionally as she sought refuge from Nick and their unfulfilled passion. She hurried into the house and picked up her purse lying where she'd left it on the hall table.

As she turned to leave, she noticed an arrangement of photos she'd missed seeing when she'd arrived. Some were of Billy at various ages, but most were of Nick and Vicki. One was of their wedding and another showed them in glittering formal dress at the aquarium's grand opening. Nick stood with his arm draped over Vicki's bare shoulder, and he was looking adoringly into her eyes.

Betsy turned and ran out the door, tears flooding her eyes. How could she have been so stupid as to fall in love with a man who was probably still in love with his late wife?

OVERCOMING the raw emotions that had washed over him, Nick cut across the yard only to see the taillights of her car disappear down the street. He turned back and walked toward the darkened water. Damn! He struck the palm of his hand on the pier. Why had he let that happen? It had been a mistake to touch her.

There was no doubt that he was enjoying his job much more these days. There was an excitement, a spark that had been lacking before Betsy had come to work at the aquarium. Her easy laughter and caring nature attracted everyone to her.

Tonight, that attraction had overpowered him. Before he'd realized what had happened, he'd wanted to carry her back to his bedroom and make love to her. That had been his undoing. When the image of making love to her on the bed he'd shared with Vicki had flashed into his mind, guilt engulfed him.

Guilt. Now, *there* was a familiar emotion. It had been almost two years since Vicki's accident, and he still couldn't rid himself of its constant companionship. Being honest with himself, he realized that he hadn't tried, choosing instead to wallow in the strange comfort of his grief. He turned and started toward the house, and, as an idea grew in his mind, his steps quickened until he was bounding up the steps purposefully.

Upstairs, he went to the master bedroom and threw open the door to the closet. He began to pull Vicki's things from the shelves and hangers. In silence he carried them across the hall to the guest bedroom. Tomorrow, he'd have Janie take them to Goodwill or the Salvation Army where they'd do some good.

On one of his trips, he picked up the photo of Vicki from the top of the chest of drawers. The familiar sadness tightened around his heart as he studied it, and tears filled the corners of his eyes. He'd loved Vicki once, but slowly that love had faded. He wished he had loved her more during the last years they lived together. That, he knew was the root of his guilt. If he'd been a better husband and loved her enough, she would be alive now. And Billy would have a mother. Finally, he slipped the picture into the top drawer.

A half hour later, he was through. He'd made a physical separation from his intimate life with Vicki. Now, he had to tackle the memories. They wouldn't be so easy to overcome. He closed the door to the guest room and leaned against it, feeling as if a weight had been lifted.

"BE CAREFUL, NOW," Betsy said as she led her grandmother, Agnes, and the other members of the Corpus Christi Senior Citizens' Quilting Club slowly up the long concrete ramp to the aquarium for the Fourth of July celebration. The ladies had been thrilled when Betsy had not only invited them but had offered to come by and pick them up.

"It's much larger than I remember," Virginia said. "Of course, I only came during its grand opening, and it was so crowded."

Era looked at her watch. "It's six o'clock. Where should we meet after the party? Just in case one of us gets lost."

"We'll meet here at the waterfalls after the fireworks if we get separated, but the aquarium is not as intimidating as it looks. The public visitor area forms a loop along the outside edge," she explained to the ladies when they'd gathered in the center of the multi-storied lobby. "Everything leads back here, so you can't get lost. Now, the work area—insiders call it the wet area," she whispered conspiratorially behind her hand, "is in the center of this building. That's where the filtration system, the kitchen, the chemist's lab and Nicholas Lupton's office are located. Some of the large fish tanks are there, too."

"Where's your office?" Bertha asked.

Betsy pointed to the balcony that ran around the upper level of the foyer. "It's up there."

Era clapped her hands together. "Oh, my, what a pretty view you have. This is so exciting!"

Betsy smiled. She was glad the ladies were enjoying themselves. "Now, let's go outside and I'll show you around." She opened the door and allowed them to precede her onto the observation deck. "From here, you can see the Marsh exhibit, the bay and the lawn where we'll watch the fireworks."

"Do we have to walk down these stairs, dear?" her grandmother asked, surveying the long flight of winding stairs that led to the patio below.

"No, there's an elevator inside."

"Well, let's use it," Bertha said, leading the way. "I'm too old for stairs. Besides, my knees would balk." As they rode down, she informed all the occupants of the elevator about her latest cortisone injection not working.

Betsy smiled and shared a look with her grandmother. "I've taken care of that problem. We've got chairs ready." Betsy directed the ladies to the patio.

"Oh! Look at all the food," Bertha said, forgetting about the chairs.

The ladies were commenting on the spread of barbecue, chicken, and seafood when Billy walked by and sneaked a piece of chicken.

"Is that the little boy you've told me about?" Agnes asked in a low voice.

"Billy? Yes, that's him. He's been ignoring me." Later, she would catch him and explain why she had told Nick what the boy had confided about the death of his mother. "Why don't all of you fill yourselves a plate and eat. Then I'll take you to one of the special diving shows and tours."

"I'd like to see the river otters, too. I read about them in the paper today," Virginia said as she selected some shrimp from the buffet table.

"They will be the main attraction tonight. Nick wasn't sure their compound was going to be completed in time, but the last touch was put on yesterday."

Betsy mingled with other visitors while she waited for the women to eat. "Are you ready to go see the otter compound?" she asked when she saw Bertha dump her plate in a bin.

"Most of us have been ready a while," Agnes said, looking meaningfully at Bertha.

"Great. Let's go." Betsy ignored her grandmother's veiled reference to Bertha's second helping.

"Ohhh!" Bertha whispered loudly when they joined a crowd gathered around a tall man. "Is that Nicholas Lupton?"

"Yes," Virginia answered. "He looks just as I remembered."

"Where are the otters?" Era asked, craning her neck. "I can't see."

One of the visitors, obviously annoyed at the disruption, turned around and gave the ladies a pointed look.

Nick nodded slightly when he noticed Betsy and the cluster of women join the group, then continued to explain, "We have a pair of otters. The smaller one is Emily Morgan named for the yellow rose of Texas because of the yellow cast to her brown coat. She and her mate, Sam Houston, enjoy an enclosure that is made to look as much like their natural habitat as possible. The den is monitored by a camera so that we can watch them even when they're sleeping."

Betsy loved listening to his voice, particularly when he assumed the professorial role. It was warm and knowledgeable with no hint of arrogance. And it lacked an identifiable Texan accent, unless he was joking, which was when he usually affected one.

He continued, "River otters are found along the drainage basins throughout southeast Texas. They avoid areas populated by humans and are rarely seen in the wild." Nick's speech lasted about ten minutes. Then he walked over to the ladies and gave Virginia a hug. "Except for Mrs. Black, I don't believe I've met any of you. I'm Nicholas Lupton."

Betsy introduced Era and Bertha. "And this is my grandmother, Agnes Johnson."

"Pleased to meet all of you."

An older gentleman came up and said, "Dr. Lupton, there are some people I'd like you to meet."

"Okay. Will you ladies excuse me? For me, this is more than a social occasion."

"What did he mean by that?" Bertha asked.

"Money, Bertha, money," Agnes answered.

"Grandmother, that sounds a little harsh." She turned to the other ladies. "He has to circulate among the members and their guests. The aquarium depends on donations from its members." Betsy knew the importance of creating interest in the operation but was still disappointed that Nick had left.

At nine o'clock, she helped direct the people out of the aquarium to the lawn near the bay where they spread out to watch the fireworks. The ladies from the Senior Citizens' Quilting Club and Nick's mother were seated on webbed chairs drinking lemonade. Betsy was glad that they all seemed to be enjoying one another's company and she smiled when she heard Agnes invite Barbara Lupton to the quilting club.

She would have liked to emulate the laughing people lounging in chairs or relaxing on quilts, and share a blanket with Nick, but he was seated with VIPs a short distance away.

As evening fell, anticipation of the upcoming fireworks display increased. The weather had cooperated completely. The temperature at this time of year was usually sweltering, but it was graciously comfortable as Betsy walked through the crowd to a spot where Billy was busy spreading a blanket. "May I sit with you?" she asked.

"I don't care," he mumbled, not looking at her.

She sat down, tucking her legs under her, and looked off to the bay where the barge with the fireworks floated. "I missed seeing you when I came to your house Friday evening."

"I was at my grandmother's."

"That's what your daddy said." She looked up as the first Roman candle split the night sky. "He said you were angry."

"Do y'all talk about everything?" Billy said, glancing at her for the first time.

"We do if we think it's best for you."

"You don't know what's best. You're not my mother."

"No, I'm not, and I'm not trying to be. But I do want you to be happy, and I thought that you would be happier if you understood about your mother's death."

"I understand all right."

"You do?"

"Yeah. Daddy didn't care if she died or not."

"Billy, that's not true. How could you possibly think that?"

"I heard him tell her. They thought I was still asleep, but I heard them fighting that morning."

"Adults fight and say things they don't mean all the time."

Billy glowered at her. "They shouldn't."

"No, we shouldn't. But just because we're grown-ups doesn't always make us smarter when it comes to the way we treat each other. We make mistakes. And I may have made a mistake by betraying your confidence and telling your dad what you said, but I did it because I care about you. It wasn't because I wanted to get you in trouble." Betsy took his hand that lay on the blanket between them. "I'm sorry that it made you angry."

Billy continued to watch the fireworks lighting up the sky without responding, but he didn't pull his hand away from her grasp.

"Betsy," a voice behind her said.

Startled, Betsy jumped before she turned and saw Renee.

"Oh, I'm sorry," Renee apologized. "I didn't mean to scare you like that. It's been a lovely celebration, but we need to rescue the baby-sitter from Michael junior, so I came to say good-night."

Betsy pushed herself to her feet. "I think it's wonderful that you got out at all." Betsy hugged Renee.

Billy interrupted Betsy by tugging her sleeve. "I'm going over to where Grandmother is."

"Okay, I'll see you later, Billy," Betsy said, and turned her attention back to Renee. "How's little Michael doing?"

"He's a three-week wonder. Really thriving. It's the mother who's tired."

"Well, it doesn't show. You really look marvelous."

"So do you. Stunning, in fact. Those red sequins have generated a lot of interest tonight. I've never seen them worn with jeans before. No one else could carry it off but you," Renee said.

"Thanks." She'd had a lot of compliments during the night, but not one from Nick.

"Betsy, is something wrong?" Renee asked. "You've laughed a lot, but it doesn't sound genuine."

"I'm fine," Betsy insisted with a quick smile while she scanned the thinning crowd for Nick. "Really."

"You're not telling me the truth. I don't believe I've ever seen a more forced smile on anyone in my life." Renee looked around. "Quit looking. He left a few minutes ago with Tom."

"Who left?"

"Batman! Who do you think I'm talking about?"

Betsy groaned. "Am I being that obvious?"

"No. I just think the two of you'd be a perfect couple."

"Well, I think I can forget him."

"Why?"

Betsy shrugged. "He's still in love with Vicki."

"Nonsense," Renee retorted. "He wasn't in love with her for the last year they were married, so he surely wouldn't be now."

Betsy was stunned by Renee's words. "What do you mean?"

"Oh, I don't know that he realized what was happening," Renee replied. "But anyone who was around them could see that things were becoming strained. Living with Vicki couldn't have been a picnic."

"But I've been told by practically everyone that she was perfect—a saint."

"Sure. One whose halo was held up by horns." Renee frowned. "I know it's not nice to speak ill of the dead, but she and I didn't get along—at all."

Betsy tried to reconcile what Renee was saying with what Mary Alice, in particular, had said. She had to know more. "Why not?" she asked.

"Let's just say that she often used her position as 'wife of the director' to undermine others."

"Nick wouldn't allow that," Betsy said, jumping to his defense.

"He wouldn't have if he'd known, but no one told him, including me." Renee lowered her voice, "And, speaking of Nick, here he comes, and he doesn't look happy."

Betsy turned. Tom tagged along a few feet behind. Both men were frowning.

Sensing something had happened, she started toward them. "What's wrong?"

"One of the otters is gone," Nick said. "Emily Morgan has disappeared."

CHAPTER EIGHT

"HOW COULD THAT have happened?" Betsy thought of all the construction designed to keep the otters out of harm's way. It would have been difficult, if not impossible, for Emily to have escaped from her enclosure on her own.

Tom jumped in with an explanation. "Someone probably wanted a threatened species for a pet. You know how that guy was caught with a chained panther in his backyard last summer."

"Maybe so. The outer door to the otter compound was unlocked and the inner one was standing open. It's a sure thing that Emily didn't unlock them." Nick looked around. "Betsy, have you seen Sue or Chester, by any chance?"

"They're over there." Betsy nodded toward a cluster of people.

"Can you quietly get them over here without alerting the others? We don't want to ruin the end of their evening."

"Well, I think the best way to get the otter back is to make an announcement," Tom said. "Someone here may know something."

Betsy didn't want to hear Nick's reply to Tom. "I'll get Sue and Chester," she said. As she started to hurry off, Nick's voice took on a sense of urgency. "Betsy, get anybody else from the staff over here as soon as you can."

Betsy found her grandmother visiting with Mary Alice. "Grandmother, Mary Alice, I hate to break up your gabfest, but Nick needs some help." She briefly explained the situation.

"Oh, dear, the poor animal, she must be so scared," Mary Alice said, voicing her dismay as she searched in her hip pack for a tissue.

"May I help, too?" Agnes asked, pushing herself up from the lawn chair.

"I'm sure you can. Nick is getting together a search party," Betsy said.

With the group clustered in the aquarium lobby, Nick explained the problem. "She's probably still here in the aquarium, so we have a good chance of finding her tonight."

Betsy heard Tom grunt as he folded his arms across his chest, but he didn't say anything else.

"Michael and I will stay a while longer to help with the search," Renee offered. "Where do you want us to start?"

"If you'd look through the public areas of the aquarium, then, Tom, you and Mary Alice could search the wet area. Chester, would you and Sue search the Marsh exhibit? Oh, and Mrs. Johnson, would you and your friends stay here to see if the otter heads toward the bay?"

Betsy was pleased that Nick made her grandmother feel useful. Now, though, only she and Nick had no assignment.

He continued, "Betsy and I will search the ground level."

Betsy followed him into the elevator. Not having been alone with him since she'd left his house in tears, she could almost feel the tension in the enclosed space as they each stared at the closed doors. Finally, she decided to make the first move. "I don't make a habit of kissing the fathers of my students."

"I never thought you did." When the elevator came to a halt, he took her elbow to guide her in front of him. He continued the intimate contact as he said, "I owe you an explanation, but now isn't the time."

Betsy nodded, acutely aware of the pressure where his fingers heated her arm.

"Let's start over there." Nick pointed to the rear of the ground-level loading area.

They spread out and threaded their way through holding tanks full of quarantined fish. After several minutes, Nick caught up with Betsy. "I don't see any sign of her. I thought she might be down here hunting for food."

"Maybe she has already gotten a fish or two."

"I don't think so. She'd have left telltale signs." Nick looked around. "She'd probably have climbed onto a table and knocked things off, or water would have been tracked around. But, she could be playing with us. I'll circle around the pickup truck if you'll watch to see if she runs out."

Betsy considered Tom's doubt that the otter was nearby. When Nick came back, Betsy asked, "Do you think there's a possibility that Emily could have left the grounds by now?"

"She could have headed for the bay, but she's familiar with this area and steady food. I think she'd stay here."

Betsy helped him search behind large gray plastic shipping crates stacked near the elevators. A maze of water pipes leading to the tanks snaked overhead. "Could she have gotten up on the pipes?"

"She could get just about anywhere. Let's check them. You start on this end, and I'll start down there."

When they met back in the middle of the holding area with no success, Nick and Betsy leaned up against a tank to assess the situation. Betsy noticed Nick clenching his jaw as she'd seen him do in other tense situations. He was obviously very upset, though he was trying hard to appear calm. "Where do we look now?" Betsy asked.

"Who knows?" Nick removed his jacket and slung it across his shoulders as he started off. "Let's check the tables and chairs."

Betsy followed Nick across the concrete compound to where the picnic lunch had been spread earlier in the evening. The caterers had cleared the food away while the guests had watched the fireworks. Now, the white plastic chairs were stacked neatly on top of the tables.

While Nick searched the dimly lit nooks and crannies around the edge of the patio, Betsy looked through the rows of table legs toward the darkened marsh that lay twenty yards beyond. Flashlight trails danced back and forth across the two-acre wetland as the other searchers combed the tall grass and reeds. Finally, the lights stopped and focused on one spot.

"Nick," Betsy called, "they've found something."

Nick practically ran to her side, took her by the elbow and propelled her in front of him as he headed for the beam of light.

Sue met them at the chain-link fence that surrounded the marsh. "Nick, we've spotted Emily. Chester's keeping an eye on her."

"Good. Is she okay?"

"She seems to be fine."

As the news spread, the other searchers began to converge in the area. Betsy spotted Emily trying to hide among the tall reeds, confused by all the commotion. "Nick," she asked, "how are you planning to catch her?"

"First, we'll fan out and try to herd her back toward her den and entice her into it with food." Nick explained the procedure, then pointed to the back side of the marsh. "If all of you will circle around, we'll put pressure on her... gently now, we don't want to frighten her."

Tom said, "I think we ought to just net her."

"If she doesn't want to cooperate, we'll try that."

"I'll go get a net just in case." Tom started after a pole net. "I don't want to get bitten."

Betsy could almost see the muscles in Nick's jaw work as he ground his teeth, this time to keep from losing his temper. Tom had deliberately defied Nick for several days, and Betsy didn't want to be in the same room when Nick exploded.

Meanwhile, she hoped Nick's way worked. It would be less stressful on the animal. After rolling up the legs of her jeans, she stepped into the marsh. Nick led the way and directed Chester, Michael, Sue and Renee to form a large semicircle. "Just go easy," he cautioned again. The birds cawed their displeasure at having their evening roost disturbed.

Mary Alice and the ladies from the quilting club sat on the bench and offered whispered encouragement as the others quietly urged Emily out of the marsh and toward her own enclosure. The otter was obviously tired and bored with her adventure. The only thing she wanted was home. Within thirty minutes, Emily was safely eating cat food with Sam Houston.

Nick locked the door to the otter exhibit and pocketed the key. "Thanks, everyone."

The searchers mumbled their concerns as one by one they wiped off their muddy shoes and prepared to leave.

"This is just so exciting," Era said.

"They need to put in a better security system." Bertha tucked a wisp of white hair back into the bun at the nape of her neck.

Betsy explained as she watched Nick double-check the enclosure, "They have a watchman on duty at all times, and the only key to the marsh door is kept in Nick's office."

"Oh! You mean someone had to break into Nick's office to get it?" Agnes whispered.

"It looks that way." Betsy glanced at Nick one last time, noting the sag in his shoulders. She wanted to talk to him, to help him, to let him know that she cared. The memories of the kisses he had burned on her lips and her heart were fresh and she yearned to hear the explanation he'd promised a little while ago. But she knew that tonight he would be focused on solving the mystery of this latest accident.

Besides, she couldn't stay to talk to him because she had to take her guests home. She turned to her grandmother and asked, "It's been a full evening, and I'm sure you're tired. Are you about ready to go?"

THE NEXT TWO DAYS, Nick worked even longer hours at the aquarium trying to keep everything running smoothly. He noticed that although Betsy stayed late, too, she kept her distance. It was as if she knew that he had to reach some decisions on his own. He wanted to approach her about the kisses they'd shared the other night, ease the tension he felt every time he saw her.

Finally, on Wednesday evening, he stopped by her office on his way out.

"When are you going home?" he asked, sticking his head in the room. "You don't have to stay this late. It's almost nine o'clock."

"I know, but I got wrapped up reading all about the otters. At first, I didn't think I would like your big weasels."

"And now?"

"They're beautiful, and so comical it's impossible not to like them."

"I knew you'd come to your senses." Sitting on the side of her desk, he said, "Betsy, thanks for stepping in and bailing us out."

"I'm enjoying it. The work is fascinating."

He idly played with a pencil as he watched her flick back the wayward lock of hair that occasionally fell across her forehead. More than once, he'd had to cram his hands into his pockets to keep from brushing it back for her.

"Nick?" Betsy twirled her chair around to face him head-on.

He looked into the depth of her eyes. They were curious but slightly wary. "Hmm?"

"Have you learned any more about how the otter got out?"

"No." He stood up. "But I think someone on the inside is responsible because no one else could possibly have access. The problem is, I just can't imagine why anyone would want to do it."

"I can't, either. I know you're worried, so if there is anything at all I can do, please let me know."

"Right now, I can't think of anything. Just keep your eyes and ears open. Maybe somebody will let something slip, or they'll get careless and screw up." He stuck the pencil in a souvenir cup. "Betsy, I...about the other night."

"Nick, you don't have to explain if you're not ready."

"I don't know whether I can, but I want to try. It may not make any sense to you. Most of the time it doesn't to me."

Betsy quietly waited for him to continue.

"The other night on the dock when we kissed...."

"Yes?" she prompted.

"That was the first time since...." He stopped and took a deep breath. "Since Vicki's death that I've gotten that close to a woman."

"And it didn't feel right?"

"Oh, yes, it did," he said and took Betsy's hand in his. "At first, that is. Don't you see? I realized that I wanted you to stay the night." He hesitated while he tried to clarify his thoughts. "I wanted to make love to you right then."

"And the memory of Vicki wouldn't let you?"

Nodding, he let go of her hand, turned his back to her and crossed the tiny room so that she wouldn't see the confusion he still felt.

He heard her walk up behind him and felt her lay a gentle hand on his shoulder. "Nick, don't beat yourself up about it. I understand. It's okay."

Facing her, he said, "No, it's not. Right now, I'm having the same feeling—wanting you again. I've had it every time I've seen you for the past two weeks." As he talked, he stepped closer, backing her against the wall until only a fraction of an inch separated their bodies.

She raised her hand to his face and touched his cheek. "Nick," she whispered.

He silenced her with his lips, cutting off any explanation or protest she might have. He raised his head and looked into her eyes before reaching over and closing the office door. He encircled her with his arms and pulled her close. As her fingers crept up his shoulders and neck to mingle in his hair, he felt the impact of her caress in every muscle.

He wanted to make love to her there in her office, to hold her and take comfort from her nearness. But he didn't get what he wanted. A knock on the door interrupted them.

Tom called, "Hey, Betsy. Nick. You in there?"

Nick pulled away and moaned, then getting control of himself, he opened the door. "Yeah, Tom, what do you need?" He could see Tom's mind turning as he assessed the situation.

"I saw the light under the door and, well, I...." Then, finally, he seemed to remember why he'd knocked on the door. "I...the turtle we got in for rehab last week isn't responding to treatment. I thought you might want to take a look."

Nothing I'd like better, Nick thought wryly. "I'll be right there." He turned to Betsy. "You want to see a sick turtle?"

She ran her fingers through her hair and nodded. "Sure. I might as well keep you company."

As Nick hurried down the hall with Betsy at his side, he thought that she was one of the few women he knew who could keep up with him stride for stride.

In the wet area, they caught up with Tom, and the three of them stared into one of the holding tanks where a hawksbill turtle swam lethargically, its eyes half-closed.

Tom said, "He's been off his feed. I didn't think he looked too good when I left this afternoon, so I decided to come back and check on him, seeing as how we've been having so much bad luck lately."

Nick sighed, wanting to add that someone was making their bad luck, but he didn't make the comment. He didn't want anyone but Betsy to know what he suspected.

"You were right to come back," Nick said to Tom. "Let's check him again for parasites and disease."

When Tom hurried off to get a syringe, Nick turned to Betsy. "I need to stay here a while. You're welcome to stay if you want." It was time to quit playing defense and go on the offense. Even if there was nothing happening that was worthy of reporting to the police, he was determined to report the incidents to the board. The directors might have some ideas.

BETSY SPOTTED Renee across the crowded restaurant and hurried to meet her. "Whew! Sorry I'm late. Grandmother and I went to church this morning and I didn't think the preacher was ever going to finish."

"Maybe he thought everyone needed a little additional edification," Renee quipped, unrolling her napkin and placing it in her lap.

"He's probably right," Betsy agreed. "It's a fact that Grandmother believes I need lots of edification."

"Sermons?" Renee asked.

"No. Advice. She loaded me up with it on the way to church." Betsy chuckled when she remembered how her grandmother had casually mentioned that she'd heard Nick Lupton would make a fine husband for some deserving woman. "She's afraid that I'll overlook Nick's single status."

"She sounds like a smart woman. If I weren't married...." Renee shrugged suggestively.

"Then I'm glad you're married." Betsy picked up her menu and just as quickly put it down. She hadn't asked Renee to meet her for lunch because she wanted to eat. "I hope Michael was as understanding about your meeting me for lunch as you said he would be. I know Sundays are for families."

"No problem."

They were interrupted by the waitress. After placing her order, Betsy squeezed lemon into her water and took a sip. "How are things going for you?"

"I love staying home with the baby, but occasionally I miss adult talk. How have things been at the aquarium this week?"

"Not so good. That's why I called you. There's been another incident. One of the hawkbills got sick."

"That's strange. Though the animals we get in for rehab sometimes don't make it. They're too sick to begin with. A few things have always gone wrong, but it's like these accidents are rolling off an assembly line."

"I don't think they're accidents. Your falling is an example. Nick suspects the walkway was tampered with, but not to harm you. I think someone is out to get Nick."

Renee's eyes grew large. "I just thought I was clumsy. Oh, that's frightening. Who would want to harm Nick?"

"That's what I intend to find out." Betsy picked up her fork and scooted the shrimp around her salad. "You may know something that would be helpful."

"I doubt it, but ask away. It seems I have a vested interest in this. What do you want to know?"

"Well, let's start with the staff. Can you think of anything? Any gossip? Grudges? Anyone who could cause problems?"

"I guess just about anyone could harm the animals, but I can't think of anyone who would," Renee said. "Now, Chester, for instance, could mess with the water easily. He works alone in the lab with all those chemicals. But he's as loyal as they come. He lives and breathes water quality. It's not just a job. It's something he takes a lot of pride in—turning plain water into seawater."

"Every time I see him with that pocketful of pencils, I think of a mad scientist," Betsy said. "Who else?"

Renee pursed her lips. "Sue could definitely poison the animals through feedings, but she's a highly reputed nutritionist. Besides, she's as good as gold. For a while last year, I thought Sue was a little sweet on Nick, but he never led her on. Both she and Chester have worked at the aquarium ever since it opened. I can't think of any reason either of them would want to hurt Nick."

"I figured you'd say that. But somewhere along the line Nick may have unwittingly done something that would make someone want revenge. Maybe he fired someone."

"What about Steve, the night-duty operations officer?" Renee asked. "He's new."

"He could have poisoned the birds," Betsy said, "but he couldn't have contaminated the shark's water because the shark was shipped during the day. And Steve couldn't have had anything to do with the otter's escape because he was on vacation the Fourth."

"You're right. That rules him out."

"How about Tom?"

Renee rolled her eyes and snickered. "Tom is a royal pain. You name it, and he's the expert. I've never known a human to embellish stories like he does."

"I wonder if any of his tales are really the truth."

"Who knows? He tells some real whoppers, like the one when he was diving with Cousteau on the *Calypso.*"

"Cousteau?"

Renee chuckled. "Tom even said that he had to rig up their breathing equipment."

"His stories may be a bit farfetched, but they seem harmless enough."

"Uh-huh." Renee took a bite and chewed slowly. "You know, though—" she pointed her fork at Betsy "—he applied for the position of director of animal husbandry at the aquarium in New Orleans but didn't get the job. Grapevine gossip has it that Nick didn't give him a good recommendation. That was two years ago."

Betsy straightened her shoulders. "So Tom might harbor some resentment against Nick?"

"Could be, but you'd think he would have done something before now if he did."

Betsy pushed her food away, too concerned about Nick to have an appetite. "Maybe, but the resentment could have been brewing all this time."

"Could be."

"What about the front staff or the volunteers?" Betsy asked.

"There's so many volunteers, who knows."

"How about Mary Alice? She's always around, a lot more than the other volunteers."

"That's because she's the volunteer in charge of the volunteers. She was overprotective of Vicki. She'd do anything for her, and I think she's probably transferred that devotion to Nick. Other than being a little eccentric sometimes, she's harmless."

"I've noticed that she wears that hip pack like a second skin," Betsy said. "She's always bruising her arm on it."

"I know it's in her way, but she's afraid someone will steal it. I used to try to get her to lock it up, but she refused."

"I doubt she has it filled with a lot of money, so what do you think she carries in it?"

"I've only seen her get out the usual things a woman carries in her purse. A compact, tissues, medicine. And lots of keys."

Betsy sighed as she mulled over the gossip she'd heard. "Renee, I think I may know something about Mary Alice. Grandmother couldn't wait to tell me she'd heard 'from a reliable source' that Mary Alice had an illegitimate child who would be about fifty now."

Renee looked surprised. "Mary Alice has never mentioned having a child. In fact, Betsy, I'd nearly swear on the Bible that Mary Alice has said she doesn't have children."

Betsy inquired further. "Has she ever mentioned a husband or any family?"

"No," Renee said thoughtfully. "I just assumed because she called herself Mrs. that she was a widow. She's never talked about her home life."

"Don't you find that kind of odd?"

"I've never really thought about it. But, no, I don't. I know a lot of people who are private and selfless. She babies me."

"She babies me, too." Betsy felt a pang of remorse for repeating Agnes's gossip. "She can't seem to be helpful enough. Maybe my grandmother was mistaken. In any case, I asked her not to spread it around—not that she'll listen. Mary Alice doesn't deserve to be hit with any unkind talk."

Renee leaned back and gave Betsy an appraising look. "No, she doesn't. But what are we going to do about Nick?"

At the mention of Nick, Betsy sobered. "He's so worried about the animals that he's practically slept at the aquarium the past four nights hoping to catch the—the culprit."

"Where's Billy while Nick's playing detective?"

"He's staying with his grandparents which, although they're wonderful people, I don't think is such a good idea. Nick needs to be with Billy more."

"How are things between you two?"

Betsy waved her hand dismissively. "Who knows."

"Nick and Billy need each other, and they both need you," Renee said. "Nick was a zombie for a year after Vicki's death. He worked out of instinct, nothing more."

"That's another thing I don't understand. You told me that he wasn't in love with her."

"I really don't think he was—I don't know how anyone would have put up with her temper, she'd gotten so volatile. But that doesn't mean he didn't feel responsible for her or miss her when she was gone."

Betsy knew Renee was making sense. Regardless of how weak or solid Nick and Vicki's relationship was, they had been husband and wife. Nick always erected a barrier whenever Vicki's name came up, leaving Betsy with unanswered questions. "Renee, exactly how did Vicki die?"

"I don't know what happened the day she died. I'm not sure anyone does but Nick. Something happened to her oxygen supply when they were diving. At the time, there were a lot of rumors."

Betsy's heart constricted, thinking about what Billy said. "About Nick's being at fault?"

Renee lowered her eyes and nodded. "Yes," she whispered. "But no one who knew him believed it."

CHAPTER NINE

July meeting of the Quilting Club

"I FIGURED ALL ALONG Emily was in the marsh," Bertha said as we adjusted the tension on the quilting frame.

I knew good and well she hadn't had any idea where the otter had gone. "Betsy said they still don't know how she got loose."

Virginia looked up and said, "It was so kind of Elizabeth to give us a lift. I don't feel comfortable driving at night anymore."

"Please tell her we appreciated it," Era said, threading her needle and settling down to work.

"I'll tell her."

After several seconds of silence, Bertha spoke up. "That Nick Lupton fellow was everything Virginia said he was. When do you think he and Betsy are going to get married? They didn't look like they were sparkin' to me."

"Looks can be deceiving." Actually, I didn't know what had gone wrong with that relationship so I changed the subject. "Wasn't Barbara Lupton nice?"

Virginia smiled. "She is a gracious lady. I thought it was such a good idea to invite her to quilt with us."

"I'll bet she doesn't come," Bertha said.

Bertha has to find something negative with everything. If I weren't such an easygoing soul, I'd dump her friendship in a moment. *"What did y'all think of Mary Alice Garrett? She's been such a help to Betsy."*

"I thought she was a little standoffish," Bertha said.

Era looked up. *"I remember."*

"You remember what?" Virginia asked, continuing her quilting.

"Mary Alice's daughter's name was Catherine. A little blond thing. She used to sneak out her bedroom window and meet a sailor who parked around the corner from our house." Era shook her head and went back to work. *"That was nigh on thirty-five or more years ago."*

She had our curiosity piqued now. *"What happened?"* I questioned.

She looked up again, her forehead creased in thought. We all waited while she collected her memories. *"All of a sudden one day, he didn't come back. Maybe he shipped out. I don't rightly know. Good-looking young man, the best I remember. We didn't see much of Catherine after that, two, maybe three times. She looked awfully sad."*

CHAPTER TEN

WHILE SHE PREPARED for the Sea Schooler class the morning after her conversation with Renee, Betsy thought about what her friend had told her. It was obvious that all of the aquarium's employees had opportunity and perhaps even motive for antagonizing Nick, but Betsy was placing her bet on Tom. He had a strong motive—revenge. She vowed to keep a close eye on him. Tom was her project for the day. After class.

Nick appeared in the doorway with two preschool-age children. The larger boy held the younger girl's hand tightly as if he'd been instructed not to let her out of his sight. Nick said, "Here are two more students for your class. I ran into their mom in the hallway and offered to deliver them personally. She'll be in a little later."

"Great," Betsy said and moved away from the origami fish she was making to greet the new students. Bending down on one knee, she said, "I'm so glad you're here today. We're going to have a lot of fun. What are your names?"

"My name's Joshua. She is Stephanie," the boy explained. "She doesn't talk much."

"Well, isn't it wonderful she has you to take care of her." Betsy led them to a table where she made name tags, all the while aware that Nick was standing a few feet away looking over her shoulder. Pinning the tags on the children's shirts, she said, "There now, you're all set. Would you like to go see the fish?"

"Uh-huh." Joshua nodded, then took off, dragging his sister behind toward the small aquarium in the corner of the room where some other children were entranced by the flashing colors behind the glass.

Nick said, "Your class is turning out to be really popular."

"After the incident the first week, I'm surprised." Betsy had expected attendance to be down, but instead it had gained four students. "Thank you for bringing them."

"Can you handle this many?"

Betsy glanced at the fourteen youngsters, not one of whom was more than five years old. "No problem. Besides, Mary Alice will be here any moment. She's a big help."

Nick shook his head in disbelief. "I'm glad it's you and not me." He turned to leave when the volunteer from the information desk arrived.

"Betsy, Mary Alice just called to say she can't make it this morning. An attack of arthritis is what I think she said." Seeing the children, the man looked sheepish and said, "I'm sorry. But since this is a morning class, there are no volunteers here to help you."

When Betsy saw Nick's frown, she burst out laughing. "Don't look that way, Nick. I can handle it. Some parents will come back soon."

He offered, "I'll stay a few minutes in case you need help."

"Thanks." Betsy was genuinely touched by his consideration and nodded toward a chair in the back of the room. "You may sit back there, if you wish." She was a little apprehensive about Nick's staying to watch her. Even though she knew he wouldn't be critical, she wanted to make a good impression.

Depressing the button on the cassette recorder, she signaled the students to gather in a tight cluster around her on the floor. When the music ended, she held up a sparkling book and pointed to the title. "This book is called *The Rainbow Fish*. Look at the cover. What do you see?"

"A fish."

"Blue." The children chimed out various answers.

"Yes. It's a lovely fish, but this fish is unhappy. Let's read and find out why he is sad." She read about the selfish little fish that wouldn't share his shimmering scales with the other fish, so he had no friends.

One of the new little boys interrupted, "He don't share. That's not nice."

"You're right. Let's see what happens."

Finally, she got to the part where the selfish fish shares one shiny scale with each of the other fish, and they all become friends. Betsy closed the book and looked over the children's heads at Nick. He caught her glance and smiled.

"I would share if I had something pretty," a little girl said.

"I'm sure you would," Betsy said. "Now let's go to the art table and put shiny scales on our fish. Dr. Lupton is going to help us."

"Him?" the same girl said, pointing to Nick as he stood up.

"Yes, he takes care of the fish here at the aquarium."

Joshua said, "Do the sharks bite you?"

"No, we are very careful," Nick explained as the crowd of children shifted from around Betsy to him.

Betsy smiled as she listened to him field questions and lead the children to the art table at the same time.

"Help me, Mr. Wupton," Stephanie said, speaking for the first time as she spread out her paper fish.

"No, me. Help me first," a boy commanded, pulling at Nick's sleeve.

Betsy intervened. "Dr. Lupton will help all of you. Now watch how we put the glue on," she said as she dotted it on the paper, "and we'll make our own rainbow fish."

As soon as Betsy set the bottle of glue down, little Stephanie grabbed it and dropped a large blob on Nick's pants.

Betsy watched him slide the glue off his pants and onto Stephanie's paper. The little girl watched him adoringly as he helped position her glittering scales.

He wasn't half-bad with children, Betsy decided. He just needed a little more practice.

Stephanie wouldn't let Nick out of her sight for the remainder of the class. If he went to help another student, she followed.

Joshua and Stephanie were the last to leave because they had to show their mother everything in the room.

"Bye, Mr. Wupton," Stephanie said waving good-bye.

Betsy said, "I think you have an admirer."

Nick looked embarrassed. "She's a little doll. I'd hate to be her father in ten years. He's going to have to beat the boys off with a stick."

She laughed as she put away the glue bottles.

Nick came to stand behind her at the cabinet. "I enjoyed watching. You're good with children."

"Thanks." She turned to face him. "I've had a lot of training."

"Training doesn't give you that natural empathy." He consulted his watch. "I've got a couple of calls to make. If you have time, why don't you come by my office when you're finished here and we'll go somewhere for lunch."

"I'd like that." She watched him close the door. It didn't take long for her to finish straightening the room and walk to Nick's office. His door was open, so she peered inside and saw him talking on the phone. He motioned for her to come in and mouthed, "Just a second."

Betsy listened quietly as he made final arrangements for a boat to take a crew diving the next day. She sat down on the edge of his desk because that was the only available surface that wasn't covered with paper and studied the white metal cabinet on the opposite wall. Through its dual glass doors, she could see that it contained syringes and medicine. Below its padlock hung a clipboard holding a sign-out sheet. She didn't understand how the accidents could keep occurring when so many safeguards were in place in every area. Chester took the same precautions in his lab, and Sue did the same in her kitchen.

NICK HUNG UP the phone, twirled his chair around and smiled at Betsy. "Do you mind if we grab something here at the snack bar and sit in the courtyard. I kind of need to stick around. I'm expecting a call about the dive tomorrow."

"That sounds like fun. The dive, not the phone call." Betsy couldn't resist the hint. She'd wanted to dive with Nick from the first time they'd met six months ago, but she'd been hesitant to ask partly because he'd never mentioned whether he still dived after Vicki's accident. "Where are you going?"

"Out to an oil platform."

Betsy was familiar with rig diving. She had done it numerous times, always amazed at the transformation sea life made to the steel columns submerged beneath the gulf waters. "What are you diving for?" she asked as they carried the sandwiches and drinks they'd selected to the courtyard.

"Amberjack, snapper and maybe some tropicals." Nick bit into his sandwich. "The Gulf water has warmed up enough that we can take some pretty good specimen without having to go to Florida or Cozumel."

"A friend and I dived at Cozumel several weeks ago, but it was just for observing. I would like to learn to collect sometimes."

Nick took another bite of his sandwich without responding. Betsy changed the subject. "How're your mother and Billy?"

"Mom's fine, particularly when she can keep an eye on Billy. She's not exactly sure she should entrust her only grandchild to me."

"I doubt that's true."

Nick shrugged. "Vicki always insisted on taking care of Billy herself, so I missed out on a lot of things. I don't have that training you mentioned."

"You're learning. You were great with Stephanie this morning," she said. "You can't expect to be a good parent overnight. I've heard people say that raising children was the one task you did without any prior practice, and when you finally had some experience, the job didn't exist any longer. The children were gone from home."

"That sounds about right." After piling his trash on the tray, Nick leaned back in the white molded plastic chair and crossed his arms behind his head to stretch.

"I need to call to see if I can get another volunteer to dive tomorrow. One of the guys canceled on me."

"Nick, if you can't find anyone, I'd like to volunteer," she said hopefully. "I don't have anything to do tomorrow that I can't catch up on later. No tours or anything. I'd love to see how you collect new fish for the aquarium. I've heard so much about it."

Nick sat forward. "No."

"What do you mean no?" She had not expected such a definite rebuff.

"What I said. No."

"Why not? I'm a good diver. I'm certified, in shape and willing."

He stood up and pushed his chair in with his knee. "I'm sure you are. I saw your credentials when you were hired."

The simple gesture of dismissal confused her. He wasn't even giving her a chance. "Is it because I'm a woman?"

"No. That has nothing to do with it."

"Then what is it? The least you could do is give me a reason."

"I don't have to give a reason because this is my expedition, and I pick my people. You're not right for it, Betsy. Sorry."

Betsy's eyes narrowed to shield her hurt. "I see." She turned and strode away, stuffing the remains of her lunch in the trash can as she walked by. What had happened? They'd been having a nice conversation until she'd asked to accompany him on the dive, then he'd cut her off cold. Why?

A SOFT GLOW was barely visible on the eastern horizon the next morning as Nick boarded the charter catamaran in Port Aransas. He was still berating himself for being so short with Betsy. For some reason, he'd responded to her request before he'd given it any thought. He could have given her a number of polite reasons that she couldn't go. All he knew was that he didn't want her diving. Not today.

Despite the rolling waves, he tried to sleep on and off for much of the four-hour trip to the oil platform. Each time he awoke, he reassured himself that this was no place for Betsy.

The captain, steering the boat carefully, tied up to the man-made reef of steel and coral. Hastily, the men prepared their gear and were ready to dive by ten o'clock. Between ten and two, the light penetration into the water was at its best, making specimen collecting easier.

Nick checked his equipment one last time before putting on his tank and buoyancy compensator. For the past two years, he'd almost had to force himself to dive in deep water, Vicki's death looming up in his mind each time. But he had to do this again and again. For himself. To prove that he still could. His stomach was in knots and his hands felt clammy as he adjusted his mask and regulator.

His diving buddy signaled that he was ready to go, and, one after the other like acrobats in a circus ring, the men jumped into the blue waters of the Gulf. As the water closed around him, Nick became all business. Because he was in such good physical shape, he could consciously slow down his pulse and breathing to a rate that would conserve air and compensate for his anxiety. Within minutes, he lost some of his tension as the beauty of the vertical reef began to work its magic.

Once deeper than twenty feet, the current of the Gulf ceased its pull, so he could relax even more. Nick continued his downward dive until he spotted a small school of barracuda threading its way through the barnacle-clad platform legs. He thought of how he'd first called Betsy, Ms. Barracuda.

Now that name didn't fit because his image of her had changed since he'd gotten to know her better. She wasn't a predatory barracuda at all. She was a porpoise—the most beautiful, graceful and intelligent of all marine life. Thinking of Betsy, he visualized how much she would have loved this dive. But so had Vicki, and she was dead because she loved it. The details of her death were stamped in his memory.

"Vicki, don't you think you should stay home today? We can dive next weekend," Nick had said as he stepped out of the shower and reached for a towel.

"No, I'm not staying home. I'm fine. If we don't go today we might not get another chance for months.

You never have time anymore for us to do things together.''

Ignoring her not so subtle dig, he'd watched her wash down a handful of decongestant tablets before grabbing her elbow and turning her to face him. "You had an asthma attack last night. You know that it's dangerous for you to dive.''

"Quit being such a worrier. I'm a big girl, and I say when I dive and when I don't.''

"As your husband and diving partner, I think I should have a say in it, too. And I say it's foolhardy.''

Vicki had twisted away from him and slammed the package of tablets on the countertop. "Nick, I'm tired of you telling me what to do and acting like you know everything. I have as much education and as many hours in the water as you. And I dive today or. . . .''

"Or?'' He'd hated her ultimatums.

She'd flipped her long blond hair and walked away from him into their bedroom. "Or maybe I'll find another husband and diving partner.''

"Fine. Have it your way,'' he'd yelled after her. "Kill yourself diving or get another husband. I don't care which one you do.'' He was tired of the constant bickering over anything and everything.

Even now, his guilt was unassuaged as he watched the shadowy figures of the divers going about collecting specimen and placing them in perforated plastic containers. Soon they'd begin a gradual ascent to the surface, thereby minimizing the risk of getting decompression sickness, something he'd been unable to do for his own wife.

ALTHOUGH HE MIGHT have deserved it, Nick decided two days of being ignored were enough. He pulled up beside Betsy standing at the bus stop in front of the aquarium. Her red jacket swung easily over her matching tank top and covered most of her walking shorts, which stopped at midthigh. She looked good in red, but she looked good in anything, he'd discovered.

He knew he'd hurt her because he'd refused to allow her to accompany him on the dive. He was sorry for that. But he stood by his decision.

Betsy looked up when he asked, "Why don't you get in? I'll give you a ride home."

"Grandmother's supposed to pick me up," she said, adjusting the silver bangles on her wrist.

"She called a few minutes ago. She said she couldn't make it. Something about it taking longer at the doctor's office with Bertha than she'd thought." The message he'd been entrusted to deliver had given him an excuse to talk to Betsy alone, to try to make amends.

"I'll wait for the bus."

"Your grandmother explained that you're having your car worked on, and that it won't be ready until tomorrow. I assured her that I would give you a ride home."

Betsy moaned. "She didn't ask you to, did she?"

"No, I volunteered." Nick leaned over to open the passenger door. Betsy slid onto the seat and closed the door. "You've been avoiding me."

"I didn't have anything to say."

"I see." He pulled out of the parking lot and onto the highway. "Look, I'm sorry for the way I reacted about the dive, and I want to make it up to you."

"How? Are you going to buy me dinner or send me flowers? I like roses. Two dozen at a time."

"I'll remember that." He knew she was being flippant to hide how she really felt. "What I had in mind was that you come sailing with Billy and me tomorrow. I'd like to hear about your upcoming trip to the Flower Gardens, and Billy said he'd like to see you, too."

Betsy sat quietly for several seconds while she made up her mind. "Only if you're sure Billy won't mind. He might still be upset with me."

"I think he's over that. He asked about you and mentioned that you were a 'narly dudette.' That's about as much of a compliment as you can get from a ten-year-old," Nick explained, pulling into her driveway.

"That *is* a compliment." She smiled for the first time since getting into his Jeep. "What time tomorrow?"

"Eight or nine. I'm packing all the food. Just bring yourself and sunscreen."

"I'll be there at eight."

BILLY WAS RUNNING up and down the front porch while waiting for Betsy the next morning, when she drove up. "Great!" He was almost hopping up and down in his excitement. "Daddy's already got things ready. I helped him unpack the jib and pump the bilge and stow the gear. The *Odyssey* is ready to go. That's her name. We're going to Aransas Pass."

Betsy laughed at Billy's enthusiasm and the way he threw out sailing terms as he led her around the house and toward the dock. He was so happy. Maybe today, she could close the gap that had developed between them.

She could see Nick breaking out the mainsail in the distance. She would have liked to stop and watch him. Clad in white, he was like a picture in a magazine as his graceful movements prepared the yacht to set sail.

Nick turned to greet her when he heard them approaching. "Hi, come aboard."

Billy jumped aboard the sloop, but Betsy grasped the edge of the boat for security before she stepped aboard. "Good morning, Nick. I do have one question before we leave. Considering the name of this boat, it's not going to take ten years to get home like it did Odysseus, is it?"

"I hope not. I don't expect any whirlpools, either, but I do expect adventure."

"I'm game." Without being told what to do, she slipped into the role of crew member. She, too, was eager for the day's adventure with Nick and Billy who was scurrying about self-importantly.

"Hoist the mainsail," Billy ordered in his best skipper voice as they got into the mood of the occasion.

"Watch the boom," she warned, joining the mood as she hauled on the halyard. This was going to be nice, seeing Billy have fun. She caught Nick in her peripheral vision as he smiled at Billy's antics. She could see the affection he felt for his son.

Nick cast off and unfurled the jib as they slid away from the dock. They were soon under way and Betsy began to adjust the sail trim. It had been a while since she'd sailed, but it all came back soon enough. Slowly, she brought in the sheet and watched the sail billow as it filled with wind. The boat heeled slightly as it picked up speed and headed across Corpus Christi Bay.

The clear sky overhead forecast a perfect day for sailing, and a gentle breeze blowing at eight or nine knots provided not only energy to push the boat, but a refreshing reminder of the power of nature. For a while, they were able to run with the wind, but Betsy knew it would require more effort on the return trip to manipulate this same breeze.

For the first two hours, they worked easily as a crew, getting the feel for the boat and the water. Talk was limited, but Betsy and Nick exchanged smiles as he steered the craft. She still didn't understand why he'd refused to take her diving. But she admitted that sailing was a good alternative.

The sailing under control, Betsy and Billy sat with their backs to the wind and watched the undulating waves. The morning light reflected off the water, causing Betsy to adjust her sun visor. The sea breeze rustling through her hair made her think of all the thousands of other sailors who had enjoyed this same feeling of freedom and adventure. "Have you ever heard of Thor Heyerdahl, Billy?"

"Thor who?" Billy squinted.

"Heyerdahl. He wanted to prove that the early inhabitants of Peru had sailed across the Pacific, and that the people who now live on Tahiti are their descendants."

"By himself?" Billy was agog.

"No, he had a small crew."

"Did they make it?"

"No, the raft named *Kon-Tiki* sank." Seeing Billy's expression turn to one of wide-eyed concern, Betsy quickly added, "But the crew survived. Most people thought they were foolish, but Heyerdahl was well prepared."

"Daddy's prepared, too."

Betsy patted Billy on the knee. "I'm sure he is."

As they neared Aransas Pass and the open Gulf, Betsy pulled herself out of her peaceful lethargy to help Nick. Amid heavy boat traffic, both motorized and wind-driven, he steered the sloop through the pass. She was impressed by how easy he made it look.

"You want to take the wheel out for a while?" he asked after they entered the Gulf of Mexico.

"Sure." Betsy planted her feet firmly on the deck and took the helm. Nick lingered beside her for a few

minutes observing her efforts. Betsy was amused at
Nick's protective behavior. "Are you afraid I'll sink
us?"

Nick grinned. "Sorry. Tell you what. To show you
how much I trust you, Billy and I'll hustle up some
lunch." He and Billy disappeared below deck, to re-
emerge twenty minutes later with enough food for a
crew of five.

Watching the wheel, they drifted while they had a
leisurely lunch of sandwiches, fruit and soft drinks.
Betsy watched in amazement as Nick ate.

Taking his third sandwich, he noticed her expression. "Salt air works up the appetite. Besides, I'm
lucky. Good metabolism."

"It's a good thing." Not an ounce of fat was no-
ticeable on his muscular frame. Satiated by the delicious meal, she leaned against the back of the seat and
applied more sunscreen. "Billy, let me put some sunscreen on you. Your face is going to blister."

"Naw, I don't want any. Daddy already made me
put some on this morning. I was prepared."

"It doesn't last. Are you sure you won't let me put
a little on your nose?"

"Aw, okay. Don't get it in my eyes, though, 'cause
it burns."

"I'll be careful." As she applied the lotion, she noticed how much better Billy looked than he had at the
end of school. His eyes weren't so sunken and dark,
and his skin, once sallow, was beginning to develop
some color. He was beginning to joke a little rather

than take every comment as an invitation to fight. She patted his cheeks with the sunscreen one last time. "Now, you're safe."

"Am I next?" Nick asked from the helm.

"Sure." Betsy stood up and squeezed the white liquid into her palm to warm it before sliding it over the arm he held out as he steered with the other. The muscles of his arms were hard and well defined. She took longer than necessary rubbing the lotion along the contours. "The other one?"

He turned slightly so she could reach his other arm, their bodies only a few inches apart. She was conscious of his chest rising and falling with each breath as she worked the lotion over his skin.

She tried to control her reactions because Billy was watching each move closely. "What about your neck?" she asked. "Do you want me to do it?"

"Of course." He tilted his head so she could apply the cream.

When she finished, she looked down at his legs. Good-looking legs, but she wasn't about to touch them. Not with Billy present.

He must have read her thoughts. "What about my legs?"

"You get to do your own legs." She snapped the cap closed.

"Chicken?" he taunted.

"Smart." She tossed him the bottle.

He caught it with one hand. "Maybe later."

Betsy wondered if he meant they would have time together later? Nick didn't take much time away from the aquarium for pleasure. Today was one of the few times Betsy had seen Nick allow himself to relax and have fun.

Much too soon, it was time to head back and Nick made ready to bring the boat about. "Hard-a-lee."

The bow of the boat swung into the wind and as the jib started to flutter, Betsy released it. And Billy moved to the windward side of the boat as it heeled on the new tack.

"You're more fun to sail with than my mom was. She didn't like it because she always got sick. So we didn't get to go much," Billy informed her when she sat down beside him.

Surprised that Billy felt safe enough to mention his mother to her, Betsy also felt uncomfortable at his revelation. She looked up to see if Nick had heard the comment. If he had, he didn't indicate it as he stared straight ahead.

Finally, Billy's head began to nod, and he leaned against her. She stood him up and gingerly led him to the cabin below and put him in one of the berths.

"He's fast asleep," Betsy told Nick once she'd come above deck. "It's been a full day."

"He's had a good time."

"I've had a wonderful time, too," Betsy said as she joined him in the cockpit.

With few words, they sailed first on one tack, came about, then on another tack, slowly making their way upwind past oil platforms.

Betsy wanted to clear the air, to rid herself of any residual hurt she felt because he'd refused to allow her to dive with the team. "How did your dive go?"

"It went well. We got a few grouper and a small shark. They're in quarantine for flukes and external parasites. Which reminds me... Did any of the staff mention staying late Wednesday?"

"Not that I know of. Why?"

"I would have sworn I saw someone behind one of the tanks when I unloaded the fish. But I searched the area. *Nada.*"

"Your imagination?"

"Maybe." He peered out over the green water for several seconds, then turned and looked at her. "I don't have an excuse for the way I behaved when you asked if you could go on the dive. All I know is I didn't want you there."

When she didn't look at him, he caught her upper arm. "I was afraid something would happen."

"I don't know why you were so worried. I'm a good diver," she assured him.

He turned back to stare at the ocean. "So was Vicki."

Betsy stood quietly and waited for Nick to continue. She could tell it was painful for him to talk about it.

"She'd been bothered by asthma off and on all her life, but for several days it had been worse than usual, so I didn't want her to dive that day."

Betsy whispered, "But she chose to go anyway."

He nodded.

"Nick, I don't know what to say. Losing someone you love like that must be terrible."

"I didn't want you to dive Wednesday because *I* couldn't handle the risk, not because I thought *you* couldn't handle the dive."

CHAPTER ELEVEN

BETSY SHUFFLED the papers scattered across her desk into one big pile and leaned back in her chair. Everything was ready for the photography trip to the Flower Gardens. She only needed to review the preparations with Nick before going home. He'd mentioned that he would come by to see her after work. She'd been foolish to think that would be sometime soon. The man seemed to be cursed with loving his job so much that he was never finished.

Earlier in the day, he'd also mentioned some business that had to be taken care of but hadn't told her what. As a rule, he let the staff know where he was in case he was needed. Today, he said nothing. She'd asked around to see what he was doing, but no one seemed to know. Then, when he'd returned, he'd skirted her questions.

Tired and feeling tense, she shook her head to get the kinks out of her neck, kicked off her shoes and propped her feet up on the desk. She was about to doze off when she felt someone looking at her. Turning, she saw Nick leaning against the doorjamb smiling.

"Nice legs," he said.

"Thanks. I'll pass the word on to my parents that you approve of my genes." Swinging her legs off the desk, she straightened her purple culotte, stood up and motioned toward the papers before her. "Are you ready to go over the dive information?"

"Now's as good a time as any." He pulled up a metal chair beside her, turned it around and straddled it. Leaning forward, he rocked onto two legs of the chair to get a better view of the schedule she pushed toward him.

She could feel the heat from his body a few inches away as he bent over her desk. "I thought we'd leave by at least four o'clock in the morning. It takes eight hours to get to the West Flower Garden, so we should get there about noon. That will allow for...at the most, two dives...say, forty-five minutes each." She ran her finger down the itinerary as she talked. "Everyone's responsible for his own breakfast, but the caterers will prepare lunch and a light dinner."

"How many people did you end up with?"

"Seven and myself." She leaned back against her desk and faced him. "You're going, aren't you? I was counting on you to answer questions about the reef. Having a doctorate carries some responsibilities, you know."

He tilted the back of the chair toward his chest and leaned away from her. "Can you find anyone else?"

She raised a leg and placed a bare foot on the back of the cool metal chair as if to tip him over backward.

She jiggled the chair while raising her eyebrows in a dare. "You were saying...?"

"I would love to answer questions." He grabbed her foot, making Betsy wonder if he were planning to tip her over or bite her toe. Her stomach tightened at the thought. All he had to do was touch her to make her lose coherent thought.

When he glanced up, his eyes connected with hers. She could see the desire there before he released her ankle and cleared his throat. "Feet hurt, or is this the new style?" he said, motioning toward her shoes lying under her desk. "I haven't seen you wear those red things again. You know—the ones you were wearing when you came that day to chew me out."

"Those were designed more for fashion than comfort and my tootsies like to breathe." She wriggled her toes.

"Is there anything else you need to discuss with me about the trip?" he asked, glancing at the high-pressure dive watch on his wrist.

"I'm sure there is, but I can't think of it right now." And it was true—she couldn't think. Her heart seemed to miss beats every time he touched her. And he had only touched her ankle. No, he was touching her soul.

"Betsy, I'm sorry to rush out, but I've got to go. There's someone I need to meet about business."

Betsy didn't move for several minutes after he left, her excitement erased as quickly as it had developed. Nick's mood had shifted so swiftly that she wondered what had happened. A memory? Vicki? Did he really have an errand or had he needed to get away from her?

NICK FINISHED his business with the security firm he'd hired, then hurried to his parents' house to pick up Billy. As he and Billy were walking in their own front door, he asked, "You want to play a game of catch before we eat?"

"Ooh, I guess. It's kinda dark, though." Billy looked out the large window at the twilight.

His son wasn't athletic and resisted every attempt Nick made to get him to play baseball. He needed to quit trying to make Billy into something he wasn't. "I suppose it is a little too dark. How about video games, instead?"

"Yeeaah!"

"Fine." Nick followed Billy to his room and sat on the edge of the bed. It was a good thing he loved Billy more than he hated video games, Nick thought.

"Prepare to meet your fate." Billy leered at his father when he handed him a controller.

Nick's fate was a good tromping by the ten-year-old. He put it down to his being unable to concentrate on the game. Betsy was on his mind. In one sense, it was wonderful to want a woman again, to feel alive after being cocooned in misery for so long. In another way, it was unsettling, the feeling of adrenaline being pumped directly into his veins. He had such a mess going on at the aquarium, he couldn't afford to be sidetracked right now. He needed to stay focused.

"Hey, dude," Billy reprimanded. "You're not paying attention. I just beat you again."

"You're right. It's hard to concentrate on something when you're getting beaten, so I let a thought or two about work creep in. You'll be staying the night at Mom and Dad's on Friday. I won't be in 'til late."

"Where you going this time?"

"I'm going on a dive."

He could feel his son tense. Usually when he dived, he didn't tell Billy. He hadn't consciously thought about it, he just instinctively knew Billy might be upset if he was aware. He reached over and grasped his son's knee and gave it a little shake for reassurance. "Everything will be okay. I'll be careful."

His eyes focused on the monitor while his fingers danced over the controls, Billy asked, "You gonna get some more fish?"

"No, this is just a photography excursion."

"Oh, who's going?"

"About eight of us. Several amateurs, a couple of professionals, me...oh, Ms. Johnson's going, too."

"Yeah, she likes to dive." Billy didn't look up from his game. "She went off somewhere one weekend with her boyfriend." The *bong, boom, thud* as he knocked off his opponents on the small screen was suddenly invasive.

"With her boyfriend?"

"Yeah. I heard them talking on the phone all slurpy, slurpy."

Nick didn't like that idea at all.

THE SALTY AIR invigorated Betsy as she and the others loaded their gear on the boat Friday morning. Darkness surrounded the gently rocking vessel tied close to the pier as they hurried about, talking in muted tones as though noise would disturb the still of the morning. Gear stowed, they all found seats and settled in for the long trip to the reef, which lay one hundred and eighty miles out in the Gulf.

Appearing to be asleep, Betsy watched Nick through half-closed eyes as he chatted with the captain and a professional underwater photographer named Brian, who appeared to be an old friend. When Nick finally selected a seat, he chose the one facing her across the deck rather than the one beside her. He'd been kind of cool to her ever since he'd abruptly left her office. What had she done?

The only thing that had changed was the blond woman that Mary Alice had mentioned seeing Nick sneak into the aquarium. At the time, Betsy hadn't given a lot of thought to the older woman's concerns. She'd figured Mary Alice was embellishing the truth a little, that Nick and the blond had business to take care of. But maybe it was more than that.

She tried to sleep but Nick's legs stretched out in front of her were a distraction. They were long and lean, his thighs corded with muscles. Healthy tanned skin shone through the light brown hair covering his legs. She raised her eyes to the owner's face and caught Nick looking at her.

After several seconds, a slow smile spread across his face before he rose and crossed the gently rocking deck to the seat beside her. "How does the song go about 'looking back to see if you were looking back at me'?"

When Betsy hummed a verse of the song—off-key—Nick groaned.

"I never said I could sing." She pretended to be offended. "Do you think I'd be working at your measly fish tank if I had latent singing talent?"

"Trying to hurt my feelings? Of course you'd work there—" he grinned a big Cheshire smile "—because you love otters."

"You're right." Never one to let a problem build if it could be avoided, she asked, "All morning you've been avoiding me. What gives?"

"Truth?"

"You're welcome to tell me a lie first if you can make up a good story, but I'd like you to get around to the truth eventually. We've got seven hours."

"I, ah...in your office the other day, I didn't know you already had a man in your life."

For once, Betsy didn't know how to react. "Who told you that?" She felt like a little girl fishing for a tattletale.

"Billy."

"Billy told you I had a man in my life?" Betsy asked incredulously. A frown crossed her face. "Ohhh...." She recalled Billy being at her house when she'd played the message from Robert on her answering machine and had returned his call. "Robert is just a friend and sometime escort. And while we're at it, who was that blonde you hosted in your office the other night?"

"Blonde?" Nick's face revealed surprise.

"Yes. The one with the tight T-shirt. The one who tried to camouflage her identity with gigantic sunglasses. The one who everyone's been speculating about for a couple of days."

"Oh, that one. She was there for business."

"Yeah, sure."

"Betsy, I can't tell you much. I hired a security firm because I'm determined to find out who's behind the so-called accidents."

"I see." She could tell from the tone of his voice that he'd said all he was going to on the matter, so she changed the subject. "Don't you get tired of taking care of business?"

"Depends upon the type of business. In college, I started out majoring in business—finance. I was going to be a wheeler-dealer investment banker like my father and grandfather."

"What happened?"

"It was the early seventies, and at the time, even at the University of Texas, the capitalist ethic wasn't too popular amongst the student body. I guess I was giving in to peer pressure when I switched my major to marine biology. Never regretted it, though." Nick leaned forward, elbows on his thighs and cocked his head toward Betsy. "What about you?"

"I was going to be a famous actress, so I majored in drama." She chuckled at her memories. "Unfortunately, I didn't like memorization or taking direction all that much. I like to improvise and be the boss."

"I can believe that."

"So, after about fifteen minutes of soul-searching and a little nudging from my grandmother who thought acting was not a fitting occupation for a young woman, I changed my major to education."

"Did you like teaching drama? I mean, you're not doing it now?"

"That's what you think. You have no idea how much acting is involved in administration."

"Were you acting that day you came to persuade me to let Billy go to summer school?"

"Truth?"

"I don't know if I like the way you said that. How about half-truth."

Betsy shifted on the bench so she could see Nick better. "I guess there was a little acting, because what I really wanted to tell you was that you were being pigheaded."

Nick snorted. "I wanted to call you a barracuda."

Betsy laughed. "We agree on animal imagery."

They spent the next several hours talking, and getting to know each other. They discussed their childhoods and laughed about the stunts they pulled in college.

"You know, I thought I was going to make a big difference in the world." Nick's voice had a wistful quality.

"All of us did," Betsy agreed. "That's the nature of youth. And who knows. Maybe we are. At least, I like to think I am, one child at a time." She looked into his eyes. "And you're saving marine species. I'd say you're making a difference."

When they neared the dive site, the captain signaled to them. Betsy stood and introduced Nick to the group of people congregated on the deck. "Dr. Lupton will tell you a little more about the dive and answer any questions you may have."

Nick stood up. "First of all, call me Nick. 'Dr. Lupton' makes me feel old. Now, most of you read the literature Ms. Johnson sent you so I won't bore you with all the details, but the Flower Gardens are the result of two salt domes pushed near the surface during the Jurassic period. Coral polyps from Caribbean reefs five hundred miles to the south found their way...."

Fascinated, Betsy listened to the music in his voice as he explained how the ancient reefs were formed.

"When we dive today, try not to touch the coral. It's made up of tiny carnivorous polyps. When one is touched, it may die. The reef you are about to dive is still one of the healthiest in the world because it is so isolated. You will see some major damage caused by oil tankers that dragged their anchors and slashed large gorges across the coral."

An audible moan came from the rapt listeners as he described the harm caused to the reef by lack of education. "Today, the Flower Gardens are protected.

Among other restrictions, you can't gather coral here or fish."

He continued to give instructions for the dive as the boat came to rest. "If you'll notice, we are anchoring with soft fiber line rather than chain. This is to prevent further damage to the coral. Larger boats are no longer permitted to anchor here at all."

When Nick had answered all the questions, the divers scurried about donning wet suits and myriad colored canisters. Betsy felt like a clumsy sea lion on dry land as she adjusted the air tank Nick held for her. The long flippers on her feet made walking awkward as she helped Nick with his gear. Though nothing had been said, it was understood that the two of them would be partners.

The divers left the boat in pairs, three pairs, then it was Nick and Betsy's turn. They sat on the edge of the boat and rolled backward into the ocean. Immediately, the heavy weight of her air tanks and weight belt was lifted from her body. No longer awkward or clumsy, Betsy glided through the water.

Nick swam a few feet away. With their movements slowed by the force of the water, they descended the fifty feet to the uppermost portion of the Flower Garden. Each breath they took was audible when they exhaled and it left a tiny trail of bubbles that ascended toward the surface. Below, the bottom crackled with the sound of invertebrates and fish.

Nick motioned to her. Gently kicking, she followed as he led the way over and between the reefs of cavernous star and giant brain coral. The vista before her was breathtaking. Living purples, greens, reds and coppers clung to the multicolored skeleton. A red-and-yellow Spanish hogfish flitted away into a crack as Betsy and Nick approached.

Rolling over in unison like floating ballet dancers, they cut through the clear waters in search of new wonders. Hovering a few feet over the reef, Nick pointed out an eighteen-inch-long scorpion fish hiding among the sponges. Without his aid, she would have never spotted it as it lay motionless on the bottom waiting for an unsuspecting meal. Betsy saw the red feather worm first. Its feathers and abstractness made her think of a Picasso dandelion. But no human could reproduce the beauty and peace of this underwater sanctuary formed millennia ago. Here the shapes were soft and rounded, any straight lines and sharp angles a sign of man's invasion by wreck or castoff. The Flower Garden was still pristine with gently rolling coral boulders ten feet high.

Farther on, Betsy found a brown-and-white sea anemone, its tentacles gracefully swaying in the current, beckoning to the unwary. When she turned to see if Nick had seen it, she noticed his black-sheathed legs also swayed in an underwater dance, not unlike the anemone's. It was seductive, drawing her toward him, into his lair, just as fish were drawn and snared by the anemone's tentacles. Edging closer, she joined Nick in his dance, their bodies swimming in arcs to the left, to the right, to a gentle descent in a primitive ritual. Seventy feet below the water's surface, she felt more at one with Nick than she ever had with anyone else.

AFTER THE SECOND DIVE, the underwater mood of tranquillity was filed in memory as the divers stowed their gear and all talked at once, trying to describe the beauty they had encountered. The excitement prevailed through dinner but began to abate as the group broke up and people wandered about to enjoy evening settling over the green Gulf waters.

Nick and Betsy found a quiet spot along the port side of the boat. Moved by the intimacy they had shared underwater, they were content not to talk as they leaned against the rail and studied the gentle waves.

Nick wasn't sure what had happened on the reef. But he did know that Betsy Johnson had a hold of his heart and her fingers were stroking it seductively.

He turned so he could see her. She was beautiful with the breeze blowing her hair away from her face, as beautiful as she was underwater when the currents playfully rearranged her locks. Still wanting to make amends for not letting her go on the dive to the oil platform, he said, "You really are a good diver."

"Thank you."

"Am I totally forgiven for not letting you go on that dive?" Her forgiveness and approval were important to him. Over the past few weeks, he'd experienced a happiness he hadn't felt for two years, and he knew it was the result of being with her, watching her patience with Billy and listening to her comforting words of encouragement. "Well?"

She smiled and waited for the couple strolling the deck to get out of hearing distance. "I don't know. You've taken me sailing and you came along to help with this dive. Do you think we're even?"

He enjoyed the way she turned what had caused them both pain into something they could kid about. "What else would it take to get your forgiveness?"

"You're a resourceful man. I'm sure you'll come up with something."

Nick leaned into the rail to allow someone to pass, then turned to face her. "Well, for starters, I'd send you two dozen roses. Then, assuming we're alone...." The thought of what he would do with her if they were not surrounded by people was enough to increase his pulse rate.

"Assuming we're alone," she prompted, leaning closer.

"I'd probably kiss you." He watched her reaction, recalling the night when he'd taken her into his arms and felt her sensuous response. "Long... Slow...." He drew the words out, his voice deep with building desire.

"Mmm. That sounds nice. Do I get to kiss back?"

Nodding, he said, "I hope so." He looked deep into her eyes before sweeping her body with his gaze. He fought the urge to reach out and stroke the swell of her breasts visible in the unbuttoned front of the white shirt she had tied over her bathing suit. He couldn't touch her. Not on an aquarium excursion. "But," he added hoarsely, "your shirt is definitely an obstruction of beauty."

Her eyes narrowed and darkened. "There are laws against obstructions," she whispered.

"In that case, we'd get rid of obstructions." He stopped, hoping that his state of arousal wasn't apparent as he nodded to the captain when he walked by.

"And then what would you do?" Betsy's voice was low and husky.

"What would you want me to do?"

"I'd want to feel your hands on my skin. I'm not a coral reef. I can be touched." She looked down at his hands as they curled around the metal rail in frustration.

Memories of times when he'd run his hands over her shoulders and bare arms flooded his senses. "Your skin is so cool, so smooth, so soft when I touch it." This verbal foreplay was getting to be more than he could take.

"Your hands are so warm, so sure." Her eyes returned to his and she swallowed. "I'd want to trace the muscles of your chest with my fingers."

"Oh, God," he groaned. He felt as if he were about to burst. He couldn't ever remember being this aroused, ever wanting to make love to a woman this much and he hadn't even touched her. All he knew was they had to stop, or he was going to have her down on the deck and they would both lose their jobs.

The remainder of the trip, Nick planned how he could be alone with Betsy. Billy wasn't going to be at home tonight. Tomorrow was Saturday so neither he nor Betsy had to work. Even though it would be late when they got back to port, he would invite her to his place.

But his plans were ruined when he stepped off the boat.

"Hey, Nick," a grizzled old sailor from the charter boat office greeted him. "A woman named Keefer called from CC Security and wanted you to get in touch with her, and I quote, 'The second he gets back.'"

Damn! Something must have shown up on the cameras she had installed at the aquarium. He hurried back to where Betsy was unloading gear. "There's a problem at the aquarium. I've got to go." The last thing he saw before tossing his tank and flippers in the back of the Jeep was Betsy holding her gear, bewilderment on her face.

CHAPTER TWELVE

THE SWEET AROMA of fresh roses greeted Betsy when she opened her office door Monday morning. In the middle of her desk was a lush bouquet of salmon-colored roses, not red, not yellow for Emily Morgan—the yellow rose of Texas—but salmon. At least two dozen. She searched among the thorn-clipped stems for a card but found nothing. Yet, she knew they were from Nick. They were a peace offering.

She needed one, too, from this man she was falling in love with, from this man whom she'd once thought loved fish more than he loved any human. At the time, she'd meant Billy, but she felt as if she was as much a victim as Billy. After the intimacy they'd shared on the return from the Flower Gardens, she was disappointed when he'd hurriedly left. She'd been sure he'd call later and explain but he hadn't. She'd called his house once during the weekend but got his answering machine. Pride kept her from calling again.

Burying her face in the sweet cluster of the salmon-colored velvet petals, Betsy sensed his apology was deeper than this token of flowers.

Mary Alice knocked on the open door and without waiting for an answer, walked in. "Good morning,

Betsy. I saw the florist bring in a big box a while ago, and you know me... I wondered what was going on." Her eyes widened when she caught sight of the flowers. "Who sent all these roses?"

Her reverie broken, Betsy greeted Mary Alice. "I'm not sure, but I think Nick probably sent this whole flock of flowers."

Mary Alice studied the blooms, then shook her head and started for the door. "They're nice, but it's a pity to spend that much money on something that's going to die in a few days."

"Now, Mary Alice, didn't you ever get flowers?" Betsy regretted her question as soon as it was out. From the gossip she'd heard, maybe Mary Alice had never had the joy of receiving flowers.

A misty look veiled the woman's eyes as her mouth formed a weak smile. "Once."

Relieved that she hadn't unwittingly hurt Mary Alice, Betsy said, "It's a special feeling. I'm going to find Nick and thank him."

"Yes, you should do that." Mary Alice straightened her rounding shoulders and started out the door. Clutching the door facing, she stopped and turned back with a questioning look on her face. "Betsy, did Nick explain who the blonde was he sneaked into his office last week?"

Betsy's heart flinched at the question. "No, Mary Alice, he didn't." The glow from having received the flowers faded a little.

"He's always had a soft spot for blondes. Vicki had beautiful blond hair, you know?" She made a point of looking at Betsy's black hair.

"I've heard." To mask any effect the words had on her, Betsy picked up a rosebud and studied it. She didn't want to hear about Vicki.

"But your hair's lovely, too, dear. I wouldn't let it worry me any." Mary Alice shuffled out the door, her right hand resting on her fanny pack.

Debating whether Mary Alice was being malicious or just thoughtless, Betsy carried the rosebud to the wet area as she went in search of Nick. Her own grandmother was often guilty of the same type of comment, totally unaware of its impact on people. Once it was pointed out to her, Agnes would simply comment, "Well, I didn't mean it that way. Besides, it's the truth." Was that what Mary Alice had done? Told the truth.

Betsy hesitated approaching Nick when she spotted him conferring with Chester. She wanted to hurry to him, but feared that Nick might not want Chester to know that he and Betsy were more than just co-workers. She discarded the idea as quickly as it had popped into her mind. Had Nick wanted secrecy, he would have had the roses sent to her house, not where the staff would undoubtedly get wind of it. She smiled, and with eyes closed, the aroma of the rosebud became sweeter.

When he saw her watching him, Nick lifted his hand in a wave, said something to Chester and headed her way.

"You found the roses?" A tentative smile touched his eyes in a quest for her reaction.

"Yes. They're beautiful." Betsy lightly stroked the velvet petals as her blue eyes met his in a tender acknowledgment of the message that lay behind the roses. "Thank you."

"You're welcome. I do want you to know that although my work is demanding, there aren't many work emergencies that force me to skip out like I had to the other night." He lowered his voice. "The problem turned out to be a false alarm, but it took a while to check it out. The roses, they're a way of apologizing. Again."

"I understand." Betsy rolled the stem in her hand, the bud brushing the tip of her nose. "Their color is so unusual."

"And hard to find."

A single flower, a simple bouquet would have done, but Nick had wanted his offering to commune with her on a deeper level. She looked into his eyes, eyes reflecting the same emotion she'd seen on the boat when he'd promised her flowers. "Now, what did you say was the next step?" she reminded him.

Emotion spread over his face, erupting into a smile that went all the way to his eyes. This time, there was no shadows lurking in their depths. "Ah, I remember well," he said, moving toward her with deliberate slowness.

Betsy stepped back and glanced around the work area at the staff going about their tasks. "You can't kiss me here," she warned.

"Then let's go somewhere else."

The warmth of his hand as he took her arm spiraled through her body. "I can't." She wanted to so badly, she would have been willing to forfeit her job to do so. But, like Nick, she had an obligation. "I have a tour in a few minutes."

"Tell 'em you came down with beriberi."

Betsy chuckled at his suggestion as she reluctantly withdrew her arm from his caressing palm. "You're impossible. Besides, you can't get away, either."

Nick glanced around the wet area. "You're right. Then, I guess I'll have to take you to dinner tonight. Someplace fancy. Say eight o'clock."

"I'll be waiting."

AT THE TIME, she didn't know the words were prophetic. By seven forty-five, she'd clipped on her heavy silver earrings. Their matching necklace lay over her simple royal blue silk dress. She was ready. At five after eight, she retouched her makeup and rearranged the dozen roses she'd brought home. Something must have come up to delay Nick. As usual, he was on call at the aquarium, but surely there hadn't been another accident.

She turned on the television and flipped through several channels. A documentary about sharks was on the Discovery channel. Strange, she didn't know if Nick ever watched television, but if he did, this is what he'd probably watch. By eight-fifteen, she was getting anxious. She adjusted the pillows on the sofa for a second time and rearranged her flared skirt over her knees. Glancing at the telephone, she willed it to ring.

Finally, it did.

Nick's voice was clipped as he explained. "Betsy, something's come up at the aquarium. Sorry, but I'm not going to be able to make it tonight."

"Has something happened again?"

"Yes. A jewfish is in trouble. I've got to go."

"Good luck," she murmured into a receiver that echoed a click. She sighed, disappointed that she wouldn't get to see Nick tonight. Then she berated herself for her uncharitable attitude—she really did understand that at times his work had to come first. With the accidents at the aquarium, this must be one of those times. Still, it was hard to be happy about how often Nick's work took him away from Billy. And from her.

Shedding her clothes and the silk underwear chosen with special care, she stood naked next to her bed, thinking about turning back the white comforter, crawling between the perfumed sheets and moping. No, she thought. She was too frustrated to feel sorry for herself, much less read or sleep.

Yanking open a dresser drawer, she pulled out some black leotards and a lime green workout suit. She finished slipping them on as she strode down the hallway to the living room. A fast tape would help. Finding what she wanted, she stuck the video into the VCR.

She understood. Of course, she did. Nick had an emergency. She kicked to the left, to the right. Bring the feet up higher, girls, the tape encouraged. He had lots of emergencies. Would this be standard procedure if they did become seriously involved? Night after night? For an ugly old jewfish.

She'd never seen an uglier fish although she'd refrained from telling Nick that. It actually had lips—lips that were turned down in a perpetual frown. He'd broken their date for a motley brown, warty looking fish. Betsy kicked higher.

Stopping, she bit her bottom lip in reflection. *"What am I thinking?"* she said aloud. *"Betsy, gal, get a grip. If Nick's important to you, so is that fish."*

ONE MINUTE AFTER Nick hung up the phone, he was in his wet suit and grabbing a snorkel. He couldn't believe his misfortune when the night-duty operations officer called just as Nick had finished knotting his tie, and told him that one of the aquarium's bread-and-butter fish—one of the fish that drew crowds—the three-hundred-pound jewfish, was in trouble.

Before he'd called Betsy, he'd assessed the situation, hoping he could still make his date. There was no way. He didn't know how long the salvage effort was going to take, or even if it would be successful.

"You ready, Eric?" he asked the second diver who would act as rear guard against the sharks in the tank.

"Let's go."

At the acknowledgment, Nick slid into the water first. The large fish was gagging and rolling in the tank as it choked. It had attempted to swallow a gray triggerfish tail first. Seldom did a fish make such an error. The triggerfish's spreading pectoral fins were wedged in the jewfish's throat, preventing the prey from going up or down. The expression of the seemingly bewildered stuck fish made Nick wish he'd brought a camera.

Taking a deep breath from his snorkel, Nick eyed the jewfish's gaping mouth, then half submerged his body in the giant fish's mouth. Wrestling with the triggerfish, Nick dug the offending meal out of the jewfish's maw. Loosened, the triggerfish shot through the water to hide amid the rocks. The second diver had a wedge ready to allow Nick to escape from the hungry, but stunned jaws of the jewfish.

Once more, success.

By the time he got dressed and assured himself that the jewfish was suffering no ill effects from the ordeal, it was after ten o'clock. Too late to go by Betsy's. He'd explain everything in the morning. At least it appeared that this crisis hadn't been engineered by someone.

BETSY DIDN'T GET to talk to Nick much for the next two days at work. He was in and out and she was very busy. But he had come by early the next morning after his bout with the jewfish and explained what had happened. Afterward, she'd gone to stare at the slow-moving sea creature and felt proud of Nick for having saved it.

That pride lasted until she got in from work Wednesday afternoon and began sorting through her mail. She plucked the one personal piece of mail from the others, noting it had no return address. Wondering who it was from, she turned the envelope over and slit it open. Extracting the single piece of carefully folded white paper, she opened it and read:

Be careful. Nicholas Lupton killed his first wife.

Betsy dropped the note as if it were contaminated, then bent down, and, with her fingertips, picked it up by the top edge. Frowning, she turned the paper over and over while searching for any clue as to who might have sent it. The block printing, done in black ink, looked rather childish. The plain white twenty-pound copy paper could be picked up anywhere. She checked the postmark hoping to pinpoint the station, but it was posted at the main post office downtown.

Bewildered, she paced the floor for a few minutes trying to decide what to do. Ignore the note or investigate it. She was certain there was no truth to the accusation, but she remembered Renee saying there had been ugly rumors.

The disturbing letter seemed to glare at her from atop her desk as she dialed Renee's number. She glared back. All she'd heard about Vicki's death had been piecemeal rumors. Now, she needed details about these rumors. Renee answered on the sixth ring, just as Betsy was about to hang up.

Betsy quickly explained about the letter. "I don't believe Nick had anything to do with his wife's death, but can you imagine anyone sending such a nasty note?"

"Actually, yes. The world is full of crazy people. Just tune in to television talk shows for proof."

"I'm well aware of that, but this isn't *Geraldo*. It's real. Why would someone purposely want to turn me against Nick?"

"Maybe for the same reason things keep going wrong at the aquarium."

"That thought occurred to me, too. There could be a connection of some type."

"Could be." Renee paused. "I've been trying to remember the specifics of Vicki's accident, and what was said afterward. Most of it was contradictory, but it seems like they were on a friend's boat... Yeah, I remember now." Renee's voice got louder with excitement. "Vicki and Nick both surfaced too fast and both got the bends."

Betsy groaned in sympathy. An experienced diver would do anything to keep from getting decompression sickness. It was excruciatingly painful—and it could be fatal.

Renee continued, stringing her sentences together in her rush to tell the story. "There was only one oxygen mask on board too, and Vicki got it. He may have put it on her... I'm not sure. So when Nick got back to Corpus, he was hospitalized... at the naval station, I think... for several days. He didn't even get to go to the funeral. I know that for a fact because I was there. Mary Alice and I went together, and she took it really hard." Renee paused for a breath. "And Nick hasn't been the same since the accident. He used to joke around and stuff, but now he's all business."

Not all business, Betsy thought briefly, before she began thinking about the pain Nick must have gone through. If he'd had access to oxygen immediately upon surfacing, it would have lessened his sickness, but according to Renee, he'd given the only tank to Vicki. Betsy couldn't even begin to fathom the psychological pain he went through at losing his wife in an avoidable accident. "What do you think went wrong?"

"Look, why don't you just ask him," Renee advised. "I'd show him that letter, too."

Betsy sighed. Advice was always a lot easier to give than to take. But she knew Renee was right. It was time to speak to Nick.

HE STARED AT the note Betsy handed him, then leaned forward and carefully laid the sheet of paper on the coffee table. "You believe this?"

"No, Nick, I don't. That's why I wanted you to see it. What I'm concerned about is that someone obviously wants to discredit you. With all the screwed-up things happening at the aquarium, and now this, it's obvious that someone's out to get you. Who'd do such a thing?"

"I don't know." He leaned back against Betsy's sofa and closed his eyes. "I don't have a clue." Vicki had been dead almost two years. Why would someone wait until now to renew suspicion about him? Obviously, they wanted to interfere in his burgeoning relationship with Betsy. His head reeled with the possibilities.

Betsy sat beside him and touched his arm. "Do you want to talk about it?" she asked.

He looked over at her. The trust in her eyes was what he needed to see more than anything. It was a great relief to know she didn't think there was any basis to the accusation.

For the first time, he wanted to talk about the accident. He wanted Betsy to know what had happened the day Vicki died. He'd talked to the investigators at the inquest and to his mother, but had dared anyone else to ask. Their opinion hadn't mattered, but Betsy's did. He took a deep breath and slowly the words began to form. "Vicki and I fought that morning. I didn't want her diving that day because of her asthma, but we went anyway." He remembered how she had put her arms around him and begged for forgiveness. Her last words had been her standard make-everything-all-right "I love you" before she stepped into the water.

Betsy sat silently, her hand still touching his arm.

"The first dive went fine. But on the second one, she developed some breathing problems. When she signaled to me, I thought she was out of air. I swam over and handed her my octopus." The image of Vicki trying to get a breath from his secondary regulator still haunted him. She'd panicked. "The water was clear when we started the dive, but by that time it was getting murky. Visibility was only a few feet, so when she became disoriented—from the asthma medicine maybe—and twisted away from me, I couldn't see her. I searched and searched. When I couldn't find her, I headed for the surface."

He leaned forward and buried his head in his hands. "I found her floating. She'd inhaled a lot of water so I dragged her to the boat and gave her oxygen. She died without ever regaining consciousness."

After massaging his forehead as if trying to rub away the guilt, he took another breath and turned back to Betsy. "I tried, damn it. I tried to save her."

"I'm sure you did."

"You don't understand. I do blame myself. For a moment that morning, before we left the house, I was so angry I didn't care what happened to her."

"That doesn't make her accident your fault."

"I wish I believed that." He gently grasped her shoulder and stared into her eyes searching for some comfort, some reassurance that her words were gospel.

"You're not to blame, Nick." Betsy's voice was soft but forceful. "Vicki was an adult who made her own decision to dive."

"In my mind I know that, but in my heart I still feel responsible." He shook his head in self-disgust. "It's even affected my diving for the past two years. I break out in a cold sweat if I have to go deeper than fifty feet."

"You seemed fine the other day at the Flower Gardens," she reassured him.

"Yeah. But it took effort—and you were there. It was a beautiful experience—diving with you."

He could see tears gathering in the corners of her eyes as he pulled her to him. The tenderness he felt for Betsy swelled to near pain. While he'd loved Vicki once, there'd been a perpetual test—he always felt he had to prove himself to some degree. Their marriage had been free-spirited in the beginning, but the last year had been beset with constant challenges caused by Vicki's mood changes.

Love should be free of threats. That was the way he felt with Betsy. She accepted him, head-on at times, but she accepted him. She was what he needed to get his life back on track.

"Betsy, I'm falling in love with you." He whispered the words against her hair, burying himself in its fragrance.

Betsy pulled back and stared at him. "What did you say?"

Nick could hardly believe the words had slipped out. Words expressing an emotion that he thought was lost to him until he met Betsy. "I love you. I wanted everything to be just right when I told you. I wanted to take you out to dinner, have candlelight, soft music, all those things that set the mood. But things keep coming up."

Her voice caught. "You love me?"

He nodded his affirmation. Uncertainty hit him when she didn't respond in kind. What if he'd been wrong? What if she'd just wanted a casual affair? He gazed into the blue fathoms of her eyes to find an answer.

"I love you, too." She reverently caressed his cheek with her fingertips before he gathered her to him and covered her mouth with his.

Nick was hungry for Betsy, not simply for a woman to end his celibacy, but for Betsy, the one woman who could make him forget loneliness. Betsy was his catharsis.

Any space at all between them—even the tiniest of crevices was a foe, an enemy to be conquered with his hands, his lips, his body. He wanted her, not in lust on the sofa, but slowly on the large bed he'd glimpsed in her bedroom when he'd picked up Billy. He loved her and wanted her to know it. He wanted to show her the depth of his feelings.

Her lips were soft, begging to be kissed. Her mouth flowered beneath his, inviting him in. He had to restrain himself from becoming too physical, too rough. But weeks of wanting her made him impatient. As their lips kindled their desire, he tugged her blouse out of the waistband of her shorts and slipped his hand beneath the soft fabric to caress her willing flesh.

His fingers burned as if they'd touched liquid fire, engulfing him in anguish as his need mounted. His hand cupped the gentle swell of her buttocks, pulling her across his lap. He could feel the well-toned muscles of her thighs and imagined them locked over his back.

He groaned and buried his free hand deep in her hair, arching her neck to better receive his kisses, his affirmations of love, his soul. He kissed her not like the zombie he'd been, but the passionately alive man she'd made him become.

Her hands, dancing over his neck, his shoulders, his back, searching his body for fulfillment, stirred his emotions into a boiling cauldron that could no longer be denied.

He wasn't sure how they made it to her bed. But he knew that he would always remember the first sight of her body. The pure white skin, the rounded curves, the dark triangle of hair, took his breath away. Reverently, as though he were touching a goddess, he allowed his fingers to worship her form. Inch by inch he discovered her, discovered what made her moan, what made her writhe in pleasure.

When his own needs could no longer be ignored, he buried himself deep inside her where he belonged. They were one. No longer separate persons, they created another entity, a third being that would live for always.

Propped on one elbow so he could better see her, with his fingertip he traced her features, her lips swollen from his kisses, her cheekbones bright from pleasure, her eyebrows framing eyes still dark from passion.

Once he reached her hair, he brushed it gently away from her face. "I love your hair. It was one of the first things that attracted me to you." He let the strands run through his fingertips and spread out onto the pillow. "When I was a young boy, I had fantasies of the perfect woman. She was like Wonder Woman—blue-eyed with coal-black hair." He buried his face against the softness of her neck and whispered, "And I've found her. You are my dream, my fantasy, my love."

And no one, no matter how many threatening letters were written, was going to keep them apart.

CHAPTER THIRTEEN

BETSY COULD HARDLY wait to get to work to see Nick after a ridiculously blissful, but fitful night. Never had she felt so complete. At the same time, her concern for his safety intensified. She knew Nick suspected someone at the aquarium was behind the accidents. She also knew Renee thought the note and accidents were connected. While lying awake, in that dreamlike state known only to lovers, she'd come up with a scheme that she planned to implement immediately.

Happy to have a sense of direction in helping the man she loved, Betsy carefully tucked the offensive note into a small leather notebook and stowed it in her briefcase. She was going to match the handwriting on the note with that of someone at the aquarium. Then she'd know who was out to tarnish Nick's reputation.

By the time she arrived at the aquarium at eight-thirty, she was feeling apprehensive. What if Nick had second thoughts? Her stomach knotted at the thought as she walked toward her office. It relaxed when she saw him leaning on the wall beside her door wearing a dazzling smile. It spoke volumes. In spite of all the problems at the aquarium, he was happy, and she felt responsible.

Flashing him a smile as dazzling as the one on his face, she asked with mock seriousness, "Dr. Lupton, what are you doing here? I thought you were supposed to be hard at work."

Nick stepped toward her. "Unlock the door, Ms. Johnson, and I'll show you."

Betsy slowly withdrew the oversize key ring from her purse and fumbled trying to get the key in the lock.

"Come on woman, I don't have all day. I sneaked away, as it is."

Throwing open the door, Betsy waved for him to precede her, then closed it behind them and leaned against the wooden barrier separating the two of them from prying eyes. She allowed her briefcase and purse to slide to the floor. "You were saying?"

His arms gathered her to him as he covered her mouth with his. Closing her eyes to savor the sensations he was causing, she immediately lost all conscious thought of her surroundings as he moved against her, awakening the passion they'd shared the previous night. She sighed and wound her arms around his neck, pressing into him until he reluctantly ended the kiss.

"I came to say good morning and tell you how much I missed you last night in my lonely bed." He punctuated his words with a quick kiss before he continued, "There should be a law against making love and having to spend the rest of the night alone, but you were right. I needed to see Billy before he went to bed. He asked where I'd been, and I told him that I was at your place."

"How did he react?" She slid her hands from his hair to his chest and traced tiny circles on his shirt. It was very important to her that Billy accept her. The child would play a big part in any relationship she and Nick might have.

"It was comical. He looked at me like a parent would a teenager and asked, 'Is it serious?' "

Pleased, Betsy tightened her arms around his waist and leaned away from him so she could see his face better. "What did you say?"

"I told him, 'Yeah, it's serious.' " He lightly kissed her forehead and each eyebrow before looking into her eyes. "As serious as it gets. I've got to get back to work before someone misses me. Have lunch with me?"

"I'd love to."

"Billy is coming to stay with me for a few hours this afternoon while Janie is in class. Mother couldn't help today because she's gotten interested in quilting. She's taking a class at some sewing shop on Thursday afternoons. She said she didn't want to be embarrassed when she went to the quilting club."

"Grandmother got to her, I see."

"Apparently." He pulled her closer and gave her one last kiss. "Gotta run. See you at lunch."

"Bye." Betsy leaned against her desk and watched him leave before gathering together her materials for the first group of children.

THREE HOURS LATER, the heat was sweltering, with the shade provided by the umbrellas on the patio outside the aquarium offering little relief. Betsy pulled up her chair by the table where Nick sat with Billy. "Hi, guys. Where's the food?"

"We forgot yours." Billy giggled as he pulled a sack out from behind his back, apparently unable to carry through with his little gag.

Betsy wrinkled her nose at Billy. "It's a good thing you were teasing, Bub. Otherwise, I'd have eaten your hamburger."

Billy covered his food with both hands. "Oh, no, you don't. This one is good." He made a face. "Daddy can't cook worth anything. He burned the hamburgers the other night."

"Why, that's a shame." Turning in mock indignation to Nick, Betsy shook her head in disbelief. "As a dad, it's an obligation to keep young men stuffed with good burgers. Since you find it such a hardship, how about if I help out by grilling hamburgers for the two of you Saturday night."

"Narly," Billy exclaimed.

Nick chuckled. "A free meal with no work sounds good to me."

"No one said anything about free. Or no work for that matter."

When they'd nearly finished their meal, Mary Alice yoo-hooed across the patio. "Yoo-hoo, Nick, oh, Nick."

Nick pulled out a chair for Mary Alice to sit in. She plopped down and pressed a hand over her chest. "I was so afraid I was going to be late that I practically ran up that ramp. It takes my breath away." She sucked in deep breaths a few more times before she finally smiled. "Hello, Betsy." Turning her attention to Nick, she asked, "What time do you want me to have Billy back here?"

"In a couple of hours. Janie will be out of class by three, and she'll stop by here to pick him up."

"We'll be here." Readjusting her pocket pouch, she motioned to Billy. "Let's get going, young man." As they started off, she turned and looked at Betsy through the tops of her bifocals. "We may stop in and see you later, Betsy."

"Guess what?" Billy piped up as they started off. "We're eating at Betsy's house Saturday night."

"Why, that's wonderful, dear. You'll have to remember your manners."

Nick leaned back in his chair as he watched his son disappear into the building. "He can't wait to tell everyone about us."

"Good. That means he approves. I'm almost as bad. I want to call all my friends, and yell it from the rooftops. It's absolute madness. I'm not hungry. I don't want to sleep."

"I thought I was the only one who felt that way. But last night and this morning before you got here, I was scared that it would all go away, that I'd just dreamed last evening, that I'd misunderstood, and you hadn't said you loved me."

She covered his hand with hers. "I was scared, too. But when I saw you by the door of my office and you were smiling, I knew everything was all right." And it would be as soon as she found out who was after Nick. "Nick, I have an idea that I think might help us find the person responsible for the note last night."

"Okay, what is it?"

"I can draw up a form, a bogus one, asking all the staff for suggestions about participating in educational programs, here in the aquarium or even at the schools in the fall. They would fill it in and I could compare their printing to that in the note."

"Sounds like it might work."

Pleased that Nick saw merit in her plan, Betsy returned to her office and designed the form. Proofreading it, she hastily added the words *Please Print* to the instructions before she ran off fifty copies.

She went to the front desk and asked Marlene, one of the volunteers, to distribute the form to all the volunteers and be responsible for collecting them later. "I'll take care of the rest of the staff. Oh," Betsy emphasized as an afterthought, "point out that I need them to print so it'll be easier for me to read."

Satisfied, Betsy went to the food preparation area. "Sue, I'm trying to get all personnel to volunteer to help with the educational programs at school in the fall. Would you mind filling out this form? Even if you don't want to volunteer, please write your name and position and just write no across the form.''

"I'll be happy to help out. Do you need it now or can it wait until tomorrow?'' She wiped her hands on a towel.

"Now would be nice. I want to start putting everyone's responses in the computer. I have a little free time this afternoon."

"Fine." Sue took out a black pen and began to print her name in the spaces. "What would you like me to do at the schools?''

"Maybe you could explain about the kitchen and food preparation and the dietary needs of the different fish. I think the kids would find your special gel fascinating.''

The special gel, made from carrots and spinach and loaded with vitamins and minerals, was fed to almost all of the aquarium's fish. There were always several of the unappetizing trays of the mixture in the refrigerator.

"Sure, I can do that. It'll make the kids glad they aren't fish. Oh, by the way, Billy was in earlier watching me." Sue grinned in a conspiratorial manner. "He said for me not to tell anyone, but that he and his dad were going to eat at your house Saturday night."

"Yes, I... They are." Betsy didn't really know how much to tell about her and Nick's relationship.

Sue smiled across the stainless-steel counter. "I think it's great. Nick needs a boost."

Betsy remembered Renee saying something about Sue's being sweet on Nick. "You don't mind?"

"Why should I mind?" Laying the towel on the counter, she said knowingly. "Ahh, you've heard that stupid rumor. Let me explain. For a while after Vicki died, I tried to invite Nick out as a friend. I thought he was missing a lot, but he never accepted. Now, I'm not saying that I wasn't disappointed. Nick is quite a hunk. A woman would have to be dead not to be interested." Sue took a pan of the infamous gel out of the refrigerator and started to slice it into one-inch cubes with more force than Betsy thought necessary.

"Thanks, Sue. I'll be back later." Betsy checked Sue's name off her list and headed out the door to find her next subject.

"Chester." Betsy was pleased to have caught someone else so soon. "Do you have a minute?"

Chester turned and walked toward her. "That's just about all I have. I'm on my way to the airport to pick up Wynona and the kids. They've been gone a couple of weeks, and I'm running late."

"Will you be back later this afternoon?"

"I won't be back until tomorrow."

"Drop in when you get back. I have a proposal for you."

Chester laughed. "Sorry, Betsy, but I'm already married."

He hastened out the door with Betsy's words following him. "Oh, darn. Then, how about discussing a project?"

She checked off one more name and headed toward the tanks. There, she found Tom staring down into the tank where the jewfish swam unharmed.

"Hi, Tom. What's happening?"

"Just checking on the jewfish. Nick did a good job, but I should have been here to help."

"You can't be everywhere, Tom. But if you want to help someone, I'd appreciate your helping me this fall." Betsy explained about the school project she was arranging.

"Do what?" Tom asked. He flinched his freckled nose and looked at her with narrowed green eyes.

Sliding her arm through his, Betsy patted his hand. "Now, Tom, it's not all that bad. All I want you to do is agree to help out a few times at school this year."

They walked around the top of the tank, checking other fish from the topside. Tom sighed. "I really don't have the time since I'm kept busy night and day. Besides, I'm not really wild about little kids."

"No one would ever know it. I saw you with a group at the Fourth of July celebration and later I overheard a kid talking about how great you were." What she'd actually heard was the child commenting that the red-haired dude thought he was hot stuff on the end of a stick.

Tom rolled his head and eyes simultaneously. "Well, you can't expect me to be rude."

"Oh, never. Otherwise, I wouldn't have asked you. I'm asking everyone, but you are so knowledgeable that I felt you'd be able to speak about things some of

the others couldn't. How about it, Tom? Just fill in
the form for me. Once, that's all I'll ask you to come.''
She thrust the form into his hand.

Tom pursed his lips as he shrugged his shoulders. "I
guess you're right. Whatever you want me to talk
about won't be any trouble, for sure. I know all that's
going on around here.''

"Great. Could you have the form back to me tomorrow, or even better, this afternoon? Please.''

Tom smiled, obviously pleased with his largess.
"No, no. Whatever you need, Betsy, just fill it out for
me. Now, I've got to get back to work.'' He handed
her the form and walked away, a bounce in his step.
"Oh, Betsy,'' he called back, "I could talk about the
time I helped Cousteau.''

Deflated, Betsy stared at the cocky form walking
away from her.

Still trying to decide exactly what to do about Tom,
Betsy headed toward the courtyard. She'd blown up
Tom's ability so much that he didn't need to fill out a
form. One lost. Turning a corner, she saw Billy sitting
beside Mary Alice.

"Hi, y'all. What're you doing down here?''

Mary Alice pointed toward a spare chair. "Come on
over, Betsy, and sit a spell. Billy and I are having a
writing lesson.''

Betsy looked over Billy's shoulder. "That's the form
Marlene gave you, isn't it?''

"Yes. I just couldn't be happier to be asked to
help.'' Mary Alice was resting her arms on the For-

mica top, all the while stroking her right wrist with her left thumb. "Do you have carpal tunnel problems, dear?"

"No."

"It's a syndrome, you know. It can be really painful."

"That's what I've heard."

Mary Alice looked at the paper Billy was printing on and read the next question. "Now, put down Tuesday as the best day for me to go to school." She leaned toward the little boy and touched his hand. "Slow down, Billy. If you write too fast, Betsy won't be able to read it."

Betsy watched, feeling helpless.

"Don't you think this is good practice for Billy? Everybody has to fill out forms, so Billy might as well learn to do it correctly."

"You're right, Mary Alice." Nodding toward the older woman's hands, Betsy asked, "Do you need an aspirin?"

Mary Alice shook her head in refusal. "No, thanks. I don't really know if this is carpal tunnel or arthritis like in my knees. But one of them's giving me fits. I was lucky to have Billy here to write for me." Mary Alice tousled Billy's hair.

Mary Alice is so sweet, Betsy thought. She didn't want to make a big deal about the older woman's not completing the form herself. It was impossible for her to explain why it was so important that each person fill out the form themselves. "Billy's a dandy. So are you, Mary Alice."

Betsy returned to her office and spread the few forms she'd already collected on her desk, then dug in her briefcase for the note. She'd briefly looked at each form and knew almost before she laid them beside the note that none would match. Each of its letter shapes was burned in her memory.

Be careful. Nick Lupton killed his first wife.

No, it was not true. Betsy was quite sure of it. Yet, someone was out there who either meant him harm or was convinced that Nick was to blame for his wife's death. Maybe the forms she'd get later would be more revealing. She wasn't through with Tom, yet, either.

Determination restored, she gathered up all the papers and put them in a file folder. Glancing at her watch, she was surprised to see it was past time to go home. She yawned widely.

"Good Lord," Nick's voice boomed from the door. "You have some nerve talking about the jewfish's mouth."

Betsy's yawn turned into a giggle. "Don't make comparisons until you see one of those things yawn. Besides, didn't your mother teach you to knock before entering."

"Uh-huh. She also said that you might miss a lot of interesting things if you always follow the rules."

"So you always follow the rules." She flashed him a wicked smile.

"Of course." Nick nodded toward the slender folder on her desk. "How did it go?"

"I struck out." She shrugged and took a deep breath as she thumbed through the papers, showing him what she'd collected. Sticking the folder into her briefcase, she added, "But I don't have all the forms yet. Tomorrow's another day, but I'd so hoped to find out something. Today."

"You're the impatient type." He walked up behind her and put his arms around her waist and slid his hands under her shirt, pulling her back against him.

She leaned her head sideways to give him greater access to her bare flesh. "You're trying to cure me of it, too."

He kissed her neck while she sighed in pleasure. "Is this the right medicine?" He turned her around and sprinkled kisses over her eyebrows, her eyelids and the tip of her nose. "Or this?" And he covered her open lips with his.

BETSY STEPPED OUT onto her raised deck and checked her new gas grill purchased specifically for the occasion. Pots of red geraniums lined one side of the deck while a hammock hung on the other side. She loved to stretch out there with a good book on cloudy mornings and forget about the real world. And since she'd met Nick, she'd thought of other activities she'd like to try in its swaying embrace. She wasn't too sure how it would work out. She could just imagine a tangle of legs and arms ending up in a pile on the deck. So much for romance. But she knew children well enough to know that Billy would enjoy the hammock.

She had a tray of tomatoes, lettuce and pickles cooling in her refrigerator. More importantly, though, she'd rented a video and gotten some games down from the top of the hall closet so they could have an old-fashioned family get-together.

The soft, royal blue silk blouse she wore had slipped loose from the back of her white shorts. Tucking it in and securing it with a wide gold metal belt, she hurried through the house to answer the doorbell.

"I'm coming," Betsy called. With a grin, she swung the door open. Nick's face was covered with a broad smile before he leaned forward and gave her a quick kiss. But, even though Billy appeared fine, he avoided meeting her eyes.

"Billy was afraid you might be outside and not hear the doorbell."

"I'd have to have been in the next county, not to have heard it."

"That's not true," Billy mumbled, easing past her to get into the house.

Betsy stepped back and watched the little boy settle on the sofa and click the remote control of the television. She shook her head at Nick as he started toward his son, a disgusted expression on his face. She didn't want Nick to chastise Billy and possibly embarrass him in her presence. It wouldn't be a good way to begin the evening. She asked, "Billy, do you want to stay inside while your dad and I grill the meat or would you like to help?"

"Naw. I wanna watch TV."

"I was hoping you would get the grill set up since you are mechanically inclined. This is the first time I've used it and I'm not sure I know how to hook up the gas." She started for the kitchen. "But your Dad can help me."

Billy scrambled up from the chair. "I'll help."

"Good. Would you carry this on your way out?" Betsy asked, handing him a platter of meat.

"Yeah." Billy took it from her and carried it toward the back door.

"He's been in a snit ever since the other afternoon at the aquarium," Nick whispered as he picked up the drinks and he and Betsy followed Billy to the deck.

She whispered back. "We'll work on getting rid of it." Louder, she said, "Billy the pliers and wrench are on the table if you need them."

"Okay."

As Billy read the instructions, Betsy thought again of the little boy who had been failing in school. He was obviously very intelligent, but would only apply himself if he was interested in the subject.

She set the table as Nick and Billy finished hooking up the gas to the grill. They worked well together.

"Ready to turn it on?" Billy asked, backing away slightly from the grill.

Betsy nodded. "Are you afraid it's going to explode?"

"Naw. We did it right. Didn't we, Daddy?"

"Yes, we did." Nick turned the knob and the burner ignited.

Betsy clapped. "Thank you both. Now, Billy would you like to be the chef?" She offered him the tray of meat.

"Yeah." He took the tray and helped Betsy spread the meat on the rack, but soon tired of watching it cook.

"You did a good job of diffusing his snit." Nick stood beside Betsy and basted the meat while they watched Billy climb into the hammock.

"Thanks."

"Hey, this is great," Billy called as he swung from side to side. But when he tried to get out, it was a different story. Sunk in the middle of the hammock, he grasped the edges and looked bewildered. "Get me outta here."

"Just roll out, but keep a tight hold on the edge," Betsy suggested.

"No. It'll dump me."

Nick said, "Give it a try, okay?"

Billy rolled out, and true to his word, fell flat on the deck emitting a loud yell.

Betsy rushed to him. "Are you all right?"

"I busted my elbow on your ole' thing."

Nick stood nearby patiently watching. "Let me see."

Billy jerked his arm away when his dad bent to look at the scrape. "Naw. It'll be okay. I'm hungry."

"The hamburgers!" Betsy and Nick both rushed to the grill in time to rescue most of the meat from the flames.

Billy complained. "You burned them just like Daddy."

"They're perfect," Nick said, setting the tray of patties on the table.

Betsy passed the buns and meat to Billy. "Would you like some help fixing your hamburger?"

"I can do it myself."

"Okay." Betsy was hurt by Billy's sudden mood swing. And things didn't improve. He wouldn't participate in the dinner conversation without prodding. He'd be animated one minute, then become silent the next. After he'd eaten less than half of his hamburger, he jumped up from the table.

"Hey, young man. Have you forgotten something?" Nick asked.

Billy sighed loudly. "May I be excused?"

Nick looked at Betsy, who smiled and nodded. In a flash, Billy was gone.

Nick and Betsy took their time finishing their meal and cleaned up the deck and kitchen before joining Billy in the living room.

"How about a game of Pollyanna?" She picked up the worn box. When her brother was alive, they had played so many times the folds in the board were loose. She hoped Billy would enjoy it as much as she had.

"What's that?" Billy asked.

The three of them settled around the table and Betsy explained the strategy of the game, adding, "Let's try it."

"Don't you have Nintendo?" Billy asked. "This sounds boring and slow."

"That's the point, son. We'll be able to visit while we play the game." When Billy frowned, Nick leaned toward him, and in a conspiratorial whisper, said, "As soon as you learn the basic moves, I'll show you how we can team up and beat the socks off Betsy."

"You and whose army?" Betsy said, meeting the challenge.

Billy straightened his back and nodded toward his dad. "You and me can do it, Daddy."

Betsy was deliberating a strategic move to put her in the lead when the telephone rang. She would have liked to ignore it, but she was always afraid something might have happened to her grandmother.

Nick looked up. "Are you going to answer it?"

"Reluctantly," Betsy said, heading toward the persistent noise. "I have a feeling I'm going to regret this."

CHAPTER FOURTEEN

NICK THOUGHT LATER as he stared into the quarantine tank how right Betsy had been. They were both regretting the interruption.

Mary Alice stood a few inches from his elbow as she explained. "I remembered that I'd left my purse here, and when I came back for it, that's when I saw these two fish floating in the tank. With what all's happened, I just knew you'd want to come look."

"You're right."

Mary Alice placed her fists on her hips. "I just wonder why Tom didn't call you. He was leaving the parking lot when I drove up."

Nick frowned. He thought Tom was going out of town this weekend. Oh, well. Tom didn't think the aquarium could run without him. He did wonder why Tom hadn't removed the fish if he'd known about them.

"That was thoughtful of you, but remember that Steve would have called if it had been anything serious."

"Yes, but he was doing something else when he let me in, so I thought I'd save him the trouble. I did the right thing, didn't I?" A troubled expression covered

Mary Alice's face as she waited for Nick's reassurance.

"Of course, you did." He didn't know what else to say. His evening with Billy and Betsy had been interrupted for a wild-goose chase. Unfortunately, Mary Alice had been almost incoherent over the phone, so he'd been unable to find out which fish were in trouble. It was certainly not unusual to lose fish from the quarantine tank.

"These fish all have a bacterial infection. We've been treating them with antibiotics, but they were just too sick to begin with," he carefully explained to the older woman, though he would have sworn that she was aware of the circumstances surrounding the fish. She'd stood around watching them treat fish in this condition ever since the aquarium had opened.

After Mary Alice had left, he disposed of the fish, a task that he still found loathsome. Looking at his watch, he noted that a couple of hours had passed. He could still go back to Betsy's if he hurried. It wasn't too late.

As he sprinted across the parking lot in the falling dusk, Mary Alice's voice rang out, "Yoo-hoo, Nick."

Nick turned toward her car.

"I can't get my car to start." She was wringing her hands. "And it's getting dark."

Nick tried the ignition, only to be met with clicking noises. He lifted the hood to check the battery cables, but after a few minutes with no flashlight, he snapped the hood closed. He didn't want to stand out here and troubleshoot a car tonight. He wanted to get back to Betsy's house. "Look, why don't I give you a lift home, and in the morning, I'll come back and see what I can do about your car."

"Well, okay." She fretted about leaving her car. "Just let me lock it up." She went to each of the four doors and pushed the locks, trying in succession to open them. "One just can't trust people anymore," she said.

Nick checked his watch and patted his foot while Mary Alice finally got everything the way she wanted it.

Even though it was only a few yards to Nick's Jeep, it was difficult for the older woman to shuffle across the concrete. Nick went to her and gave her his arm for support.

As he headed across town, it began to shower. By the time he pulled into Mary Alice's driveway, he had the wipers going full blast. A summer rainstorm was in progress with thunder rumbling in the distance.

Mary Alice didn't move when he killed the engine, her hands clasped firmly in her lap and a worried expression on her face.

"Do you need anything, Mary Alice?" he inquired.

"It's dark."

He nodded knowingly. "Let me walk you to the door. Here, let me have your keys so I can unlock the door for you."

Mary Alice unzipped her pocket pouch, fumbled around and withdrew her keys. "Here."

When he opened the front door to her house, she peered into the darkness. Finally, she took one step forward, slid her hand inside and around the corner. "The light switch is here somewhere." When she found it, light gushed out the open doorway.

Nick stood in the living room, holding Mary Alice's arm. "Is everything okay, now?" The fear had not left her expression.

"Nick, would you mind checking all the rooms for me?"

Minutes ticked away as he checked first the downstairs, then the upstairs. "It all looks okay," he explained to Mary Alice.

"Would you check the back door, please?"

Returning to the living room where she still stood dead center, he reassured her. "The back-door lock and dead bolt are fully engaged. Everything's fine."

By the time Nick persuaded Mary Alice that she was safe—he'd even checked the storage house out back and the closets—it was after ten. He wondered if such inordinate fear came with age. He shivered when he slammed the door to his Jeep, both from the strangeness he'd sensed in Mary Alice's fear and from his rain-soaked clothes.

He needed to warm up. Ten o'clock or not, he wanted to see Betsy. If she was asleep, he was going to wake her up.

SOME OF BETSY'S earlier frustration at being abandoned again subsided when she opened the door and saw Nick standing in the tropical storm. His hair and clothes were plastered to his body and a trickle of water ran off the end of his nose onto the steps.

But she wasn't quite ready to welcome him with open arms, not after spending the past several hours evaluating what her role would be in his life. She appreciated his concern for the animals, in fact, it was one of the things she loved about him. But it was going to be hard. Would she and Billy always have to play second fiddle to the animals at the aquarium? Could she accept this?

But all her concerns were shoved to the back of her mind when she opened the door and saw Nick. He had come back. That was all that mattered. Without saying a word, she wrapped the long, white robe tighter around her and stepped back to allow him to enter.

"It was a wasted trip."

"Tell me about it while you take off those wet clothes. You'll get sick." She dragged up an area rug for him to stand on.

"You know those fish with the bacterial infection that we all expected to die?"

"Yes."

"Well—" he swayed as he unlaced a shoe while balancing on one foot "—they did. Mary Alice wanted me to come see their corpses."

"What was she doing at the aquarium?" she asked over her shoulder.

"She'd left her purse there and went back to get it." He peeled off his socks and dropped them on his shoes.

"That's strange," Betsy called from the bathroom. "She doesn't usually carry a purse." Carrying a big, fluffy, hunter green bath towel, she returned to the living room.

"The whole evening was strange. Her car wouldn't start, so I took her home. That was a two-hour chore by the time I'd checked everything." He slipped his belt out of the loops. "Betsy, I feel really sorry for Mary Alice."

"Why?" Betsy did too, but she wondered if it was for the same reason.

"She's afraid of her own shadow. I'm telling you, she was terrified. I checked her yard and storage house, all the rooms, the closets—I even checked under the beds."

"Oh, that's sad. Grandmother's nervous to go into her house alone at night, too."

"At first, I thought she was coming up with ways to keep me from leaving until I realized she was truly afraid." Nick gave his hair a final toweling. "Maybe it was because I was in a hurry to get back here."

His words warmed her. She'd been a little hard on him earlier. Even though he wanted to be with her, with all the crises at the aquarium, he did need to check out anything suspicious. It wasn't a job he could delegate to anyone else right now, she reasoned. As soon as the problems cleared up, he'd have more time for her and Billy. "I wondered if you'd come back, but after a couple of hours passed and you didn't call, I didn't know. . . ."

"I didn't think it would be appropriate for Mary Alice to hear what I'd say to you." He began to unbutton his shirt.

"Here, hand me that and I'll hang it up to dry." Betsy held her hand out as he exposed well-tanned skin.

He slithered out of the wet garment and handed it to Betsy. "Did you have any trouble getting Billy to Mother's?"

"No. We had a nice talk." She hung the shirt on a plastic hanger and carried it to the bathroom. "Did you think he seemed a little distant toward me tonight?"

"He was rude, but I thought he was just angry with me for God knows what."

Nick's answer wasn't reassuring. "Maybe it was just my imagination, but he'd be friendly one minute, then seem to catch himself. It was as though he wanted to talk but something kept him from it, especially when I tried to help him. Do you think it's because he doesn't want us to be serious about each other."

"Hmm, he hasn't said anything, and I think he would have."

"Anyway, he seemed to warm up a little after you left. He told me that your birthday is next Sunday."

Nick ran the towel over his chest. "Yes, it is."

"How old will you be?"

"Too old." He held the towel out toward her. "Would you dry my back?"

"Sure. So how old are you?"

"Let's just say I keep good company. Jack Benny and I have a lot in common."

"I'd have never guessed it. Thirty-eight maybe, but not thirty-nine." Betsy ran the towel over his back, drying the drops of moisture on his skin, marveling at what good shape he was in.

When the towel dropped to his waist, Nick asked, "Do you want me to take off my pants, too?"

"Only if you intend to sit down." She watched him work out of the soaked jeans. "I don't know why Mary Alice didn't offer you an umbrella."

"She did, but I was already drenched." He picked up the jeans and dangled them from his hand. "What do you want me to do with these?"

"I'll take them," she said, exchanging the towel she was holding for the jeans.

Returning from the bathroom, she watched him dry his legs and drape the towel around his neck. It hung from his shoulders, hiding a little, certainly not the desire reflecting from his eyes. He wasn't even trying to hide the fact that he'd come back with the intention of making love to her.

He shivered. "I think I'm chilled to the bone," he said.

Betsy crossed her arms and pretended to assess the situation. Except for the towel and his damp underpants, he stood naked in the center of her living room.

The last of her anger evaporated. "I guess I can turn off the air-conditioning and get you a blanket."

Nick looked at her with a serious expression as if considering the choices. "Just get me a blanket please."

She returned in seconds with a large green velour blanket.

Nick gathered it around his upper body and settled on the sofa. "That's better." Motioning with his finger, he said, "Why don't you join me? There's room in here for two."

"I thought you'd never ask."

He enveloped her in the blanket, tucking her head on his shoulder. "I hate that tonight ended so abruptly, Betsy." Leaning back to meet her gaze, he added, "Particularly since Billy and I were about to thrash you."

"For your information, it was important for Billy to feel successful the first time he played a game with me, so I was letting the two of you win."

"Bull." Nick teased her lips with his as his hands slithered down her back, sending warmth through her body. She felt him pull the loop out of her sash, and her robe fall open.

THE NEXT MORNING, as they lay in each other's arms, Betsy traced figure eights around his bare nipples with her fingertip. "Let's do something special for your birthday."

"What would you like to do?"

She sat up slightly to look into his eyes. "Let's go to South Padre. Just the two of us. I know where we can rent a little cottage. We won't ever have to go outside unless we want to."

"Sounds good." He raised himself on his elbow, reversing their positions. Her hair spread like a halo when she fell back against the white satin pillowcase. "Of course, I wonder what we'd do if we were house-bound." He nibbled on her earlobe. "We might get bored." He moved to her other ear, exploring her flesh with his tongue. "What do you think?"

She didn't think she would ever tire of his lovemak-ing. It would be heaven to spend hours and hours in bed with this man. Her answer to his question was an incomprehensible moan as he nuzzled her neck with his lips, kissing, biting and sucking as he edged lower.

When his warm mouth reached the dark circle of her breasts, an uncontrollable quiver gripped her. Clutching at the sheet by her side, her hands formed a fist as he suckled. A fog of pleasure masked coherent thought.

She gasped as cool air bathed her lower body when he threw back the coverlet and coaxed her over onto her stomach. He planted kisses along her spine while his hands stroked her sides and cupped the swell of her bottom. She could no longer control the cry of plea-sure that was building inside. A deep moan escaped as he slid lower, kissing her buttocks, her thighs.

"Want me to stop?" he whispered.

"No." She rolled her head from side to side. "No, I love it."

He continued stringing kisses down her side and across her rear, until unable to bear the mounting desire, Betsy rolled onto her back. She looked down to Nick's head buried between her thighs. She wanted to feel his tongue on her, but she wanted to feel him inside of her more. Her breath coming in short pants, she reached down and grasped his shoulders. Pulling his heated body over hers, she whimpered, "I need you. Now."

His mouth found hers, their tongues dancing in the eternal act of love. Nick consumed her, all questions of what they would do if they were housebound forgotten.

FRIDAY AFTERNOON Betsy slowly latched the suitcase lid. Before they'd even begun their trip, it had been wrecked. At the last minute, he'd called to say he couldn't make it. He'd been polite enough, saying he would explain everything later when he dropped by. He could drop by all he wanted, but she wasn't going to be there.

He could stop by long enough to take her to bed, but not to dinner, not to the movies. Was that all she was to him? A bed partner? She'd certainly put a stop to that. She reopened the suitcase and dug out the sexy lace lingerie she'd so carefully packed. She crammed the garments into a bottom drawer and selected more subdued cotton ones. Her grandmother wouldn't be impressed with black teddies.

A pang of guilt about being childish permeated her silent tirade, but she reasoned it away. She wasn't being childish, just practical. After all, even Ann Landers said that a person can't be treated as a doormat unless she allowed it. How would Nick feel if she never had time for him? Maybe he needed to find out how it would feel.

She went through the house gathering up her luggage, then tossed the bags in the trunk of her car. The problem with Nick was he thought he was the only person who could take care of things at the aquarium, she decided as she locked her house.

On the way to pick up her grandmother, Betsy tried to put her hurt into perspective. It wasn't just her that Nick pushed to the side—it was Billy, too. Nick expected his mother, Janie and Mary Alice to take care of Billy. And Betsy had even found herself helping out. Billy was a little boy and couldn't help how he was treated, but she could.

The front door of her grandmother's house was open with a stack of luggage clustered in the entry. Betsy called, "Grandmother?"

"Just a minute, dear," Agnes called from the recesses of the house. "I'd better go to the bathroom before we leave. I've been hurrying so, ever since you called."

Betsy hollered back, "I'm glad you could come on such short notice."

Her grandmother appeared, adjusting her skirt as she came down the hall. "It's just such a shame that Nick couldn't get away after all the arrangements you made." She gave Betsy a hug. "I know you were looking forward to this weekend. Being with an old lady just won't be the same."

Betsy grinned in acknowledgment. No, the week with her grandmother wouldn't be at all like the one she'd planned with her lover. "We'll have lots of fun. We can go to the beach and shop until we can't walk. Then, when we're dead on our feet, we'll relax at the little cottage I rented." She talked as she gathered up the luggage and led the way out of the house. "And we can eat. There's this restaurant I was telling you about. The cheesecake is just out of this world."

THE NEXT MORNING, even though it was Saturday, Nick was at work. He flipped through the papers on his desk while he waited for Tom to arrive. Nick had started a file on each of the employees. It contained his own observations, and samples of everyone's handwriting, thanks to Betsy. Everyone's handwriting except Tom's, Chester's and Mary Alice's. Somehow, they had slipped through the process.

He studied Mary Alice's file. Her form bore Billy's familiar scrawl. Nick made a note about the dead fish and her car. That had been a strange night. The next morning, after what had seemed like a futile attempt to get her car started in the aquarium parking lot, he found that the only thing wrong was some loose wires.

He looked up when Tom knocked on the open door. "Close the door." Nick leaned back in his chair and studied Tom. "I called you in because I want to know what you were doing in the storeroom for an hour yesterday afternoon when you were supposed to be working."

"I...I wasn't in the storeroom an hour." Tom's voice was hostile.

"You were seen going in and coming out."

"By whom?" Tom fidgeted.

Nick ignored his question. "So was a young volunteer named—" he picked up a paper and glanced at it "—Patricia Moore."

Tom's face turned bright red, blending with his hair. He stared at Nick in open defiance.

"I believe her husband is the night-duty operations officer," Nick said.

"So what if he is. What does that have to do with me?"

Nick held out a photograph of Tom peeping out the storeroom in a disheveled state with Patricia Moore's face showing in the shadows behind him.

Tom took the picture, studied it a second, then tossed it down on the desk.

"Tom, what you do with Mrs. Moore is my business as long as it could affect the morale at the aquarium. I'd say having two employees committing adultery is cause for concern."

Tom mumbled something about the pot calling the kettle black.

"What did you say?"

"You're doing the same thing." Tom puffed out his chest and glared at Nick. "I've seen you and Betsy Johnson together more than once."

Instantly angry, Nick stood up and glared back at the man. "There's one enormous difference. Betsy Johnson's not married, as opposed to your *Mrs.* Moore. Do I make myself clear?"

Tom seemed to shrink. He nodded.

"Tom, this is a warning. You're a good employee, so don't let your extracurricular activity jeopardize the running of the aquarium. If that happens, I'll have no choice but to fire you."

After Tom left, Nick leaned back in his chair. He was furious. He'd given up a weekend with Betsy on South Padre because for several days the hidden cameras had picked up suspicious movements by Tom and this Moore woman. After further surveillance, it looked as if the only thing they were guilty of was sneaking off together, and they weren't very subtle about it.

Running his fingers through his hair, he emitted a breath of disgust and studied the clock above his desk. There was still time. Maybe Betsy would be interested in going to South Padre or somewhere else for the remainder of the weekend. He picked up the phone to call. When no one answered, he decided to drive by her house to see if she might be outside.

SUNDAY NIGHT, Nick asked Billy, "Do you know where Betsy went? Did she say anything to you? I've tried to get hold of her all weekend."

"Naw. I don't know." Billy glanced up from the carpet where he was watching television. "Did you try her grandmother's?"

"Yes. No one is home."

"Maybe she went to South Padre with her boyfriend."

"I'm her boyfriend."

Billy shrugged his shoulders and turned back to his program.

"What's that supposed to mean?" Nick asked. "Hey, turn that thing off." He indicated the TV.

"It didn't mean nothing."

"Quit using double negatives. It drives your grandmother crazy. Now, what *did* you mean? Why do you think she might have gone somewhere with him?" He couldn't bring himself to use the man's name.

"Maybe she got tired of you having to work."

"But I had to."

"That's what you always say."

"I do not." Nick frowned, remembering how upset Billy had been when he'd found out he wasn't invited to go with him and Betsy for the weekend. He'd pouted and tried to hide the tears. If Billy really did feel neglected, Nick wanted to remedy the situation. Nick sat down on the floor next to Billy. "Do I really say that a lot?"

Billy sat up and looked Nick straight in the eyes. "Yes, you do. You're always telling me that you'll do something with me, then something happens at work and you don't do it."

"Billy, you don't understand. That's my job, and I have to make a living for us."

"No, you don't. We're rich."

Spoken with the innocence of youth, but there was some truth in Billy's words. If Nick never worked another day, the trust fund his grandfather had left him was large enough that he and Billy could live well for the rest of their lives. No, it was something other than money that drove him. Perhaps it was a need to be as successful in his field as his father and grandfather had been in theirs. He didn't know.

"Maybe not exactly rich, but you're right. I don't have to work for us to eat. I have to work for another reason, Billy. True, I enjoy my job, but I want you to understand that I also made a commitment to the aquarium. I'd be less than an honorable person if I didn't do as good a job as possible."

"Did you make a commitment to Mom?"

Nick felt as if Billy had punched him in the stomach. How could he have been so ignorant, so insensitive to his son's needs? In a flash, Billy's fears had been opened to him, something that should have happened a long time ago. "Yes, Billy, I did. And to the best of my ability, I met it." He tried to hug his son, but Billy leaned in the opposite direction.

"Billy, I love you." He hoped for the right words, words that would bridge the pain and doubt that had obviously filled Billy's psyche. "I also made a commitment to you, but I haven't been so good about doing what I should."

Billy hesitated. He looked into his father's eyes before moving into Nick's embrace. No words were necessary as they held each other.

Nick patted his son's back until Billy had apparently had all the hugging a ten-year-old boy could tolerate.

"I love you, too, Dad." Billy pulled away and sprawled on the floor to continue watching his favorite television show.

Acknowledging to himself that the mood was broken, yet reluctant to leave it completely, Nick sat down in a recliner and stared first at his son then at the television. He couldn't get interested in the sitcom that had Billy giggling. Nick's mind kept straying to Betsy. Surely, she hadn't asked Robert to go with her.

Billy interrupted his thoughts. "What are you mad about?"

"What makes you think I'm angry?"

"'Cause of the way you look. You're frowning. Did I do something wrong?"

Nick sat up. "No, river rat, you didn't do anything wrong. You did everything right." He pulled a pillow off the sofa and lay down beside his son. He grinned and ruffled Billy's hair before settling back on the pillow. "I'm just worried about Betsy."

CHAPTER FIFTEEN

"SLOW DOWN a little. I'm not as young as I used to be and it takes longer to look." Agnes withdrew a necklace made of small oval-shaped shells from a bin of similar novelties. "What do you think of this?"

Betsy laughed, unable to believe Agnes would choose such a necklace. "Where would you wear it, Grandmother? Church?"

"Mercy, no. I'm getting it for Bertha." Agnes snapped open her purse, extracted her wallet and paid the cashier. "She'll appreciate it."

Betsy shook her head.

Agnes smiled when she tucked the small paper sack in her purse. "Okay, let's head back to the cottage."

Hot air blasted from the car even though Betsy had left the windows cracked a little. She adjusted the air-conditioner as they headed toward the beachfront cottage.

After they'd unloaded their purchases, Betsy poured cold drinks and headed for the bright airy living room. She took off her shoes and reclined on the white wicker sofa which was filled with overstuffed cushions. Agnes would want the straight-backed chair and the ottoman. Being with her grandmother was a pleasure, but melancholy stole over her, nonetheless.

Agnes smoothed the skirt to her dress as she settled herself in the chair and crossed her ankles. She dropped her hand down and picked up her sack of yarn. "Now, it's time for us to have a little talk."

"What do you want to talk about?"

"You. What else is there?" They both giggled.

"I can't believe I start back to school in just nine days. It's been a short summer."

"I'd say it's been an exciting summer. Working at the aquarium and *all*," Agnes said, emphasizing the last word.

"It was fun. Friday was a little sad when everyone dropped by to say goodbye." Images of the aquarium and its employees appeared before her. "Renee came by to get briefed on where to start. That made me realize it was really over."

Agnes looked up from the blue afghan she was crocheting. "Nonsense. Not with Nick around."

"I'd rather not talk about him."

"Whatever you say." Agnes unwrapped some more yarn. "Did you ever find out any more about Mary Alice and her daughter?"

"No." Betsy knew her grandmother well enough to know she was being set up to ask why so Agnes could impart some new information. "Why?"

"Well…Era said that she saw a young man over at Mary Alice's house the other night. She said he went in and out several times and it was raining like crazy. She thought the whole thing was very strange."

"It was Nick." Betsy explained what had happened. "Nick said Mary Alice told him she'd left her purse at the aquarium. I thought that was odd. She doesn't carry a purse. She wears that pack thing. And she guards it like it's the U.S. Mint." Betsy sipped some of her cola.

"Anyway, Nick had to take her home because her car wouldn't start. So they left it at the aquarium. I went with him the next morning to get it started. The only thing wrong with it was some wires had pulled loose under the dash. She must have hit them with her foot, or something. When he took her home, he was there a long time. She wanted him to check every inch of her house. Everything was double-locked, he said."

"Era says Mary Alice is funny that way. Era said that years ago she went over to tell her about a neighbor dying. Mary Alice just stuck her head out the door, never inviting Era in out of the sun. Era said she was either hiding something or had a poor upbringing, which leads me to what I was wanting to tell you."

"What's that?" Betsy sat up straighter.

"Era said that the other day she was visiting with the old man that lives down the street from her. I think he and Era have something going, but that's beside the point. Anyway, this man, Mr. Putman, is ninety years old and he remembers Mr. Garrett, Mary Alice's father." Agnes stopped to catch her breath.

"Well, go on."

"It seems Mr. Garrett was some kind of evangelical preacher but didn't belong to any regular church. He was really strict about the way his wife and daughter dressed and behaved. They couldn't wear makeup or cut their hair. And he said that Mr. Garrett wouldn't let them go anywhere without him. It must have really been hard on Mary Alice growing up that way."

"She seems really nice at the aquarium. Couldn't be more helpful to everyone. She's good to Nick and Billy. Of course, Nick's good to her, too," Betsy said.

Agnes waved her needle toward her granddaughter. "Do you realize, dear, that you keep bringing up Nick although you insist you don't want to talk about him?"

"He's hard to ignore."

"Now, just give the young man time. He's got a lot to sort through, but he'll be smart in the end."

"Grandmother, I don't think I need him in my life, at least until he gets his priorities in order."

"I've heard the wind blow before."

"Your homilies don't apply this time." Betsy got up and refilled their glasses. Returning to the sofa, she asked, "What would you do, Grandmother?"

Agnes laid down her crocheting. "I'd help him get his priorities in order. Let me tell you about your grandfather. James was so determined to be a success that he more often than not went to sleep in the front-porch swing when he came courting because he was so tired. I had to have a serious talk with him to let him know how the cow eats the cabbage.'' Agnes leaned back in her chair, closed her eyes and smiled. ''He decided he wanted me. Your Nick wants you, too.''

Her Nick. That's the way she thought of him, too. That's what hurt so much. He wasn't her Nick. He was the aquarium's Nick. ''How much time will it take him to wise up?''

''Sometimes, Betsy, you have to take things into your own hands. Do something to help him come to his senses. Shock him, but not too much.''

''I'll think about it.'' She didn't want to try to manipulate him into a relationship. It had to be his choice.

''Have you told him how you feel?''

''Not exactly. I always say that I understand, because in many ways I do. Of course, there are emergencies with the animals and he has to go in. But Nick is just too willing to rush in at the slightest hint of trouble. He's never prepared to let someone else handle things.''

''Sounds to me like you haven't been exactly honest with him, Betsy.'' Agnes pointed her needle toward her granddaughter. ''My advice to you is not to be so hard on him until you've given him a chance to hear your concerns.''

EIGHT DAYS had passed since Nick had heard from Betsy. No one seemed to know where Betsy was, or if they did, they weren't talking.

He called her house for the fourth time that day. She had to return soon. He missed her. During the week, he'd begun to come to terms with how difficult things were for her and planned to make changes. He loved Betsy.

It was five o'clock. Time to leave if he was going to follow through with his vow to spend less time at the aquarium and more time with Billy and Betsy. As he walked down the hall, Steven Moore, the night-duty officer, called out to him. Nick turned to the man. "What's up?"

"I got this note here that says to call Tom if anything comes up tonight. That right?"

"Yeah, and if you can't find him, call Chester. I'm off for the weekend."

Smiling, he strode out into the evening sun. It felt good to walk out and know he wouldn't be back until Monday morning. He and Billy would do something fun this weekend. Looking out at the bay, he thought they might tour the new ships docked nearby. They were replicas of Columbus's ships—the *Nina,* the *Pinta* and the *Santa Maria*. Betsy might enjoy it, too, if she was home. He'd swing by her house just in case.

After he rang the doorbell, he shifted his weight from one foot to the other, waiting. From the recesses of the house, he heard footsteps. After breathing a sigh of relief, an illogical anger swept through him. How dare she put him through the torment of the previous week. The muscles of his chest tightened so much, it was hard to catch a breath as the door swung open framing Betsy in a glow of warm light.

"Where have you been?" he said, glaring at her across the threshold.

"What do you mean, where've I been?"

"Considering the circumstances, I'd say it would have been common courtesy to let me know if you were going to be gone."

"What circumstances?" She was being deliberately obtuse.

"May I come in so we can finish this in private?"

Gesturing with a sweep of her arm, Betsy stepped aside to let him in. Once he was inside, she crossed her arms, leaned against the wall and waited.

"Couldn't we sit down, or something?"

"Go ahead." She nodded toward a chair, determined to remain standing, not wanting to get too close to him lest it sway her from her objective.

Noting her stance, Nick changed his mind and turned to face her from the center of the living room. "I was worried about you, Betsy. I called every day. Where were you all week?"

"I had a cottage reserved on South Padre. Remember?"

"You mean you went to South Padre by yourself?"

"No. Not by myself."

Nick's eyes narrowed. "Not by yourself," he repeated. The volume of his voice lowered, but not enough to hide his concern. "Who…ah…who went with you?"

Betsy was pleased that he was upset at the thought of her not being alone. She ought to tell him that it was none of his business so he could speculate to his heart's discomfort. Instead, she found herself weakening by the moment and told the truth. "Grandmother."

Nick sighed. "I should've known." He nodded his head in reflection. "She never answered the phone, either." He ran his fingers through his rumpled hair, turned and walked toward the dining-room windows where he stood silhouetted against the glass in a silence broken only by the gentle clicking of an anniversary clock.

Finally, he walked purposefully to where she was now sitting, and stopped only a few feet from her chair. His eyes pleaded with her to understand. "You had every right to be upset about my canceling out on our trip. I've allowed the aquarium to be my whole life without any balance between it and home. Billy and I had a long talk the other night. He taught me something about commitment and priorities. I think he and I have our problems ironed out." He hesitated before continuing. "I hope you and I can work out our differences, too. I want you in my life, Betsy."

No amount of effort could stop the tears that formed in the corners of her eyes. She wanted to believe him more than she'd ever believed anything in her life. No matter how much she tried to deny it, no matter how hard she tried to dictate that reason rule her emotions, emotion was winning. She loved Nick. A crumb might be better than having no piece of the cake at all. "Nick, I—"

"No, wait. Let me finish." He knelt beside her chair and cradled her clinched fist with his hand. "Today, I set up a rotation so I won't be on call all the time. And the fishing, Tom can handle most of it, so I'll be around more in the evenings, too. I also put out feelers for an assistant."

Her mouth was as dry as her eyes were wet. Betsy was afraid to breathe, afraid that she would disturb the tide of emotion pulling her and Nick closer together.

"And . . . I want you to marry me."

BETSY TRIED to hide her anxiety as she followed Nick and Billy up the walk to his parents' house. She looked at the two-story white stucco house surrounded by trees untouched by a breath of wind. Only the hushed sounds of cars whisking by on Ocean Drive broke the solemnity of the three of them walking hand in hand. She hoped Nick was as happy as she was about the planned announcement. What if John and Barbara Lupton or Billy disapproved? What would she do? Could she marry Nick against their wishes?

Nick punched the doorbell at the same time the door swung open. "Come on in," Barbara greeted them. "I was watching for you."

"Hi, Grandma." Billy hugged his grandmother who had stooped over for his greeting.

"Hi, Mother." Nick gave her a peck on the cheek she tilted toward him. "You remember Betsy Johnson, Billy's principal."

"Of course, Nicholas. Betsy and I met at the Fourth of July festivities. I met her grandmother, too." She turned to Betsy and took her hand. "How are you doing, dear?"

Betsy relaxed as Mrs. Lupton continued to hold her hand. "Fine, thank you."

"I'm so glad you could join us. Sunday lunch together is something of a family tradition even though Nick has been tied up at the aquarium for the past several Sundays."

Nick sniffed the air. "That was a mistake on my part. Mmm, smells good."

"It is," Barbara stated with confidence. "Your granddad's outside, Billy."

Barbara Lupton turned and started toward the kitchen. Betsy and Nick followed. "May I help you with anything?" Betsy asked.

"It's all prepared. Cooking is one of my joys in life." Barbara crossed the room, leading the way through the large, warmly decorated living room. Its plump cushions, florals and stripes spoke of home and comfort. Barbara continued to talk over her shoulder. "John and I belong to a gourmet club, but I find cooking for two a bit boring. It's more fun to cook for a crowd."

"I seldom have to do that," Betsy said.

"Nicholas, would you roll the cart out to the garden, please?" his mother asked as she unplugged a bread warmer.

Betsy followed them to a large patio enclosed on three sides by the house. In the center of the terra-cotta expanse was a three-tiered fountain. Under a canopy of twisting vines, a glass-topped table was adorned with colorful pottery place settings and fresh flowers.

"Hello, there." A booming voice preceded a man walking toward them from a corner flower garden. "I'm John. Anything good you know about Nick, he probably got from me. If it's bad, blame it on mutated genes."

Betsy laughed. She liked Nick's dad.

"Now, Dad," Nick said, "go easy. Betsy Johnson, the shy man standing before you is my dad."

John extended his hand in a warm greeting. "Pleased to meet you for two reasons, the least of which is having a decent meal."

Barbara gave him a loving look. "Not if you don't behave. Now, why don't you all be seated," she insisted as she spooned gazpacho into bowls.

When Nick pulled out her wrought-iron chair, Betsy couldn't help smiling as she took the seat. This was the first time they had eaten a meal together at a proper table. Betsy settled back into the cushioned chair, agreeing with Nick. Something did smell good.

"What's this?" Billy groaned when his bowl was placed before him. "It looks like it has tomatoes in it."

"Soup," Nick said, looking at his son with a raised eyebrow. "Eat it."

Billy stirred it a few times, then asked, "Does it have onions in it?"

Betsy lowered her head to hide a chuckle.

"Just a few, dear," Barbara said.

"I don't like onions." He made a face and started to push the bowl away.

Nick intercepted it. "If you don't care for it, sit there quietly until the rest of us are through. It's rude to say you don't like the food."

"Yes, sir."

Betsy was impressed that Billy acquiesced without feeling he had to have the last word.

His grandmother tried to lessen his discomfort. "Now, Billy, this may be adult food, but if you're polite about it, I have something special for you for dessert."

As soon as the adults had eaten their gazpacho, and Billy had eaten two spoonsful of his, Barbara uncovered browned chicken breasts seasoned with crushed Texas pecans, lemon rice, a garden salad and homemade cheese rolls.

"This is delicious, Mrs. Lupton," Betsy said after savoring a bite of the chicken.

"Mrs. Lupton is so formal. Why don't you call me Barbara. Nick tells me you are a school principal."

Betsy clarified, "Assistant elementary principal."

"I don't think I would have the patience."

Betsy smiled. "It isn't the children I find trying. It's the adults and the government. The kids are very special."

John laid his spoon beside his bowl. "I wish they would work out the funding plan for schools. I know several of the legislators personally." He stopped and looked at Nick. "Remember Senator St. Clair. He was a friend of your grandfather's."

"Who could forget him?" Nick said wryly.

"He said that it's just a matter of time before they have to find a new way to fund education without going to the taxpayers."

Betsy grimaced. She hoped she wasn't in for a long discourse on how schools had plenty of money, and if it was used wisely, there would be no need for a tax increase.

Nick set down his fork. "That's what I've heard."

Barbara interjected, "Well, something needs to be done. It's about time every student in the state had access to an equal education."

"That's what the business community is beginning to say, too," John added.

Betsy wanted to applaud. Even though the whole issue was one that would never be solved equitably, she was glad to hear that the Luptons supported education. It would make being their daughter-in-law much easier.

While Nick and his parents continued to discuss Senator St. Clair, Betsy watched Billy out of the corner of her eye. He was picking up pecan pieces individually with his fingers and putting them on his tongue before chewing them with his front teeth. She was glad that neither Nick nor Barbara corrected him, because the boy was amusing himself and allowing the grown-ups to talk.

Finally, he'd been good as long as he could. "What's for dessert?"

"For you, dear, I made your favorite brownies." Barbara cleared the dinner plates and set a platter of chocolate squares in the center of the table. "And for us... fruit in my special cognac glaze."

When they'd completed their meal, Betsy helped Barbara clear the table. Nick's mother wiped her hands on a kitchen towel, folded it neatly and placed it on the kitchen counter. "Betsy, come upstairs with me. I want your opinion on something."

Betsy couldn't imagine what Mrs. Lupton needed her opinion on. Everything about Barbara seemed perfect. Entering a country-style decorated bedroom, Barbara went to the bed and picked up a square of fabric. "I've been practicing quilting. How do you think this looks?"

"I don't quilt, myself," Betsy said, "but it looks wonderful."

"You've seen your grandmother's work, so you know something about quilting. I've decided that I may join her quilting club. I'm really the homemaker type. I love cooking, sewing, crafts and the like. The fund-raising work is for the younger women. I'm ready to rest, and Virginia said she finds quilting a delightful diversion."

"So does Grandmother." Betsy really thought that Agnes preferred the company to the quilting. Of course, that was probably the point.

After discussing Barbara's quilting technique, they went back downstairs where Nick was pacing at one end of the living room while his father was playing a game of Chinese checkers with Billy.

Nick stopped his pacing when he saw the women enter. "Everyone, come over here and sit down. I have something I want to tell you."

"Do we hafta right now?" Billy asked. "I wanna beat Granddad again."

"Yes, son. Now. This is important."

"Adult stuff, huh?"

"Sort of." After everyone had seated themselves in a corner conversation area, Nick cleared his throat. "I have an announcement." He cleared his throat again, then flashed a smile toward Betsy. "Betsy and I are planning to get married."

Nick's mother smiled broadly and clasped her palms together. "I'm so delighted." She crossed the small area and hugged Betsy at the same time that John pumped his son's hand. "Welcome to our family," Barbara said.

Billy hung back and stared, looking first toward his dad, then toward Betsy. Then, he gave a thumbs-up signal and said, "That's narly." As an afterthought, a beam crossed his face. "Hey, Miss Johnson, I mean

Betsy, that means I'll get to do what I want to in school without getting in trouble, huh?"

THOUGH IT WOULD be two weeks before classes began, Betsy sat in her office at school with a grin spread from ear to ear. She couldn't turn it off. She was getting married. To Nick. She was going to be an instant mother. She thought of her friend and colleague Susan Bradley who'd found herself an instant grandmother nearly a year earlier and vowed to call her that night. She'd invite Susan to be her matron of honor.

She needed to call Robert and tell him. After he got over his initial disappointment, she knew he'd be happy for her.

Shaking her head to clear her thoughts, she looked down at the special programs report due in the central office that afternoon. Halfway through the report she caught herself doodling and making lists on a scratch pad. With a determined effort, she forced herself to finish the report so she could concentrate on wedding plans.

At lunch, she called Renee to tell her the good news. Before she hung up, Renee said, "Oh, by the way. Something interesting happened this morning. A tour group came in, and one of the women recognized Mary Alice's name. She said she'd lived next door to her back in the fifties. Mary Alice didn't seem too pleased to see her and said she had to rush off to take care of something. But before Mary Alice could hurry off, the woman said something about being sorry about Mary Alice's daughter Catherine dying.''

"So she did have a child." Betsy felt instant pain for Mary Alice. "How did Mary Alice react?"

"That was the strange part. She said, 'You must be mistaken. I don't have a daughter.' Then she turned around and walked off, leaving that poor lady standing there shaking her head.''

"And you're sure the lady said the name—Catherine?"

"Yes. Catherine."

"Why would Mary Alice deny that she had a daughter?"

"DO YOU WANT to rent the convention center for the ceremony?" Betsy asked after looking over the list of wedding guests she and Nick had compiled.

"No. I want to scratch out three-quarters of these."

"Well, I've got to invite everyone at school, and there's my family, plus my sorority friends, and—"

"Wait, let's get focused." Nick picked up his list. "Look at this. Everyone at the aquarium, Mom's friends, family... Okay, let's count to see how many would be involved if we only invited close—" he looked at Betsy "—*close* friends and family."

They counted. "Okay, that would get us in a chapel rather than a church," Betsy said. "Is that small enough?"

Nick nuzzled Betsy with his chin. "You wouldn't consider running off and eloping, would you?"

"What do you think?" Betsy nuzzled him back.

"Right. The chapel it is."

Betsy looked around at Billy who was organizing his new school supplies. "That okay with you, Billy?"

"I guess, but why do I have to be best man?"

"Because if it hadn't been for you, I might never have met Betsy." Nick folded the sheets he and Betsy had been working on and handed them to her.

"Are y'all finally through with that stuff?" Billy closed his notebook.

"For the night," Nick said as he headed for the kitchen. "I'm going to get something to drink. Would you like a glass of tea?"

Betsy shook her head and tucked the wedding plans into her purse. "No. I need to get home." She turned to Billy. "Are you ready for school to start?"

"Naw. I'd rather be at the aquarium with Dad and Mary Alice." Billy's voice became animated. "You need to come see us. We've got a new otter."

"I'll try to come by after work to see it."

"She's not doing too good," Billy said. "She's in rehab because she got caught in a trap. But with Dad's help, she won't die. That's what Mary Alice said."

"Mary Alice is a wise woman."

"Yeah, she told me a lot today." Billy propped up on one end of the sofa and gave Betsy a funny look. "Betsy, after you and Dad get married, you aren't going to make me call you Mother are you?"

"Of course not, Billy, not unless you want to."

"That's what I told Mary Alice. She said I might forget my mother when you and Dad marry."

"Oh." Why would Mary Alice say such a thing? Betsy wondered. She'd never want Billy to forget his mother.

The last few days had been so perfect that she didn't want to spoil the effect, so she didn't tell Nick about Mary Alice's comment when he came back into the living room. After all, Billy was a child and could have misinterpreted what the woman had said. Still, this time, she decided she needed some questions answered and decided to do a little snooping.

BETSY HAD AN HOUR to search the records at the courthouse the next afternoon before it closed. She planned to go through the birth certificates and death records to see whether the rumors about Mary Alice's daughter were true.

"Sure, honey," a red-haired assistant in the county clerk's office said. "Come back here." She swung open the half-gate for Betsy and led the way to a room where shelves of old record books were stacked from floor to ceiling. Large rectangular oak tables occupied the center of the long room where three people sat sifting through the large tomes spread before them. "What year do you need? Doing some genealogy? Looking for your family?"

The woman didn't pause long enough to allow Betsy to answer, which suited her fine, so at the end of the assistant's monologue, she answered vaguely. "Yes.

And I'm not sure about the decade. Let's try the 1950s."

The tall woman looked at Betsy over her black-rimmed bifocals. "Well, in that case, you can use the index on the computer if you want. It'll save you a lot of time. All of our records since 1950 are indexed by last name. You'll find a volume and page number next to each name, then you can go to the corresponding record book." With a large sweep of her arm, she indicated the three walls lined with books.

"Thank you." Betsy stared at the books whose spines were labeled by the year and type of record.

"Now, let me show you how to use this computer."

Betsy quickly located the name Garrett. There were several pages of transactions, but within fifteen minutes she had located a death record for Catherine Garrett dated in 1957.

She turned through the pages of the heavy book she had laid on the table before her. First she scanned the information, then went back and read it slowly. Catherine Garrett was only seventeen when she had died. Betsy closed the book more gently than she had opened it. Seventeen. Guilt at prying into Mary Alice's private life assailed her, but she couldn't stop now.

She slid the book back in its slot, then walked along the wall where the birth records were stacked and pulled out the one that housed the records for the year 1940. She found what she was searching for. Catherine Garrett's mother's name was listed as Mary Alice

Garrett with the father unknown. Genuine pity for this woman who had befriended her overwhelmed Betsy. To have had a child out of wedlock in the 1940s spelled harsh whispers and ostracism. And, if Mary Alice's father had been as tyrannical as Agnes had described, she'd had no support at home.

Betsy slowly shook her head. It had happened more than fifty years ago, and Mary Alice was still trying to conceal her shame.

CHAPTER SIXTEEN

"ARE YOU READY, Billy?" Betsy asked, staring with pleasure through the doorway at the boy. His pale complexion of a few months ago had been transformed into a warm, healthy glow.

"Yeah. Come on in. I didn't think you'd be here so quick." Leaving Betsy standing at the door, he scurried down the hallway yelling, "Janie, hey, Janie. Betsy's here so I'm leaving. Okay?"

"Hi, Betsy. Sorry Billy beat me to the door, but I was knee-deep in studying biology. I have my final exam in the morning," Janie said.

"I'm glad those days are behind me," Betsy commiserated. "Hang in there, though. Billy and I'll get out of your hair."

"Thanks. I'll lock up."

Betsy jerked her head toward the door. "Time's a wasting, Billy. Let's go."

Billy settled into the seat next to Betsy. "Janie doesn't like animals much. I told her that an otter belongs to the genus *Lutra canadensis*."

"How'd you know that?"

Billy craned his neck and looked at Betsy with disbelief in his eyes. "All kinds of junk's posted at the displays. All you've got to do is read."

"Right." Betsy smiled at this little boy who could read and remember technical information, but who'd had trouble with a fourth-grade reader last year.

Billy idly scratched the seat's plush upholstery with his index finger. "Betsy, when are you and Dad gonna get married?"

"The week before Thanksgiving."

"Oh." All the fingers on his left hand became engaged in the rhythmic scratching. "Then you'll move into our house?"

Betsy glanced at Billy. "How do you feel about that?"

Billy looked out the window, the beginnings of a scowl on his face. He didn't answer.

"Billy, if it bothers you that your dad and I are getting married, let's talk about it."

"Naw. It's okay."

"I hope it is. Neither of us would want to do anything that would make you unhappy."

The scowl softened, revealing only a concerned ten-year-old whose life had been in a turmoil the past two years. Now, he faced the prospect of having a stepmother. Betsy didn't know what the future held for them, but she'd never do anything to hurt Billy.

"I know," Billy finally said. "Really, it's okay. I won't have to have a baby-sitter, and Dad said he'd be home more now." He stopped scratching the seat. "I guess that's because you'll be there."

"That's not quite right, Billy. Your dad finally realized that he spends too much time at work. He's already made a lot of changes. He didn't wait until the wedding. He did it now. For you."

A slow smile spread across the child's face, replacing the earlier expression of concern with one of relief. "Yeah, I guess he did."

Pulling up into the parking lot, Betsy flipped off the air-conditioning switch and pushed the buttons on the armrest to lower each window an inch while they were inside the aquarium. She'd already had one window cracked by the summer's heat. "Now, let's go find him."

"Last one in's a rotten egg," Billy squealed and took off running.

"Hi, river rat," Nick greeted Billy with a head scrub and nodded toward Betsy. "What's with the huffing and puffing?"

Betsy, trying to catch her breath, explained, "I'm a rotten egg."

Billy laughed with glee. "I beat her, Daddy. But for a woman, she can run pretty good."

"She can, uh?" Nick gave Betsy a gentle hug, "You don't smell like a rotten egg."

Turning to Billy, Nick said, "I told Mary Alice you were coming. She stayed late because she wanted to see you. She's in the marsh."

"Great." Billy dashed off in search of his mentor.

"Now," Nick said, leering at Betsy and motioning toward his office. "Want to come into my parlor...."

"...said the spider to the fly." Laughing, Betsy followed him into the tiny room and closed the door. "You must think I've actually missed you."

"It's been at least eighteen hours." He eased her up against the wall and buried his face in her neck. "Mmm, for a fact, you don't smell like a rotten egg. You smell good enough to eat." He nibbled her neck.

"For someone surrounded by fish all day, you don't smell half-bad yourself. If I didn't know better, I'd think you might have put on some fresh cologne."

"You might have thought right." He nuzzled her with his clean-shaven chin. "I scrubbed one of the tanks, so I had to take a quick shower in anticipation of seeing my woman."

"Of course...." Her voice dropped to a whisper as blue eyes and green eyes met. She ran her tongue over her lips. My woman, he'd said. The scent of soap, cologne and man clouded her nostrils making her knees weak. She was glad she had the wall behind her for support as his lips sought hers.

Minutes later, she murmured, "Someone might be looking for you. This behavior is highly unprofessional. We'd better go find Billy and look at the otter."

"I'd rather do this." He leaned back and looked into her eyes. "God, I love you. This waiting is driving me crazy. I want you in my bed every night, not just when I can get a baby-sitter for Billy.''

"I'd like that, too, but we agreed that it would be best for him if we didn't flaunt the physical side of our relationship.''

"That was before I realized how addictive making love to you was going to be. I need you.''

Betsy smiled and caressed his cheek with a fingertip. "It's only three months until the wedding.''

"I don't want to wait that long. Let's move it up. To hell with the week before Thanksgiving.''

They had chosen Thanksgiving so Betsy would have a long weekend combined with three personal days. That would give them nine days for a honeymoon, but Nick was right. They could get married sooner and take a honeymoon later. "Whatever you want. We could go to South Padre for the weekend, or wait until Christmas to take a honeymoon.''

"Great! How soon can we have this wedding?''

"I'll have to check about the chapel reservations, cancel the invitations if it's not too late, check with the caterers, Susan, Renee and our parents.'' She ticked off the things on her fingers. "And Grandmother.''

Nick groaned.

"Don't groan yet. My parents would never forgive me if we eloped. Maybe we can arrange something in the next three or four weeks.''

Betsy halted, remembering Billy's reaction in the car. "Nick, no matter what we want, this will have to be cleared with Billy. We're not the only ones affected."

"He won't care. He's as happy as I am." Nick kissed her as though to guarantee his words, then took her hand. "Let's go check on Billy and that otter."

Nick led the way to the ground floor where the otter was enclosed in a special cage. "We're keeping her isolated until she recuperates," Nick explained. "It protects her and makes it easier for us to handle her."

"Billy said someone had trapped her."

"From the wounds, it looked like it was a trap for a larger animal. I'll never be able to understand how someone could allow this to happen. It looks like she was strong-willed enough to be able to tear her hind leg loose and swim away." His body radiated controlled anger. "Anyway, a ranger found her later and brought her here because he'd heard we're working on a breeding program for otters."

Betsy kneeled and studied the sleek creature. It stared back with big sad eyes. "Will she make it?"

"It looks like it. The critical period when she was running a fever is past. Now, we've just got to wait for the wound to heal. Like I said, she's got a strong will."

"I'm glad. What do you call her?"

"We named her Marie LaVeau."

Betsy laughed heartily recalling the old pop song about the witch who destroyed men who broke promises. "A witch from the swamps. Just what is Emily Morgan going to think when another female invades her territory and makes eyes at Sam Houston?"

"She'll probably be more tolerant than you would be."

"You're correct." She lowered her voice in mock warning. "I'll be more like Marie than Emily."

"Thanks for the warning." Glancing at his watch, Nick said, "It's almost five. Let's find Billy and Mary Alice and go out to dinner."

"You can leave now?" She was pleased that Nick was leaving early.

"Things are under control. I'll come by to check on things on my way home. Now, where could those two have gone?"

After a bit of searching, they found Billy and Mary Alice with their heads together outside on the patio, sipping soft drinks. They stopped talking as Nick and Betsy approached.

"We searched everywhere inside," Nick called out, "and never thought you two would choose to sit out here in the heat."

"We kept cool with our drinks, didn't we, Billy?" Mary Alice pushed and pulled herself out of the chair. "I hadn't realized the time." Covering her hip pouch with an arm, Mary Alice said, "I'd better be getting home. It's time for my medicine." She leaned over and hugged Billy. "See you in a few days, Billy. Now, you be a good boy and remember what I said."

On their way to the restaurant, Nick asked, "Billy, what did Mary Alice want you to remember?"

"Nothing."

Nick glanced over his shoulder to look at his son. "It had to be something."

"Oh, about being good." Billy squirmed in the back seat.

"Well, it sounds like good advice to me," Nick said.

Billy selected the chair directly across from Betsy in the seafood restaurant anchored in Corpus Christi Bay. When the young waiter came to take their orders, he didn't look up. "I don't want anything."

"You've got to eat something because I'm not fixing you something when we get home," Nick said.

Billy picked up his menu and glanced at it. "Okay, I want lobster." He slammed the menu shut and glared at his father.

Nick tried to reason with his son. "Billy, you won't like that. Please choose something else." When Billy huffed, Nick frowned and added, "You may have some shrimp."

Orders placed, Betsy said, "I saw the new otter today, Billy."

"So?" He began flipping his spoon over and over.

"So, I think she's going to be okay."

Billy looked up at the wall decorations, ignoring Betsy's comment.

"Billy." Nick's voice contained a barely concealed warning.

The sullen boy looked at his dad, and in mock courtesy said, "Yes, sir."

"Oh, look at this." Betsy picked up a plastic stand that pictured tempting calorie-laden desserts.

Nick appreciated Betsy's trying to ease the tension, but for all her efforts, Billy remained uncommunicative. After what seemed an interminable time, the food was delivered.

Billy just stared at the shrimp until Nick made him take a bite, then another.

"Billy, do you want to split a piece of this delicious-looking cheesecake with me?" Betsy asked him.

He kept his head down.

"Billy, Betsy was speaking to you." Nick's voice was filled with warning.

Billy shook his head.

"Billy." Nick's voice was harsher.

"No, ma'am."

"I think you and I had better have a little talk later." Why was his son being so rude to Betsy? She'd been nothing but kind to Billy, and, in turn, Nick expected Billy to treat her with respect. Just this morning, Billy had seemed pleased about the upcoming marriage. But, now, Nick wasn't sure.

He glanced toward Betsy with an apologetic expression on his face. She smiled back in understanding.

"HIT THE DECK, sailor," Nick yelled into Billy's room early Saturday morning on his way down the hall to make coffee. "Let's get out to the boat." He hoped his son was in a better mood than he'd been in last night. Things hadn't improved by the time they'd arrived home, particularly after Nick's little sermon about manners. In fact, as soon as they'd gotten inside the house, Billy had gone to bed. Nick hoped that a day on the water would cheer him up.

When Billy didn't show up for breakfast ten minutes later, Nick began to get a little peeved. Billy was pushing it. It looked as if he'd decided to be difficult, again. Had he been too hard on his son? No. He was only doing what Betsy had suggested—be a good father.

With a long, bold stride, Nick went back to his son's room and stood in the open doorway. "Billy." He said the words with slow deliberation. "Come on and get out of bed and get dressed. Your breakfast is getting cold."

There were no movements or groans of protestation. Nick shook his head in exasperation. "Son, come on. Last night's over." Nick strode across the cluttered room and pulled the covers back. He stared down at two pillows, carefully arranged to resemble a sleeping body.

Nick recognized the scenario from his own childhood. Make Mom and Dad think you've run away so they'll be sorry they made you do something you didn't want to.

"Billy?"

No answer.

Kicking aside the loose clothes lying on the floor, Nick searched Billy's closet. He made a mental note that as soon as he found Billy, the boy was going to clean up his room . . . then they could go sailing.

Nick was about to shut the closet door when he noticed the large empty space on the top shelf. At first he couldn't recall what was stored there, but then it came back. Billy's sleeping bag. What was the little rascal up to? Nick made a more thorough search of the room as his apprehension mounted. Nothing else was out of the ordinary.

After calling Billy's name several times, Nick went out to the backyard. He looked all around the house, behind the shrubs, up in the trees, anywhere a child could hide. Then he started down the wooden walkway to the boat. Maybe Billy had decided to get an early start by himself. The closer Nick got to the boat, the more he knew that this search was going to be futile, too. The yacht rocked gently in the water, undisturbed. Nick climbed aboard and made a quick search. Nothing.

Maybe Billy had decided to go to his grandparents'. If he was upset, that would be the logical place to go for comfort. Nick sprinted back to the house.

He poured a cup of coffee and sat down at his desk. If Billy happened to be at his grandparents', Nick wasn't sure how to handle the situation. What he wanted to do was give Billy a good spanking, more to vent his own frustration than to punish his son. But, in ten years, he'd never hit Billy. Vicki had always said that violence bred violence and prohibited anyone from spanking Billy. He took a sip of coffee and dialed his parents' house.

"Hello, Mother?" He tried to sound as if he were making a social call. He didn't want to worry his mother unnecessarily.

"Nicholas. Is something wrong? You don't sound good."

"Probably not." He took a deep breath. He never could fool his mother. "Have you seen Billy this morning?"

"No, Nicholas, what's going on?"

"Billy wasn't in his bed this morning, and I can't find him. He was mad because we had a little fight last night. I figured he went to your house."

"Nicholas, over two miles separates our houses."

"I know, but it is possible for him to walk that far."

"In the middle of the night? Oh, dear."

"Mother, would you please look around and call me back if you find him?"

"Yes, of course."

With growing concern, Nick stared at the receiver after his mother hung up. He hadn't realized how certain he'd been that Billy would be at John and Barbara's. He slumped back into his chair. Where could Billy have hidden? The brief satisfaction that he was getting a grip on fatherhood evaporated. He'd never felt so alone.

He needed Betsy. She might have some idea where Billy could be. She knew a lot about children and how they thought. He picked up the receiver and dialed.

He was growing impatient by the time she answered on the fourth ring. "Hello." She was breathing hard.

"It sounds like you were doing that workout thing."

"You're right. What's up? You want to come over and help me shower?"

"I'd like to but...uh, have you heard from Billy this morning?"

"No, I haven't talked to him since last night. Nick, what's wrong?"

Nick explained the entire morning to Betsy. "At first, I was disappointed that our little talk didn't help. Now, I'm worried that something has happened to him."

"I'll be over as soon as I finish showering. We'll find him."

"Thanks. I love you."

"I love you, too. See you in thirty minutes."

Nick felt a little better after talking to Betsy. She would be there for him. He hurried back to his own bedroom to take a shower and get dressed so he could go hunting for Billy.

Propped against his bedside lamp was an envelope with the single word *DAD* on it. Nick's heart flip-flopped. How had he missed it? He tore open the envelope. On a sheet of notepaper, in a childish sprawl, was written:

I don't want a new mom.
I love you.

Billy

An indescribable feeling of despair enveloped Nick. Why couldn't Billy have leveled with him? Billy liked Betsy, always wanted to include her in their plans. Then, in a matter of days, he'd become resentful. The thought of the marriage and Betsy's moving in had been too much for the boy who was still trying to come to grips with the loss of his mother. Nick bit down on his bottom lip. He sure as hell was one sorry excuse of a father not to have recognized the signs.

Swallowing back the welling emotion, he picked up the phone on the nightstand and punched in the numbers 911.

"YES, I called the neighbors," he told the uniformed patrolmen. "While I was waiting for you to get here, I called the whole damn phone book."

"Mr. Lupton. Calm down, and let's start at the beginning."

Nick recited the story again, trying to add anything he'd omitted. Knowing that Betsy would be with him momentarily, he asked the patrolmen not to disclose to her the contents of Billy's note. Betsy didn't need the hurt. But Nick did need this man's help, so he added an apology for blowing up earlier.

"Think nothing of it. If it were my kid, I'd feel the same way. Let's check out the house again. Okay?"

Nick nodded. The only place he hadn't checked was the attic and Billy wasn't strong enough to release the pull-down ladder in the garage. Still, he retraced his tracks.

"Hmph," the policeman grunted after checking all the rooms. "Well, let's look outside." He slipped his sunglasses out of his shirt pocket, shook them open with one hand and slid them on.

After a thorough search of the grounds, he turned to Nick. "We'll get this on the computer and begin a city-wide search immediately."

"Thank you."

While the policeman was calling in his report from his car, Betsy drove up. Nick took her to the living room to wait.

"Nick, did it have anything to do with our getting married?" She could hardly contain her anxiety as she paced the floor.

Nick avoided looking into her eyes, unwilling to deny or confirm her question. "Betsy, who knows what's in his mind. You know he's been having problems for the past year." He took her in his arms to comfort her. "Honey, everything will be all right." He wished he believed the words he mouthed.

Barbara and John Lupton arrived about the same time a detective showed up. "Have you found him, Nick?" Barbara asked.

"No, but it won't be long." His parents' presence reassured Nick.

"How tall's your son?" the detective asked, notebook in hand.

Nick held his hand up to midchest. "He's about this tall."

Nick was trying not to show his impatience at the policemen's slow, methodical approach. He wanted action. His son was missing.

A telephone ring interrupted his thoughts. He grabbed the receiver. "Billy," he yelled. "Oh... oh, hello, Chester." He listened for a moment to Chester explaining that the injured otter had taken a turn for the worse. "Let Tom check it and call the vet if necessary. I've got something else to tend to right now."

A sudden thought occurred to him. "Chester, Billy's run away. Look around the aquarium to see if he might be hiding there." He paced while he listened. "No. It's okay. The police are here. I'll be fine... Yeah, thanks."

A knobby-kneed man clad in Bermuda shorts walked through the open front door. "Nick, I was out watering my front lawn and noticed the police cars and everything. Is anything wrong that I can help with?"

John Lupton explained to Nick's neighbor that Billy had run away. "Have you seen him?"

"No, but old man Rivas gets up with the chickens, and that's about when his grandson gets home. I'll walk over to see if they saw anything."

JUST BEFORE LUNCH, Tom and Chester showed up. "We came to see if we could help," Tom said to Nick.

Having his co-workers show up touched Nick. Unable to speak, he nodded his gratitude. Already, he knew cars were driving up and down the streets of Corpus Christi, the drivers looking for a little boy, while other people were walking through the neighborhood searching for the missing child. Mobile and cellular phones kept them in contact.

The crowd increased, but Nick noticed when Renee entered, supporting Mary Alice by the elbow. "She insisted on coming when she heard," Renee explained to Betsy and Nick. "Is there anything I can do?"

"No, but thanks, anyway. Everyone is being terrific. People are combing the neighborhood."

Renee gave them a hug. "Then I'll get back to work. Call me the minute you find out anything. Everyone at the aquarium is concerned."

"I will," Betsy assured her.

Mary Alice stood in the center of the room wringing her hands. "Oh, mercy me."

Betsy offered her a seat. "Here, sit down. Are you going to be okay?"

Mary Alice slumped into the chair, all the while shaking her head and muttering.

Barbara Lupton stepped forward. "Mary Alice, let's go to the den. You need to lie down." With Barbara and Renee supporting her on either side, Mary Alice walked down the hallway, tears sliding down her cheeks.

Tom and Chester headed out to the dock. Chester came running back after a few minutes. "Ah, Nick, have you been out to the dock?"

"Yeah. That's the first place I looked."

"Did . . . did you hurt yourself?"

Nick tensed. "No. Why?"

"I think we need to go out there for a minute." He pointedly looked at the policeman lingering nearby.

Everyone followed Chester and Nick who hurried to the dock where Tom was squatting at the edge.

Nick knelt beside him. How had he missed it? How had they all missed it? Fresh blood stained the wooden surface.

"Oh, my God!" The words came from over his shoulder where Betsy slumped against a pier.

Nick stood up and began shucking off his clothes.

"No, I'll go in." Tom faced Nick with authority. "You're in no shape to dive right now." He turned to Chester. "Call the aquarium and have someone bring my gear."

In a matter of minutes, two divers showed up with the proper gear. Nick felt helpless as they donned their masks and dived off the end of the dock. He paced back and forth, up and down the wooden structure, watching the trails of bubbles as the divers circled in ever-larger bands.

Finally, Tom surfaced nearby and slid up his mask. "Nothing, but we're going to keep searching."

Again and again, Nick watched as the ever increasing group of divers slipped below the murky water. The muscles of his stomach knotted as the worst thoughts parents could have intensified. Silently, he bargained with God, pledging to be a better father if he were allowed another chance.

Nick felt Betsy slip her arm through his. He gave it a slight squeeze while continuing to search the water's surface. Her presence calmed him, just knowing that she, too, cared for Billy.

"Nick." He heard a voice and glanced around to see his parents coming down the path. He answered his mother's unspoken query with a shake of his head. "Nothing yet."

Quietly, Nick and his parents discussed why Billy would have sneaked out of the house when he had so much to make him happy. Betsy stood aside, eyes downcast, as she listened. The roar of motors nearing the dock broke up their conversation.

"What's that?" Barbara Lupton asked.

"Those are the boats called in to seine the Bay," John told his wife.

Nick watched his mother clench her jaw and try to control her emotions, but tears began to run down her cheeks until she could no longer hide how upset she was by the possibility that they were looking for a body. Finally, she broke down and sobbed. John tenderly led her back to the house.

As the day progressed, Nick refused Betsy's efforts to get him to eat or to rest. He had no appetite. Only Billy filled his thoughts.

IT WAS LATE AFTERNOON, the shadows deepening as the sun slid lower in the western sky, when John Lupton walked up beside Nick. "Why don't you come in the house, son?"

"I'd rather wait here."

"There isn't anything you can do out here." He guided Nick toward the house. Betsy followed a few steps behind.

Barbara had regained control of her emotions and had uncovered some food brought in by neighbors. "I know you're not hungry, but try to eat. You need to keep up your strength."

Nick took the plate she offered and took a sip of his tea. He was studying the food with distaste when the back door burst open.

The younger policeman stood in the doorway. "We found something. . . ."

Nick's heart stopped.

". . . that might belong to Billy. You want to come down and identify it?"

Forcing his legs to be steady, Nick stood up and followed the policeman to the dock. Betsy, Barbara and John were right behind him.

Nick knelt beside the wet bundle. "It's Billy's sleeping bag."

CHAPTER SEVENTEEN

HOURS LATER, heavy raindrops of the August thunderstorm pelting against the windows of Nick's home echoed Betsy's heartbeat as she looked out into the dark night. Even with the outdoor floodlights on, she saw little other than the wind whipping the rain into sheets of water.

Mary Alice, fingering a gold cross hanging from her neck, joined Betsy at the window. "It's like the gods are angry, isn't it? Neither saint nor sinner should be out on a night like this."

Betsy was taken aback by the evangelical tone of Mary Alice's voice. "And Billy? Which is he?"

"Neither. He's a child. Others are to blame for what happened to that child."

"Mary Alice, Billy ran away because he chose to, not because Nick or anyone else made him do so."

"I don't know about that." Mary Alice walked over to the shelves holding pictures. She picked up a silver-framed photograph of Nick and Vicki holding Billy in her lap.

Betsy followed her. "Mary Alice, what do you mean about someone making Billy run away?"

"Oh, that's not what I meant. I just mean that sometimes, well, others make choices for you that...." Tears gathered in her eyes.

Betsy wondered about the choices that Mary Alice's parents had made for her. Was she transferring her own past to Billy's situation? Had Mary Alice wanted to run away as a child? Or was she remembering her daughter? It was obvious that Mary Alice loved Billy as if he were her own flesh and blood. Was she making him her Catherine, her own lost child?

Betsy put her arm around the quivering woman who was trying so hard to stop the tears rolling down the creases in her cheeks. Betsy handed her a tissue and murmured, "Billy is okay. Just you wait and see."

Nick glanced at his watch. Nine-thirty. He took a sip of coffee, oblivious to the conversation going on around him. Over two hours ago, Tom and Chester and the other divers had called it quits for the night. Nick had found a new appreciation for them.

He still hadn't had the heart to tell Betsy about Billy's note. She'd been so understanding today, never pressing him, as though she understood his need to keep his own counsel. If Billy was ever found—*when* Billy was found—they'd have a heart-to-heart.

Sitting at a table just waiting was taking its toll, so Nick pushed himself up and walked out the front door. He paced under the portico, wishing all the while for something to do during this interminable wait. Down the street he saw headlights muted by the drenching rain. His heart constricted when the patrol car pulled into the driveway.

Nick stood stiff-legged as he watched two men get out of the car, their heads lowered against steadily falling drops. He braced himself for bad news. One of the men ran toward the house as the other opened the rear door of the car and helped a small child out.

"Billy, it's Billy. They found Billy," Nick called back toward the people waiting in the house before he dashed across the lawn toward his son.

He was speechless as he enfolded the soaking wet child in his arms. Conflicting emotions interplayed as he and Billy embraced. Nick wanted to reassure him and yell at him, keep him from harm and swat him. He rocked to and fro, letting the tension seep from his muscles until he broke his hold and looked into the boy's face. He couldn't tell if it was rain or tears running down Billy's cheeks.

"Welcome home, river rat. Let's go inside." He led Billy and the officers back into the house and the waiting family and friends.

Everyone talked at once, all expressing happiness over Billy's being returned safely. No one accused Billy or chastised him for his disappearance.

Barbara rushed down the hall and came back with a blanket. "Here, Nick. Get Billy out of those wet clothes before he catches his death."

Nick descended the stairs with Billy wrapped in a blanket just as Betsy emerged from the kitchen balancing a mug on a saucer. "Here's some hot chocolate topped with marshmallows, Billy. It'll warm you up from the inside."

"I don't want any hot chocolate." Billy sent her a hateful look as he turned away from his favorite drink and sat on the sofa.

Nick settled on the sofa next to Billy. He hadn't missed the look Billy had given Betsy. Now was not the time to embarrass everyone. He had to intervene. Taking the cup from Betsy, he sent her a weak smile. "You might want it later." He set the chocolate on the coffee table.

"Officers," he asked the waiting patrolmen, "do you reckon we could wrap this up in the morning? Everyone's tired."

After the police and neighbors had left, Barbara sat down on the other side of Billy. "I for one don't think I can sleep a wink until you tell me a little bit about what happened, Billy. Do you think you can?"

Billy dropped his eyes and fidgeted with the edge of the blanket as he told how he planned to sail the boat by himself. After he'd dropped his bedroll, he plunged into the water trying to retrieve it. "But I couldn't find it so I got out," he said, defiance in his voice.

"Where'd you go?" John asked his grandson.

"I just walked and went down alleys until I got tired. Then I saw a treehouse and got in it. I'd still be there, too, if I hadn't eaten all my food and it hadn't started thundering."

So hunger and thunder were to thank for Billy's return. Nick noticed that the other adults, with the exception of Mary Alice, were trying to stifle smiles.

He massaged his son's back. "What really had me worried, Billy, was the blood out on the dock. What happened?"

"Oh." Billy pulled his hand out from under the blanket and showed his father a cut. "I kind of tore it on a nail. It's not bad now because I stuck it in my mouth."

Nick took Billy's hand in his and examined the tear. "I think it will be fine with a little antiseptic dressing. I'll get some."

"Do you think he should have a tetanus shot?" Betsy suggested. She had been standing quietly nearby.

Billy's relaxing attitude stiffened again. "I don't want a shot," he said, pouting.

"I know, but if the nail was rus—"

Billy interrupted, "You're not my mother. I don't want you here."

Nick stopped him with a hand on his arms. "Billy, there's really no need to be so rude. Betsy is just trying to help."

"I don't need her help."

"I think—"

Betsy laid a hand on his elbow to interrupt him. "It's okay, Nick. He's been through a lot today. I...I think I'll go on home."

"You don't have to go."

"I know, but I think it would be best."

He watched her gather up her purse and say something to Mary Alice. He turned to Billy. "I'll be back in a minute."

He walked to the entry where Betsy and Mary Alice were preparing to leave. Putting his arm around Betsy's shoulder, he said, "I'll call you later, and thanks for being so understanding. Billy's been through a lot."

"You're welcome."

He avoided looking directly into her eyes as he drew her to him and kissed her goodbye. Her kiss was sweet as always but he could feel the tension in her body.

He gave Mary Alice a warm hug, then stood silently under the portico watching them walk through the rain to Betsy's car. He shuddered. He should have been happy that Billy was fine, and while he was relieved, he couldn't shake a sense of impending doom.

THE WINDSHIELD WIPERS of her car played a slow staccato beat in the lingering mist while Betsy drove Mary Alice home. The reduced visibility seemed somehow stifling and sinister as she searched for the turn. Perhaps it was the effects of the evening getting to her.

Betsy glanced at her passenger who was mumbling unidentifiable sounds to herself. The dashboard lights illuminated Mary Alice's face in an eerie glow, casting shadows over her wrinkled features.

"There's my street." Mary Alice pointed to the left.

Betsy turned in to one of the older neighborhoods in town where small houses lined the narrow streets. Swaying mesquite branches blocked the illumination of a distant streetlight, projecting themselves as blackened shadows fingering their way across the ground. Betsy shivered.

"This is it." Mary Alice pointed at a white-framed house with lights on in every room.

Betsy pulled up to the curb and put the gearshift in park. She remembered how Nick had searched the house and grounds at Mary Alice's request. "Would you like me to come inside with you and check things out?" Betsy asked, feeling nervous herself.

"No, I'm not scared." She opened the door and started to get out.

"I thought...." Betsy stopped before she mentioned Nick's name.

"I leave my lights on all the time now, and I've got me some good protection."

Betsy was curious. "Protection? What kind?"

"In my day, it was called a piece." The dashboard lights glinted from Mary Alice's eyes.

"You bought a gun?"

Mary Alice's lips curled into a tight smile. She nodded her head and patted her hip pack. "Carry it right here."

"You carry a gun with you all the time? How long have you had it?"

"For a couple of years."

So she'd had the gun when Nick searched the house. Why had she pretended to be afraid and asked him to search everything?

"But I just got the bullets last week. A gun's not much use without bullets, is it, Betsy?"

Mary Alice got out of the car and started to close the door before she leaned back inside. "A soul can't be too careful nowadays. It's not like it used to be. Thanks for bringing me home, Betsy. It's a relief that Billy's okay. I don't know what I'd do if something happened to that little boy."

Tension crept around Betsy's shoulders as she pulled away from Mary Alice's house. People handled problems in so many different ways, and she wasn't sure Mary Alice was handling hers properly. A gun! She'd talk to her about it later.

But right now she was tired. Her jumbled thoughts kept her from relaxing. Why had Billy run away? Was it because of her? He'd made it obvious the past few days, and particularly tonight, that he didn't want to see her.

And Nick. What must he be going through. She loved him so much, sometimes she thought she couldn't contain it within her heart.

BETSY HAD JUST SLIPPED on a red teddy and was staring at her tired eyes in the bathroom mirror when the phone rang. She settled herself on the bed and lifted the white receiver. "Hello."

It was Nick. There was so much she wanted to say and ask but she was afraid to. Afraid of the answers. "How's Billy?"

"He's fine. He was so tired he's already fallen asleep."

She heard ice clink in a glass. Nick probably needed a drink after what he'd been put through. "I'm sure he was."

"Betsy, thanks again for coming today."

"Oh, Nick. I couldn't have been anywhere else, but I was basically useless."

"You're never useless. Your being here helped me through the day."

"Nick, did Billy say why he ran away?"

Nick didn't answer immediately. She heard the ice clink again. "Betsy, he's confused. I don't think he knows why he ran away."

Betsy's eyes moistened. Was Nick deliberately keeping something from her? She could hardly concentrate on the remainder of the conversation. She sensed their relationship was in some kind of danger. After Nick wished her sweet dreams, she whispered, "I love you . . . and Billy."

After hanging up the phone, Betsy was too upset to sleep. She got up and made a cup of instant coffee and began to pace the carpeted floor.

Nick wasn't blind. He had to realize Billy was upset about her becoming part of their family. She'd seen the way Nick had looked at her today, only to glance away too quickly. She'd overheard two officers mention something about a note, but Nick had said there'd been no note. He was trying to protect her and she wouldn't allow him to do that.

She couldn't marry Nick in three weeks, not the way things were. Not if Billy objected. There would be enough problems being a stepmother without his hostility.

Stepmother.

What sinister images the term conjured up. Cinderella and Snow White. Billy?

SUNLIGHT GLINTED through the blinds Sunday morning, leaving stripes of light across the bed where Betsy lay curled in slumber. It had been almost dawn before, finally, from sheer exhaustion, she'd fallen into a fretful sleep. As the light tickled across her face, she woke feeling as if she'd never rested. Her eyes were swollen from crying and her heart ached. But her decision was made. She knew she was going to hurt Nick, but she had to tell him.

She showered and slipped on a caftan, wondering whether Nick could leave Billy just now to come over to her house. Billy needed him more than ever, but Betsy knew what she was about to do would help the boy, too. It had to be now, and she couldn't go over there. Sitting cross-legged on the bed, she dialed Nick's number.

BETSY WAS CRYING again by the time she hung up the phone. He'd refrained from asking her what was wrong even though she knew he could sense it. It wasn't fair. They had so much to offer each other. They could be so happy together if only...

She unwrapped the damp towel from around her hair and started to get dressed. She didn't want to look like something the tide had washed up when Nick arrived. After carefully applying her makeup to hide the black circles under her eyes, and brushing her hair, she donned a pair of jeans and a white shirt. She tied the tail of the shirt around her waist and rolled up the sleeves. She slipped on white sandals and surveyed herself in the mirror. Pretty subdued for her. But that was how she felt.

She heard Nick's Jeep in the driveway. Only thirty minutes had passed since she'd called him. She met him on the front porch and after a quick kiss led him by the hand through the house and out to the patio. She didn't want the intimacy of close quarters to affect her judgment. It would be so easy to abandon her intentions and end up in his arms.

It was a beautiful day, with a slight overcast from the storm the night before. A gentle breeze refreshed the air and kept the heat at bay.

"What's wrong, Betsy?" He turned her to face him.

She looked into his eyes then twisted away. She couldn't look at him and say what needed to be said. Staring across the green lawn at nothing, she leaned against a support column. "I...we...I don't think we should get married." There. Finally, the words were out.

Though she hadn't heard him approach, Nick was standing immediately behind her. "Well, I do." He put a hand on her shoulder and turned her around.

"Things have changed. Billy. . . ."

". . .will get used to the idea. I'll talk to him."

"What if it doesn't work? What if he continues to resent me? I love you too much to put you in a position where you'll have to choose between Billy and me."

"That won't happen."

"It could and deep down you know it."

Nick released a deep breath and pressed his lips together in a thin line as he studied her. "Betsy, don't do this."

Despite her best efforts, Betsy felt the tears begin to form in the corners of her eyes, and her throat felt as though someone had slipped a noose around it and was slowly tightening the rope. She could hardly talk. "It won't work, Nick."

"You give up too easily. I love you. More than I've ever loved anyone in my life. I don't want to live my life without you."

"Love doesn't conquer all, Nick. It sometimes hurts people." She sighed. "Maybe we could still see each other occasionally, without Billy knowing." Even as she said the words, she knew what his reaction was going to be.

"I'm not going to sneak around just so Billy won't get upset, and I'm not going to settle for half a loaf.

Okay, I'll tell you what. Let's postpone the wedding for a few months and give Billy time to adjust."

"Do you know what you're saying, Nick?"

"Yes, Betsy, I do. What I want is you to be my wife. I want to go to bed with you by my side at night and wake up with you still there in the morning. And I want to be there for you. We belong together."

Betsy moved away from his touch. It was too potent. Just his touch and she would recant, agree to marry him, something that would slowly destroy him and Billy. She couldn't do it.

"Damn it! What else can I say?" he asked.

She shook her head. "Don't make this more difficult. Please, Nick, I would marry you right now if I thought there was any way it would work."

"At least give it a try." He pulled her into his arms and cradled her against him. "I love you, Betsy. I love you."

She closed her eyes and tried to relax, absorbing his fragrance, his essence for later when the nights would be lonely. Finally, she was able to speak in a husky whisper. "I can't risk that love turning to hate. But I'll agree to an indefinite postponement, provided that we don't see each other for a while. You're right. Sneaking around was a bad idea. Billy would find out and resent me even more."

"He won't resent you."

"I wish I were that certain, but I've seen too many stepfamilies with all their problems." She could feel his neck muscles against her cheeks tense with mounting anger.

"Betsy, we don't have to be like everyone else."

"Sure," she said, looking up into stormy green eyes, "and Billy will run away again."

Nick's eyes searched hers. "You knew?"

Betsy nodded. "I won't have Billy running away from me, because he'll eventually take you with him." She stepped out of his arms. She'd never felt so alone, so cold. "Go to him, Nick. He needs you."

I need you, too. She watched him walk across the lawn toward the gate. *I need you, too.* His stride was measured as if he were concentrating on putting one foot in front of the other, forcing himself to leave.

There was still time to stop him. All she had to do was call his name and he would come back. What if she were making a mistake? What if she was letting go of the best thing that ever happened to her? What if he were right and they could make it work? Tears obscured her vision as he disappeared around the side of the house. When she heard the gate latch close, she collapsed in the hammock and sobbed until she fell asleep.

WHEN NICK PULLED in to his own driveway he was still angry. Angry at Betsy for not having more faith in him. Angry at Billy for being so manipulative. Angry at himself for allowing things to get into this mess.

"What did Betsy want, Nicholas?" his mother asked when she saw the storm on his face.

"She called off the wedding." Since his mother intuitively knew his problems, he saw no reason to beat around the bush.

"Oh dear, I'm sorry." She put her arm around him. "What was her reason?"

"She didn't think Billy was ready."

"I see." Barbara mulled over the information, then added, "She could be right."

Nick straightened and looked at his mother. "You think so, too?"

"Billy is still a confused little boy. He has been for two years, Nicholas."

Nick stared at his mother. "You're dying to give me some advice, Mom. This is your chance. What should I do? I don't want to lose Betsy."

"Have you considered taking Billy to a counselor?"

"Not really. I don't believe in them. Intelligent people ought to be able to solve their own problems. Besides, I don't think our problems are anyone else's business."

"But it was everyone's business yesterday. Police, neighbors, friends. And yet, you stand there and say your son can handle his problems," Barbara said. She placed her hands on her hips and eyed her son. "Well, Nicholas, you asked me for my advice and I gave it to you. If Betsy means as much to you as you say, then you'll do whatever it takes to find a solution."

Billy entered the room in his pajamas, rubbing his eyes. "What's going on?"

Nick looked at his son. He loved the boy beyond words, but he wasn't going to allow this boy to keep him away from the woman he adored. He'd find a way to bring them together. "Betsy and I are not getting married."

Billy didn't even try to hide his joy. "All right!" He shook his fist in a sign of triumph.

Barbara picked up her purse and said, "I'll say goodbye," giving her son an I-told-you-so look.

"Thanks, Mother."

"Anytime. Things will work out if problems are dealt with rather than ignored. You'll see." She gave him and Billy a peck on the cheek and closed the door behind her.

Nick turned back to his son who was spread out on the sofa as if he didn't have a care in the world. Maybe his mother was right. Maybe a counselor would understand what was going on with Billy. He sure didn't. One minute Billy said he wanted Betsy for a stepmother, the next minute he was running away.

CHAPTER EIGHTEEN

*August meeting
of the Quilting Club*

I WAS SO SURPRISED to see Barbara Lupton enter the room that I nearly forgot my manners, but pulled myself together before anyone noticed. "Why, hello, Mrs. Lupton," I said, struggling to my feet. I smiled smugly at Bertha who'd thought that Mrs. Lupton might be too uppity to join us. "You remember Bertha Clark and Era Sullivan." I pointed out the two ladies on the left of the quilting frame. "And, of course, Virginia."

"Yes, hello, Virginia. It's nice to see you again, Bertha, Era." She smiled and nodded toward them.

I could tell she was nervous as she took a seat beside Virginia. She was a nice lady and I didn't want her to feel out of place. "I'm so glad you could come. We're getting this quilt ready for...." I stopped. I couldn't very well say we were getting it ready for Betsy's hope chest since the wedding had been postponed—indefinitely, Betsy said—so I just made something up. "...Uh, for charity and we could use some help."

Era looked up. "I thought we were making it for Be—"

Bertha poked her in the side with her elbow. "Shh."

Barbara Lupton seemed to be ignoring the interchange, probably thinking we were all a little senile. "I can't say I'll be much help, but I have been practicing," she said. "Let me watch you for a while."

As we worked, we explained the way we quilted. Bertha added, "Now, the smaller the stitch the better."

I don't know why she was saying anything, her stitches were the biggest ones in the group. Virginia and I were the best quilters.

Barbara seemed to take it all in. Finally, she got out a needle and began outlining a wedding ring.

Bertha fidgeted before she asked the question we were all dying to ask. "I heard about Billy running away. How're he and Nick doing?"

"Billy seems fine after his ordeal. You know how children are, but...." She shook her head. "—Nick is taking the wedding's postponement awfully hard."

"The whole thing is just terrible. That poor little boy."

I don't know why Bertha was being so sympathetic. She'd just told me, not more than fifteen minutes ago, that what Billy needed was a good spanking for scaring his daddy like that. And I had to agree, but I wasn't going to say so. Instead, I said, "I've never seen Betsy like this. She just doesn't seem to have much life in her."

"Speaking of weddings being called off...." Era looked around. *"The other day, Mr. Putman—you know that gentleman who lives down the street I was telling you about...."*

Everyone but Barbara Lupton nodded.

"Well, last week he came over for a piece of my award-winning peach pie."

Bertha looked at me and smiled. Era had won a blue ribbon at a fair twenty years ago for her peach cobbler. You'd have thought she'd won a Pulitzer, the way she went on.

Era continued, *"His memory not being what it once was, it took him a while to recollect what happened to Mary Alice's daughter, Catherine."* She stopped quilting and fixed us with her eyes. *"It seems that Catherine had a baby before she killed herself... right there in that house where Mary Alice still lives."*

CHAPTER NINETEEN

"WHAT DID you say?" Betsy stared at her grandmother, stunned by the news Agnes had just told her.

"I said that Mary Alice had a grandchild."

"I don't understand it, Grandmother. Most people are so glad to be grandparents that they bore people to death with anecdotes. Mary Alice hasn't mentioned having a daughter or a grandchild." Betsy sighed. "In fact, she said that she doesn't have any family left."

"Maybe she doesn't now. But she did at one time."

"That's so hard to believe."

"Like mother like daughter is what I say. Neither one of them married."

"I wonder what became of the baby?"

"Era didn't know."

"And Catherine killed herself?"

Agnes nodded. "She took a straight razor and slit her wrists—right there in the bathroom of Mary Alice's house—is what Era said."

Betsy shivered. "How horrible."

"And Mr. Putman told her that Mary Alice had been a little unstable ever since."

"I can see why." Betsy noticed that her grandmother was twisting her purse straps and knew that something big was on her mind. Agnes would have been happy to discuss inconsequential gossip over the phone. Instead, she'd been waiting on the front porch when Betsy came in from school. "All of what you said makes me feel like we're prying into someone's locked-away past—which you've been known to do. This isn't the same thing, is it? Grandmother, is there something else?"

Agnes nodded. "Era said that earlier in the summer, Mary Alice accidentally locked herself out of her house. Mr. Putman tried to help her get in, but couldn't. So he waited with her on the back porch while a locksmith got the door open. He followed her into the house and while she was paying the locksmith, he glanced at an open scrapbook sitting in the middle of the kitchen table." Agnes took a deep breath and stared into Betsy's eyes.

"And?"

"This is the unsettling part. There were some newspaper clippings of Nick and Vicki in a scrapbook." Agnes leaned toward Betsy and said in a low voice as if someone were going to hear her. "Mr. Putman said that all the pictures of Nick had been crossed out."

Betsy frowned. "That doesn't make sense. Why would she keep articles, then scratch out Nick's picture? She likes him."

"I have no earthly idea, but don't you think that it's a little odd?"

Betsy nodded and stood up, suddenly too tense to sit. This seemed more than idle gossip. "I think it's strange, all right."

"Did you ever find out what she carried in her pack?" Agnes asked.

"Yes, yes I did." A chill washed over Betsy as she recalled the gun and the newly purchased bullets. "Oh, Lord. She has a gun. You don't think...no, the gun's for her protection."

Agnes shook her head. "An old woman's got no business with a gun. I don't know what's logical, but I do know my feelings, and I have a feeling," she said with deliberation, "there's something going on with her, what with the accidents at the aquarium and everything. That's why I came right over to tell you."

Betsy pecked Agnes on the cheek. "Thanks, Grandmother. Your feelings are generally on target, but I hope you're wrong this time."

"I do too, dear." Agnes pulled herself out of the chair.

"I think I'd better call Nick and tell him what you've told me."

"I agree." Agnes patted Betsy's arm. "Things will work out with him. You'll see. Oh, I forgot to tell you—today at quilting, Barbara Lupton was a surprise visitor. And she said Nick had a long talk with Billy and was going to take him to see a counselor."

Betsy felt some of the tension flow out of her muscles at the only good news her grandmother had told her. Maybe, just maybe, Billy would come around and things would work out. If Mary Alice didn't do something crazy first.

After her grandmother left, Betsy tried to call Nick several times. He wasn't at home or at the aquarium, so she left a message for him to call her as soon as he could. She paced the floor and thought. In her mind she outlined everything she knew and none of it made sense. Mary Alice was in her early seventies, Catherine had a baby and then committed suicide when she was seventeen. That would make the baby an adult in his late thirties. *His?* Betsy wondered if it was a boy or girl and what had happened to it.

More important, how did all of this tie in with Nick and Billy? Mary Alice acted as if she cared for them deeply. She acted as if she was Billy's grandmother. Could that be it? Vicki had been a late-in-life only child and her parents had died shortly after she and Nick had married. Maybe Mary Alice had transplanted her love to Vicki. Yet something niggled at Betsy's mind.

She hurried to her desk and dug out the pictures of the Fourth of July celebrations Nick had given her. Quickly she pawed through them searching for a picture of Vicki. Finally, she found the one she was looking for.

Betsy carried it to the sliding doors leading to the patio where the light was better. She studied it. As she imagined Vicki forty pounds heavier with graying blond hair, she wondered if she really detected a facial resemblance between Vicki and Mary Alice, or if her desire to find an answer to this puzzle was putting one there.

Betsy tossed the picture on the desk and picked up the phone, unable to wait for Nick to return her call. When there was still no answer at Nick's house, she called his private number at the aquarium. After five rings, she hung up. There was no need to leave another message on the answering machine. As a last resort, she called Barbara Lupton.

"Mrs. Lupton, do you know where I might be able to find Nick?"

"Yes, he got a call about some emergency and had to go to the aquarium."

Betsy's heart sank. "I tried the aquarium and no one answered. How long has he been gone?"

"Maybe twenty minutes."

"Is Billy with you?"

"Yes, dear. Why? Is something wrong?"

Betsy didn't want to excite Nick's mother when there might be nothing to worry about. "I'm not sure, Mrs. Lupton. It's probably nothing."

"Does it have anything to do with that Garrett woman? I've been worried ever since this afternoon at the quilting club. Your grandmother's friend was discussing her."

"That's what I wanted to discuss with him. Did you say anything to Nick?"

"I didn't get a chance. He dropped Billy off without coming in the house. I thought I'd talk to him tonight when he got back."

After hanging up, Betsy was more apprehensive than ever. She dialed Mary Alice's number. There was no answer. Betsy's apprehension turned to panic when she recalled the way Mary Alice had patted her hip pack. Unstable was what Mr. Putman had called her.

Once more she rang the aquarium on the outside chance that Nick hadn't gotten to the phone in time earlier. Still no answer.

Betsy ran to her bedroom and grabbed her purse. She fumbled for the car keys as she raced out the front door. She wished she had on something other than the heels she had worn to school, but she sensed that Nick was in trouble and she had to get to him.

NICK CUDDLED the otter in his arms as he inspected the gunshot wound in her thigh. Then he laid her on the examining table and administered a small dose of morphine to ease her pain, before gently removing the bullet.

He picked up the bullet and tossed it in the air and caught it. Clinching his fist around the offending piece of metal, he studied the resting otter. Who could have done something like this to Marie? None of the previous attacks had made sense and could have been accidental, but a gunshot was deliberate. With sudden clarity Nick realized that he could be in danger.

He glanced up at the security camera hidden among the pipes and wondered what it would show when the tape was played back. Maybe now he would find out who was responsible for the accidents. Now he would have something to show the police, not just some wild stories or suppositions.

Where was Steve? He'd been on duty and had telephoned Nick about the otter. As Nick searched the darkened meeting rooms and foyer of the aquarium he called, "Steve?"

No answer. The night-lights cast eerie shadows as Nick jogged through the deserted corridors looking for the night-duty officer. Several times he thought he heard footsteps, but when he'd stop and listen there would be silence. Leaving the public areas of the aquarium, Nick headed through the water control system and back toward his office to call the security company. Something was wrong. He could feel it in the air. The animals were nervous. Their sleep had been disturbed by something before he'd arrived. When he opened the doorway to the wet area, he saw Mary Alice standing by his office.

"What are you doing here, Mary Alice? Did you forget your purse again?" He wasn't too happy to see her. If something was going on at the aquarium tonight, he sure didn't want her to be at risk.

For the last two months, he'd given instructions that no one was to be authorized entrance after hours except those on duty. This was the second time she'd been here after hours. Then he recalled that he hadn't locked the back entrance when he'd come in.

"No, I've got it right here." She began unzipping the ever-present black pouch on her hip.

"Good. Have you seen Steve? He called me a while back and I. . . ." He froze when he saw Mary Alice remove a gun. She slowly raised the revolver and pointed it at him.

"What are you doing?"

She didn't answer, but stared at him without speaking for several seconds.

"Mary Alice, what is going on? Why do you have a gun?"

"You killed my granddaughter."

"I did what?"

"You killed my Vicki." Mary Alice's voice cracked as her eyes hardened.

"Vicki?" Nick realized he had to placate the irrational woman, calm her down until he found a way to disarm her. "Vicki was your granddaughter? Neither you nor Vicki ever said anything. Why?"

"She didn't know." Mary Alice's eyes clouded with remembrance. "My father was ashamed. He locked us in the house and wouldn't let us go out. Not even to a hospital. My Catherine, she had Vicki in that dark house with only me to help." Mary Alice raised the gun warning Nick not to move. "He got rid of the baby in a week. Said she was being adopted. No more shame was to be in our house."

"Vicki was adopted?"

"Yes."

"I didn't know. She never told me."

"She didn't know it, either. My cousins raised her, but I kept track of her. I knew everything she did." Mary Alice waved the gun again. "And you killed her."

"That's not true, Mary Alice. I didn't kill Vicki."

The crazed woman acted as if she hadn't heard a word he said. "'An eye for an eye and a tooth for a tooth' is what my father said. You killed Vicki, so I'm going to kill you." Her finger tightened on the trigger.

"Nooo," a scream rang out from the back entrance.

Nick turned toward the noise and watched in horror as Betsy raced across the concrete floor toward Mary Alice. He had hardly a moment to wonder why she was there before Mary Alice whirled and fired a wild shot at Betsy.

Betsy stumbled and caught herself by grabbing the railing of the steps that led to the top of the largest tank.

His heart in his throat and with no concern for his own safety, Nick rushed to help her as Mary Alice recovered and aimed the gun at him again.

"Stop," she yelled, waving the gun, "or I'll kill her!"

Nick froze. Several yards still separated him from Betsy. He couldn't see any blood on her clothes. Her face was white but she appeared to be okay as she straightened up.

Nodding toward Betsy, Mary Alice spoke again as she took a few steps backward to get a better aim at both of them. "I'm glad you came. Get over here and stand by your lover."

Betsy didn't move.

"I said to come over here, now, or I'll shoot him. You can watch him die."

Nick shook his head at Betsy. He didn't want her too close. Mary Alice wanted to kill him, not Betsy. "No, don't...."

The sound of a bullet ricocheting off the metal fish tank brought him back around to face the woman head-on. Out of the corner of his eye, Nick watched Betsy slowly walk up beside him. He had to do something before Mary Alice killed them both. "Put the gun down so we can talk."

"Wouldn't you like that?" The look on Mary Alice's face was demonic. "I know you killed my granddaughter so you could be with this whore." She motioned with the gun toward Betsy.

Nick tried to remain calm. "Mary Alice, you know that's not true. I didn't even know Betsy then. And you know Vicki drowned because she had an asthma attack and surfaced too quickly."

"No, you killed her."

"Mary Alice, you're sick. You need help."

"No," she was almost hollering. "No. No. You killed her and I'm going to kill you." A wicked laugh escaped from her lips. "I will, you know. I killed all the others."

"The others?"

"The birds and the shark and the otter. You loved them, so I killed them just like you killed what I loved. Now it's your turn. Both of you. You both deserve to die for what you did to my Vicki and Billy."

"Billy?" Nick thought of all the times Billy had spent with Mary Alice. What had she been telling him?

"Yes, you hurt him. He didn't want a stepmother taking the place of Vicki."

Maybe she could be reasoned with. She loved Billy. "It will hurt him worse if you kill me. He needs me."

"No. He doesn't need you. I'm all he needs."

"But if you kill me, he won't have you, either. He'll be all alone."

"After I kill you tonight, I'm going to get Billy and go away where we'll be safe."

Nick sensed Betsy's tension. There was no time left. Mary Alice's eyes were growing wilder by the minute. He stepped forward and at the same time shoved Betsy behind him and yelled, "Run."

Mary Alice aimed the gun with both hands. "Don't come any closer."

He watched her shaky finger tighten around the trigger as he took another step.

"Nick!" he heard Tom yell. He looked up and saw him running toward them, followed closely by Steve.

Mary Alice, startled at the sound of voices behind her, squeezed the trigger as Nick lunged and knocked the gun to the floor. He fell to his knees as the impact of the bullet hit his arm.

Tom closed the space quickly and grabbed Mary Alice from behind, and with assistance from Steve, subdued her.

Betsy was immediately on her knees by Nick's side. "Oh, Nick. I tried to call you. I was so afraid." She pulled back, looked at her hand and gasped. "You're bleeding."

Nick looked down. A red line showed where the bullet or its heat had etched a path over his skin, bringing blood to the surface. "It's not purple-heart quality," he tried to joke.

"Thank goodness." Betsy offered him a weak smile as he pulled her into his arms.

Tom led Mary Alice to a chair and stood nearby with the gun pointed at the floor while they waited for the police to arrive.

Steve looked stunned as he surveyed the group and told his story. "I . . . she held a gun on me and forced me into a closet, then she locked it. That was after I called you about the otter being shot."

Mary Alice talked as though she were in another world. "You see, I didn't have a choice. I had to shoot her when the poison I gave her last weekend didn't work."

Nick shook his head. "Why? Why did you harm the animals if all you wanted was me?"

Mary Alice smiled sweetly. "You needed to suffer for what you did. I wanted you dead, but I wanted to ruin you first."

Nick shook his head as he realized how close Mary Alice had come to achieving her objective. "Tom, it seems you came through again."

"Well, it seems I was being discredited, too," Tom said. "I got to thinking. Everything pointed to me. I looked guilty as hell, so I decided to do a little nightly surveillance of my own. That's why I was here to hear Steve's pounding. In fact, you nearly caught me behind one of the tanks a few weeks back." He shook his head in disbelief. "Mary Alice . . . who'd have thought it?"

Nick heard the sirens as the police pulled into the parking lot. "Let's go meet them."

Nick and Betsy watched sadly as Mary Alice was led to the police car. She had no family, no one to help her. While they were glad to be alive, there was no joy or relief in their victory.

Nick noticed that Betsy was pale, so he gathered her against him. Even though things were strained between them, he loved her. That she had endangered her life to save his proved she still loved him.

She began to tremble as she whispered so low he had to strain to hear. "I really did try to warn you, but you weren't home."

"You knew what was going to happen."

She looked up. "After the quilting club met today, Grandmother dropped by." She explained how she had reached the conclusion that Mary Alice was going to harm Nick.

"And you walked straight into harm's way." His arm tightened around her. "Come on. I'll take you home before I go to the police station. They're going to want some answers. You can wait until tomorrow to give your statement."

"I'd just as soon get it over with."

"Are you sure?"

"Yes. And I'll drive." She straightened as if willing herself to be strong. "You're the one who's hurt."

"It's only a scratch, so I'll drive. Let's leave your car here. We'll take care of it tomorrow."

She walked by his side, their fingers entwined. Maybe some good would come from the horror of this night. With Betsy beside him, with the two of them drawing strength from each other, anything was possible.

THE FOLLOWING WEEK passed quickly.

Betsy stood in the hall the first day of school and listened as the building filled with the sounds of eager children searching for their rooms. She checked the roster to see whose room Billy was in, then avoided it all day, afraid he would be upset if he saw her. The child had gone through enough turmoil to last a lifetime. Finding out Mary Alice was crazy must have been really hard on him. They had been so close.

The day passed quickly, and after the final bell rang to dismiss the students, Betsy sat at her desk reviewing permanent records. Hearing a shuffling sound, she glanced up to see Billy standing in her doorway, his head hanging. "Can I talk to you, Miss Johnson?" He shifted from one foot to the other.

"Yes," she answered, wondering how long he'd been standing there. "Come in."

Billy trudged over to the brown, straight-backed chair and slumped down on it.

Betsy greeted him with a tentative smile. "What's on your mind, Billy? Don't you like your teacher?"

"Yeah, she's going to be okay." He put his elbows on Betsy's desk and picked up a pencil. "That's not what I came in for." He rolled the pencil back and forth over the wooden surface. "I came in...I guess," he stuttered, then the words rushed out. "I'm sorry."

She let out the breath she'd been holding as a bud of hope began to form in her heart. "About what?"

Billy sighed, still unable to look at her. "About running away and saying I didn't want you for a mother. I didn't mean it."

"You didn't?" The hope began to flower.

"No. I... was afraid that... Mary Alice said...."

"What did Mary Alice say?"

"She said that my dad killed my mom so he could marry you and—"

"She told you that?" Betsy was no longer surprised by anything Mary Alice might have said. Nevertheless, she was distressed that Billy had been used as a pawn.

"Yeah. You know the day when you took me to the aquarium to see the otter... Well, she said that you wouldn't have time for me." Billy sucked his bottom lip in under his teeth. "She said that you would want to get rid of me."

"Billy, no! You know that isn't true." She came around the desk and knelt beside Billy. One arm circled his shoulders in a gentle hug. "I love you and your dad."

Tears began rolling down Billy's face, dropping off his chin onto his shirt. "That's what Miss Webster, my counselor said. She said none of it was true. That Mary Alice was a sick woman. Dad said she tried to kill you and him."

Betsy nodded. "Miss Webster is right. Mary Alice is sick. She loved you in a strange way, Billy. She couldn't share you, and with most people, love is best when it's shared."

"I know that now."

"Had Mary Alice been telling you things all along?" Betsy probed. "Do you remember when you told me that your dad had let your mom die?" When

Billy nodded, Betsy continued. "Was she the one who told you that?"

He nodded, then looked at her with glistening blue eyes. "It made sense because they used to fight."

"That doesn't mean he wanted her dead, Billy. He loved her very much."

"He loves you now. I know because he's really sad you won't marry him. He just sits and looks at the TV at night. He doesn't want to play or anything. It's just like when my mom died."

"I'm sorry, Billy. I thought it was best if you didn't want me."

"But I do. That's what I came in here for... to ask you to marry my dad."

Tears began to run down Betsy's cheeks as she wrapped her arms around him.

There was a knock on the door frame and Nick stuck his head inside. "The secretary said you two were in here."

Betsy stood up but kept her arm around Billy's shoulders. "He came to ask me to marry you."

Nick stopped and looked at her. "Well?"

"If the offer still stands, I would love to be your wife and Billy's mother."

Nick gathered both of them into his arms.

CHAPTER TWENTY

*September meeting
of the Quilting Club*

ALL THE GOINGS-ON *at that aquarium had just about
worn me to a frazzle. If it weren't for the support of
my quilting club, I just might have broken down. Just
as Barbara Lupton did every time she thought of what
could have happened to Nick and Billy.*

"Are you sure you didn't cry just a little?" Bertha
asked.

Virginia snipped a thread. "I certainly would have."

I pride myself on being strong, not like Bertha who
cries during every television show. And sometimes
commercials. "To tell the truth, I did shed a tear or
two when Nick and Betsy rescheduled the wedding for
next month."

"Well, the timing's just about right," Bertha said.
"We'll finish this quilt next week. Just in time for a
fine wedding present."

"What are the wedding plans?" Virginia asked.

"They've decided to keep it simple and invite only
a few close friends and family," Barbara Lupton said.

Bertha's face fell in disappointment. "Where will it
be," she asked.

Barbara smiled. "I had to stifle Billy's creativity a little. He wanted Nick and Betsy to get married at the aquarium. I finally convinced him that my backyard is the perfect setting. I do need some help though. Can all of you help?" she asked.

Bertha's jaw dropped open, but I must say she recovered nicely, offering to do anything. After missing my neighbor Susan's wedding back in the spring, she'd been a bit huffy. I'd bet ahead of time that her arthritis wouldn't act up on Betsy's wedding day.

Era looked up. "Now who's getting married?"

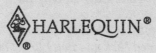

THE WEDDING GAMBLE
Muriel Jensen

Eternity, Massachusetts, was America's wedding town. Paul Bertrand knew this better than anyone—he never should have gotten soused at his friend's rowdy bachelor party. Next morning when he woke up, he found he'd somehow managed to say "I do"—to the woman he'd once jilted! And Christina Bowman had helped launch so many honeymoons, she knew just what to do on theirs!

THE WEDDING GAMBLE, available in September from American Romance, is the fourth book in Harlequin's new cross-line series, **WEDDINGS, INC.**

Be sure to look for the fifth book, **THE VENGEFUL GROOM,** by Sara Wood (Harlequin Presents #1692), coming in October.